STUMBLE & FALL

A LEGACY OF SILENCE
BOOK 2

AMY RIVERS

Compathy Press, LLC

For Jessica, my best friend
&
Stephanie, my mother

Two women who have taught me about strength, vulnerability, and grace in times of adversity

PROLOGUE

Lucy finished her filing, carefully closing the drawer so the noise wouldn't disturb the clerk working in the next room. The quiet set her nerves on edge, reminding her of walking on eggshells around her father before he passed. As an intern for the City of Alamogordo Lucy was used to menial assignments, but she preferred being out in the office where she could observe the inner workings of the city government. Where it was never quiet.

She turned to find Sam Garrett, the Assistant City Manager, hovering near the door. Blood rushed to her cheeks as she jumped, unable to contain a small squeak of alarm.

"Didn't mean to startle you," Sam said, flashing a charming smile. She hadn't heard him approach. Now embarrassment had her wishing she could stuff herself into the filing cabinet and disappear.

"Sorry, Mr. Garrett," she said. "I was just finishing up." She picked up her backpack from the floor nearby and held it close to her chest, feeling more awkward by the second.

"No need to apologize," Garrett said, taking a step into the room. The gray in his hair betrayed his age, but his otherwise-youthful appearance and demeanor made him a favorite among the staff and student interns. Two of Lucy's friends had huge crushes on Sam Garrett, and Lucy could see the appeal. If you ignored the fact that he was old enough to be her father. Maybe even her grandfather.

"I hear you've been doing a great job," Sam said, drawing Lucy's mind back to the conversation. She was surprised that the department head even knew who she was, much less keeping tabs on her. A bit of an introvert, Lucy had to push past her desire to remain invisible every day as she pursued her goals. The unexpected attention, even if it was positive, was unnerving.

"Thanks. I'm super grateful for this opportunity," she said, smiling while she tried to coax her breathing back to a normal rate. "I'm applying for the Public Administration program at UNM. This internship will go a long way toward helping me get in."

"That's a strong program," Sam agreed. "And a competitive one. What are you hoping to do after you graduate?"

Lucy's mom worked three jobs to support her and her siblings, her dad having died shortly after Lucy's youngest sister was born. As the oldest, Lucy spent all her free time helping with her sisters and brother. She loved her mother desperately, but she didn't want to end up in the same position.

"I want to be a city planner," she said.

"That's *my* field," Sam said. Of course Lucy knew that. She'd researched each city official thoroughly to make sure she got the most out of her internship by having meaningful interactions with everyone she got the chance to meet.

"You know, I just had a great idea," he said, taking a step closer and making the room feel smaller. "Maybe you could come do some work for me in my office. I can write you a killer letter of recommendation if you show me what you can do."

Lucy's heart leapt at the possibility, but something made her pause.

His words?

The tone of his voice?

For a moment she hesitated, hugging her bag more tightly, but the reality of her situation necessitated that she take advantage of every opportunity given her. She couldn't afford to attend college without a full scholarship and she wouldn't get that scholarship without help.

This was an opportunity she couldn't pass up.

And anyway, what did she have to lose?

"That sounds great, Mr. Garrett. Thank you." She hoped he couldn't hear her voice shaking.

"You can call me Sam," he said with a wink. "I'm sure glad I ran into you today, Lucy." He held the door open, inviting her to exit first. Despite her best efforts, her arm brushed against his as she passed by.

CHAPTER 1
KATE

Kate wiped her brow, grateful that the autumn sun wasn't nearly as intense as its summer sister. She didn't know how they would have finished work on the house in the sweltering heat. It was hard enough with a cool breeze.

She climbed down the ladder, returning her paintbrush to a bucket of water. She tucked a few stray curls that had escaped the scarf she'd wrapped around her head to keep her hair off her neck.

"I need a drink," she called out. "Are you ready to take a break?"

In record time, Roman walked out of the house with two cups of iced tea. He handed one to Kate and she drank it fast, giving herself a brain freeze. "I don't even care that it hurts," she said, laughing as she pressed her palm against her forehead waiting for the pain to subside. "You're my hero."

Roman smiled, then turned to appraise her work. "It's looking great. Do you want me to finish up?"

Kate laughed. "Sure, volunteer when it's almost done." She punched him in the arm playfully, noticing how dark his skin had turned from being in the sun. "How's the gate coming?"

"All finished," he said, taking her hand. "Let me show you." They walked through the adobe arch to the front entrance. Roman had taken down the old wooden gate and replaced it with a thick wrought-iron monstrosity that looked medieval, complete with decorative spikes at the top that left no room for someone to squeeze through. Between the iron gate and the thick wooden door, the entrance to Kate's new home was impenetrable.

"Looks amazing," Kate said, turning to wrap her arms around Roman's neck, her glass dangling from her hand behind him. "Thank you." She kissed him, noting his saltiness. They both needed a shower. They'd been working all day.

Kate had purchased the hacienda—the first home she'd ever owned—using the money from the sale of her father's house in Alamogordo. Her new home was located in the desert outside Tularosa, just a fifteen minute drive from Alamogordo. Close, but still far enough away from her hometown to help her breathe a bit easier. It was too big for her alone, but from the start, Kate's intention had been to create a safe haven for victims of abuse. She ran her hand along Roman's side, letting her fingers bump faintly along the scars near his ribs.

For nearly four months she and Roman had worked tire-lessly to fix the house, replacing broken fixtures and plastering the entire interior to keep the adobe from further erosion. They'd installed a state-of-the-art alarm system complete with perimeter cameras, but the natural defenses created by brick and iron were what really made Kate feel safe at night—though not enough to stave off her panic attacks entirely. She'd finally finished up the master bedroom, and had officially been living in the house for about a week.

There was still a lot of work to be done.

Sealing the brick in the courtyard was taking longer than she'd expected, and the work was grueling. The adobe fence that enclosed the property was six-feet tall. The outer edge was thick with cacti and mesquite trees, making it nearly impossible to reach but Kate insisted on cameras just in case someone risked it. The effect was like living in an old-time fortress.

"Did you talk to Tilly today?"

"Yes." Kate released her hold on Roman and massaged the sore muscles in her shoulder. "She and Jim are still trying to work out the details of their move."

"Is he still looking at the DA's office in Las Cruces?"

"No. Actually, that was today's big news. He accepted a job with the U.S. Attorney's Office. He'll be working at the Las Cruces branch."

"Wow, that was fast. Didn't think the Feds moved that quickly."

Kate smiled. "Tilly says that Jim leads a very charmed life. I guess she's right."

"Maybe his good luck will rub off on me," Roman said, absentmindedly touching the same spot on his side where Kate's fingers had been—the spot where he'd been stabbed a few months earlier. He tried not to complain but Kate knew the injury still ached, especially after a long day of manual labor.

"Tilly's getting restless," Kate continued, knowing her sister wasn't the only one chomping at the bit. She hoped Roman's job hunt wouldn't last too much longer. He'd been so helpful with repairs on the new house, but she knew he needed something more to give him purpose.

"Never thought she would be anxious to get back to New Mexico," Roman said with a laugh. "Though I suppose living an hour away isn't the same as moving back home."

"It's going to be a big adjustment for her." Kate leaned her head against his shoulder. "But I guess things change."

"I'm glad they do," Roman said softly, making her shiver.

After being estranged for nearly twenty years, Kate and Roman had not only rekindled their friendship but they'd become romantically involved. Unfortunately, they'd reconnected while working on a murder investigation. Kate had lost her position as a high school psychologist as a result of her involvement with the police, and Roman had resigned as a detective before his department had a chance to fire him. The situation had brought them closer, but Kate worried that the circumstances of their reunion would cause problems moving forward.

Having spent his entire career with the Alamogordo Police Department, Roman was now at loose ends. He'd applied to state and federal agencies, but the hiring process was slow. Kate had encouraged him to apply with the sheriff's department, but he was worried about working with an agency so closely associated with his previous employer. They both knew that the Chief of Police in Alamogordo was involved in criminal activity, and he had done everything he could to thwart Roman's investigation while staying off the radar. Roman hadn't left on good terms, and still wasn't sure who among his former colleagues he could fully trust.

For Kate, the investigation had been a wake-up call. Being a school psychologist had never been her life's ambition, and uncovering a thriving sex trafficking ring in her hometown had been the driving force in her decision to buy the hacienda and use her psychology background to to help stop the violence. The decision had come at great cost to her own physical safety, and Roman had been a reluctant ally in her project despite his feelings for her.

"Not gonna lie," Roman said, as if reading her thoughts. "I couldn't picture how this was going to turn out, but now that we've cleaned the place up it's like a little slice of heaven."

"It's pretty great. I just hope opening up a psychology practice will be enough to keep this place running." Kate had used her savings and the money from the sale of her father's house to purchase and renovate the hacienda. With funds running low she'd decided a return to work was necessary, but she wanted to keep her schedule flexible. She'd never worked for herself and she had no idea if she could make ends meet on her own. The fear that she might not succeed was a thorn in her side. She knew Roman would help—he'd said as much—but the idea of having to rely on someone else still chafed.

————

"How'd it go?" Roman asked when Kate arrived home later that afternoon.

"Good. I signed a lease for a place on White Sands Boulevard near downtown. I'm still planning on putting in a security system, but it's an interior office so I feel pretty good about it. The property manager is Ken Nichols. Ring any bells?"

"Nope," Roman said. Kate sighed with relief. Working in Alamogordo was a calculated risk. Though she hadn't seen Allen Parks since his nephew's sentencing hearing, and had cut ties with her former employer, Kate was still on high alert. She knew it would only be a matter of time before everyone knew where to find her. Living with her father and working at the high school, she'd kept herself distant from the goings-on in Alamogordo, which left her short of information and unsure who to trust.

"How was your day?" she asked, putting aside those uneasy feelings.

"Good," Roman replied. "I got a call from the FBI." Roman had been applying for both local and federal law enforcement jobs, and though Kate knew the FBI was basically Roman's dream job, she never seriously considered him working there.

"What did they say?"

"They have an opening in Las Cruces. I'd have to go through their training program, but then I'd be working here. Maybe some occasional travel, but mostly regional work."

"And you want the job," Kate said. It wasn't a question. She could see the fire in Roman's eyes as he spoke about the position. Her stomach twisted "Are you going to meet with them?"

"Yes. On Monday."

Kate swallowed hard. She'd gotten used to having Roman around. Even though he still had his house in Alamogordo, he spent his nights with her. She hadn't been alone at night in months and even though she had Rusty—her very hyper watchdog—she wasn't sure she was ready to be left to her own devices just yet. This unpleasant truth gave her a sour taste in her mouth.

Roman put his arms around Kate, pulling her to him and holding tight. "I nearly had a heart attack when I got the call. I don't think I ever would have pursued this job before now." He took a breath. "Yeah, I want the job."

Kate rested her head on his chest. "I'm happy for you, Roman." she said. "And I appreciate everything you've done to help me make this place livable." She couldn't keep the quiver out of her voice, but she fought hard to keep her tears at bay.

Roman pulled away so he could look at her. "I'm not going anywhere, Kate. Don't sound so worried." His smile melted her heart.

"I know," she said, but she couldn't shrug off the discomfort she was feeling. Kate was still grieving her father's death. That coupled with the trauma she suffered at the hands of Benny Parks and his goons had thrown her into a depression. And she was still having nightmares. If she were a patient Kate would have called out these telltale signs of PTSD, but she stubbornly clung to the idea that if she kept moving forward she would find herself on the far end of her grief and trauma. It irked her that every time she started to feel settled, something came along to rattle her.

CHAPTER 2
KATE

Kate woke up struggling for air that night. She sat up and reached for her water, thinking calming thoughts even as she sweated, the panic attack battling for control. She took deep breaths trying to slow her heartbeat. A warm hand rubbed her back in circles.

"Breathe," Roman said, his voice heavy with sleep.

Kate focused on her breathing, counting each inhale and exhale until her body began to relax. Slowly she laid back down, resting her head on Roman's bare chest. He ran his fingers through her hair, brushing loose strands away from her face. "Nightmare?"

"Yeah,"

"Want to tell me about it?"

Kate hesitated. She still had a hard time talking about her dreams, though she knew it would help dull their effect.

"The usual," she said flatly.

Kate had been attacked and raped in her prison job. For years, she woke up with images of her attacker still fresh in her mind. Lately those nightmares had been less frequent. Instead of her prison attacker she now saw Benny Parks, whose violence against one of Kate's students had brought her into the case and made her a target. Knowing that Benny was behind bars didn't make him any less scary. He had connections, and one of those connections was still at large after attacking Kate in her father's home.

Kate and Roman both knew Benny Parks had been made a scapegoat by the organization responsible for trafficking girls in the area. Kate knew that her sister had been a victim decades earlier. She knew that Allen Parks, Benny's uncle, was involved. And according to her sister, several other prominent local businessmen were as well.

Knowing all that didn't help because Kate couldn't prove it.

When Roman began investigating the disappearance of Gabby Greene last year, neither he nor Kate had known that the investigation would uncover something so horrifying. Evidence had been tampered with and the Chief of Police had impeded Roman's ability to do his job, eventually forcing him to resign. Roman had brought in contacts in the State Police to apply pressure. The result: Benny Parks was arrested and found guilty of Gabby's brutal murder.

Case closed.

Everything went back to normal. Supposedly.

Except that now Kate had no inside connection. As much as she'd hated her job at the high school, she'd been in the right place to see things. Roman, of course, had been tied into the local law enforcement community. But after leaving his job, he distanced himself from his friends on the force, never sure what information was being fed back to Chief Gunnison. Roman suspected that Gunnison was directly involved in the trafficking ring, and his behavior with Kate seemed to support that assumption. However, Roman was cast out before he could even begin his own internal investigation.

The State Police had been called in to help, and Kate had consulted with them briefly after leaving her job at the school, but now even that connection was frozen. At any other time Kate might have resisted the urge to ask her next question, but the image of Benny was still fresh in her mind.

"Have you talked to Angela lately?" Kate asked, not surprised when Roman stiffened. Angela Lopez was Roman's contact with the State Police. She'd also been his lover on and off through the years. She and Roman had been "on" again when Kate finally confessed her feelings for Roman.

"No," Roman said with a sigh. "She's still not returning my calls."

"Mine either," Kate said. Angela had signed Kate up as a consultant with the State Police. Kate received occasional work from the department, mostly analysis requests, and she had handled each case with care. She wasn't sure whether she was trying to impress Roman's ex, or if she was covering her own ass in case Angela became vindictive. It didn't matter because Angela hadn't contacted Kate in months, and Kate wasn't surprised.

Kate sighed. She had truly liked Angela, and she hated that her own happiness came at the detective's expense.

At present, Angela was the only person they knew they could trust to get information about the sex trafficking investigation. Kate wondered if the investigation had been closed after Benny's arrest. It was a terrifying thought, and one that she simply had no way to resolve.

"She'll come around," Roman said, his voice barely more than a sad whisper.

"I'm sorry, Roman. I shouldn't have brought her up," Kate said. She laid back on her pillow, wondering why she'd been thinking about Angela. The detective's face was clear in Kate's mind, as if she'd just seen her. It reminded her of something just outside her grasp, but the goal of getting back to sleep forced her to clear her mind. She began breathing steadily, counting her breaths until she fell back asleep.

———

As soon as Kate fell asleep again, the dream returned with a vengeance. She was back in that visitation room, her assailant gripping her neck so hard she felt like she would die. The pain in her neck had almost overshadowed the other violence her body was enduring, but in her dream she felt a tearing sensation somewhere low in her body.

She looked up into the sneering face of Benny Parks, but she was distracted by a sound nearby. A miserable, keening cry. The sound was familiar, like something she'd emitted herself before, but she wasn't making it now. No sound could escape the stranglehold her attacker had on her. Without warning, Benny released his grip on her neck and she turned her head slowly, feeling the injured muscles in her neck protest at the movement. Her heart beat so fast in her chest it felt like it would explode. She was absolutely certain that the source of that hideous, tortured sound would be her sister, Tilly.

But when Kate finally located the source of the sound, she screamed. Kate saw herself lying on the ground, bloody and bruised. Her clothes were torn and she didn't move. Her mouth was frozen wide open, gaping, and despite the stillness of the broken body, the figure was vocalizing a pain so raw that even in her dream, Kate felt like she would pass out—escape mentally from something too horrible to contemplate.

A few steps away was a dark doorway. Benny Parks had disappeared. Kate was alone, pinned against a wall, unable to help the form on the floor. Dark figures loomed in the doorway. Kate pressed her back into the hard wall, shrinking away from those threatening figures. They didn't make any move to come closer, which made them all the more terrifying.

Kate awoke with the first light of dawn. She was drenched in sweat, but she wasn't in her usual anxiety spiral. Instead, she was alert and curious about the dream.

Though she'd made a lot of progress in coping with her assault, Kate's mind still had no trouble replaying the incident in graphic detail. Tonight's dream, however, had touched on a deeper fear. The unknown. Kate had never been good at handling uncertainty and her life now was full of just that. She was returning to her career as a psychologist, but in a radically different environment than her previous work. She and Roman were half a year into their relationship, but it still felt fragile sometimes. Roman's announcement about the FBI job was bringing many of Kate's insecurities to the surface, and it was just the beginning. Once she was in the public eye again, would he be targeted?

Kate thought she knew what she signed up for, staying in town, but the truth was she didn't know anything. She only knew that she couldn't turn a blind eye now that she saw just how far back the abuse stretched. And as she lay in bed, listening to the soft sound of Roman's steady breathing, she wondered how long it would take before the shit hit the fan.

CHAPTER 3
KATE

Setting up her new office was both a satisfying and tedious experience for Kate. With all the work she'd put into her new house, more cleaning and moving wasn't exactly high on her priority list. On the other hand, she'd never had so much control over her professional surroundings. The work she was doing on the house was more functional than stylish. Her working space in both the prison system and the school had been heavily regulated. Here, Kate could express her personality and focus on her therapeutic style.

Which led to an existential crisis.

As a psychologist in private practice, Kate had no idea who she was. Working with incarcerated inmates required a certain mindset. Working with adolescents was also a narrow focus. Kate's passion for abnormal psychology had driven her in her educational and professional pursuits, and while she hoped she'd eventually build a client base that allowed her to flex her academic muscle she knew that the majority of her work would be in family counseling. That was the way with small towns.

Kate was sitting in her stark office, stuck in the mire of her own lack of direction, when Roman knocked at the door.

"How's it going?" He looked around the office. Kate had cleaned and vacuumed. She'd purchased a used desk and couch. Both pieces of furniture were sitting where the delivery men had left them. "Is everything okay?"

Kate sighed. "I'm stuck. I have no idea who I am."

Roman sat beside her on the couch. "This isn't a pass/fail situation, Kate. You don't have to have all the answers. And you can change your mind as you go along."

"I know," Kate said. "I've just never had to consider what my work would look like outside the criminal justice system. I've been so focused on the house, but I'm realizing how much I've been avoiding this moment."

Roman took her hand. "I know how you feel. I can't believe I interviewed with the FBI. The thought that I could actually work there is overwhelming."

"Really?" Roman's career as a law enforcement officer had made him an expert at not showing his emotions, and she'd been distracted by her own mounting panic. "I'm sorry, Roman. I've been so focused on the house and now this."

"You don't have to be responsible for everything, Kate." He was looking at her now, his expression serious. "I'm capable of tending to my own emotions." He softened his tone. "And I know who I can trust if I need help processing."

He was throwing her a bone, but Kate still felt conflicted.

"I want the girls to come to me for help. Girls like Gabby and Mandy. And Tilly. How do I make it clear that this is a safe place for them?"

"It's not just the space, Kate. It's you. You're the key to making them feel safe." Roman was silent for a few minutes. "I've been thinking—and you're not going to like this—but just hear me out." Kate sat up straight and scooted a few inches away so she could look at Roman while he spoke. "You have to play the game."

"Meaning?" Kate asked, her voice full of disgust.

Roman kept his tone even, "We have no access right now. Not to information. Or to a viable means for reaching out to the victims. I know how much you want the abuse to stop, and I'm right there with you, but I don't think we can win this battle from the outside."

Kate forced herself to relax a bit. She knew this was a tender subject for Roman, and no matter how much she hated to hear what he was saying she knew he was right. "You're hoping a federal job will give you a way to get back into the system?"

"Yes, but I'm talking about your practice right now. We know that several of the people involved in the trafficking operation are connected through their businesses. You're opening up a new business. It might be a good idea to join some of the local organizations. The Chamber of Commerce maybe. Network. Begin working the system from the inside."

Kate laughed bitterly. "Lovely. My career just became subterfuge."

"That's not what I meant," Roman said, taking her hand. "You're going to help these girls. *We* are. But it's going to take time, and in the meantime you can leverage your new position as a business owner to infiltrate . . . ."

"You make me sound like a spy," Kate said ruefully. "You're right. I don't like it, but there's something to be said for thinking like a criminal to catch one."

Roman's expression turned serious. "Remember Kate. Not everyone in town is a criminal. It might be good to find some allies. Maybe even make some friends."

Friends, Kate thought. Friends had never been her strong suit, and she couldn't imagine how to make friends when she felt so much suspicion. But Roman was right, she'd have to try.

———

"This isn't going to work," Tilly lamented. She'd called Kate in a panic, and nothing seemed to help. Kate had been listening to her sister's continuous stream of nervous rambling for nearly an hour. At first she'd tried talking Tilly off the ledge, but ran into a wall of stubbornness. Now her sister's anxiety was starting to spread.

"Okay, Til. You've got to calm down. You're going to give me a panic attack, and it's not even my life." Kate laughed to soften the blow, but she slowed her breathing. They hadn't even gotten to her problems yet.

"Sorry," Tilly muttered. "I'm freaking out over here."

"Um, yes. I got that," Kate said. "Listen. Jim is a good guy. You guys are good together. This move is going to be fine. You've already been living together for how many years now?"

"I know," Tilly groaned. "And look how that ended up. Things got too intense. I ran away, if you'll recall, and he basically had to drag me back kicking and screaming. And now we're moving to New Mexico. It's literally my worst nightmare come true."

"First, that's not exactly the way I remember it. You went back quite happily. And you're not going back in time. You're moving forward, and you're in a strong relationship. Anyway, it could be worse. You could be moving to Alamogordo."

Tilly didn't agree, but Kate knew she'd made her point. Lately her conversations with Tilly had gone in circles, and she wanted to change the subject before they rounded another bend. "Did I tell you about my new office?"

"No. You told me you were going to look at spaces. Did you find something?"

"You remember where that Chinese restaurant was on White Sands? Across from the zoo?"

"There's an office space there?"

"A nice one, actually. Back behind the restaurant. Several office spaces. I rented out a two room suite." Kate and Roman had finished decorating her office. It was tasteful, had soothing colors and abstract art. Kate was actually looking forward to seeing clients.

"How have things been?" Tilly asked hesitantly. Kate knew she wasn't looking for commentary on the weather, but it took some effort not to deflect. Everytime Kate went to town, she felt eyes on her. Occasionally she'd look up quick enough to make eye contact. It was never the same person, but if the goal was to make Kate paranoid it was working beautifully.

"Quiet," Kate finally replied, picturing her sister's expression. "I'm going to a women's networking meeting later this week. Should be fascinating."

"Sounds awful."

"Probably. But Roman makes an excellent point. I need to start figuring out who I can trust. He even suggested I might make some friends."

Tilly snorted. "And here I thought he knew you."

"Thanks a lot." Kate had spent most of her teenage years hanging out with Roman, and most of her adult years thus far focused on her career. She'd never been a "drinks after work" kind of girl and now that she was working on her own again her chances for social interaction were slim.

On the other hand, she'd been thinking a lot about what Roman said. Despite living in Alamogordo for more than five years, Kate had been reluctant to see it as home. She'd looked at it as more of a temporary stop on her way to better things.

Her decision to stay in town and put down roots meant that she'd have to stop thinking of herself as passing through. And her recent run-ins with the dark side of town had her viewing everyone as inherently bad. She knew this wasn't true, but it was easier to stay detached when she could lump everyone together as "other."

It was going to be a hard habit to break, especially when the PTSD she suffered made her over-cautious and suspicious.

She glanced at her watch. "I have to let you go, Til. But please take a few minutes to sit with your feelings. I know this move is a big change—and a scary one at that—but you're a solid, capable, professional woman. Jim is starting a kick-ass job. And between the two of you, it's going to work out. Don't be so afraid to try."

Kate braced for some snide remark, but Tilly just sighed. "Thanks, Kate. I needed a sisterly pep talk. I'll see you this weekend."

After disconnecting, Kate thought about her relationship with her sister. They'd come a long way from barely speaking less than a year ago. Moments like these made Kate hopeful that they were building a strong foundation. Yet, with Tilly spiraling over her impending move, Kate's decision to avoid adding to her sister's worries was mostly self-preservation.

Having Tilly close would be wonderful, as long as they could resist being pulled into each other's orbits of anxiety.

CHAPTER 4
TILLY

Tilly didn't know how long she'd been sitting there, staring at the photo in her hand, but when Jim touched her shoulder she jumped. She opened her fingers and let the paper flutter to the floor, determined not to touch it again.

"What's this?" Jim said, picking up the photo. She could see the creases in his forehead as he studied the picture. His lips turned down slightly at the corners.

"It fell out of a stack I dropped. I didn't know I had it," Tilly offered, but she couldn't bring herself to say more.

"Is this you?" Jim asked, pointing at the teenage girl laughing in the photo. Anyone else might have smiled at seeing Tilly's cheerful young face, but Tilly's distress must have been written all over her because Jim's expression stayed neutral.

"It was our first date."

In the photo a dark-haired boy stood beside Tilly, carelessly wrapping his arm around her shoulder. It should have been a fun snapshot—a bit of harmless nostalgia. But the look on the boy's face betrayed a violence and entitlement that Tilly would fall prey to. How could she not have seen it then?

"This is him?" Jim asked.

"Yeah."

Tilly had told Jim every disgusting detail of her so-called relationship with Jacob Copeland and the aftermath—countless instances of abuse at the hands of his father and his father's friends.

"Throw it away," Tilly whispered. Her body felt heavy, making it difficult to move or breathe. She was stunned at the visceral reaction to simply seeing his face. The way her body betrayed her. How all those years of therapy and struggle and avoidance amounted to nothing when it came right down to it.

Jim tore the picture in two and left the room. Tilly could hear his footsteps on the stairs. The door shutting behind him. He was gone for a long time. Each moment that passed brought Tilly closer to regaining her composure but progress was slow. She had to remind herself that she wasn't that naive girl anymore.

When Jim returned, she'd returned to packing. He seemed to sense that she didn't want to talk, so they worked side-by-side in silence. Tilly had learned to control her emotions while working with patients. She employed those skills now, pushing down the rage and grief until it was a dull roar inside her.

———

The trip had been uncomfortably silent. For the last few days Tilly had kept her head down, working so hard at packing the house and running trips to the thrift store with donations that she'd hardly had time or energy to dwell on the feelings lingering since she'd picked up that photo of Jacob Copeland. Jim had given her space at home, but the car created a captive audience and the silence was deafening. Tilly didn't know what to say, and she could feel the tension growing. As they passed through Raton on their way south, Jim finally broke.

"Are we going to talk about it?" he asked gently. She could hear a hint of desperation in his voice.

"There's not much to say that you don't already know," Tilly answered, knowing it wouldn't be enough. She'd given Jim a very clinical run-through about the abuse she suffered as a teenager. She'd watched Jim's face turn red and then drain of color as the story continued, but she'd been detached. Recounting the details at a safe distance from her own emotions. Like the story wasn't hers.

And maybe her detachment had given him the sense that the pain wasn't so near the surface. That triggering a panic attack took more. Maybe she'd even convinced herself of that.

"What's changed?" he asked, throwing her off-guard. She sometimes forgot how observant he was. "Because we've been together for three years and I've never seen you react this way. Not even when you were with Kate last year."

Tilly sighed. "It's been brewing. I'd almost convinced myself that I'd moved on. Then my dad died. And Kate got mixed up in the middle of the same shit that ruined my life."

"Then we decided to move to New Mexico," Jim finished for her. His eyes were on the road, but she could see the worry. "I feel like I'm driving you to your execution."

"I didn't think it would be this bad, but that's the thing about processing trauma. You're never done." Tilly felt so weary. The conversation was depleting what little energy she'd mustered. "So the answer to your question is yes, we need to talk about it. But I definitely don't feel up for it now. I'm going to try to take a nap, and then I can drive some if you want."

"Get some rest," Jim said, stroking the top of her hand where it rested on her lap.

Tilly settled back and closed her eyes, letting the car's vibration lull her to sleep. She awoke with a start when Jim said, "We're here." Her neck ached, and she silently cursed Jim for letting her sleep so long.

As Jim wound through their new neighborhood, Tilly noticed a lot of basketball hoops and children's toys worn down by the intense heat and wind. The houses were mostly stucco in shades of tan. The lawns mostly xeriscaped with desert plants bringing color to an otherwise monotone palette.

They pulled into the driveway of their new home, where the property manager was waiting to hand them the keys, all paperwork having been signed electronically. The sun was starting to dip below the mountains, the sky a radiant band of color.

Tilly opened the door, and marveled once again at the interior of their new home. She hadn't lived in an actual house since her childhood, preferring apartment complexes with good security and less upkeep. Having all this space felt strange, knowing that it would only ever be her and Jim occupying it. Another reminder of a life that she'd never have.

"What do you think?" Jim asked, smiling. He wrapped his arms around her waist from behind, and then rested his chin on her shoulder so they could survey the new terrain together.

"It's huge," Tilly said. She'd seen pictures online, but they hadn't quite done justice to the high ceilings and tiled floors.

"I'll start unloading," Jim said, heading back to the car. The moving van wouldn't be coming for a few days, so they'd be camping out on an air mattress. Tilly's body was tired from the drive, but she knew it would be a while before she could relax enough to sleep.

———

Jim left the house early the next morning to fill out paperwork and get his credentials for his new job, leaving Tilly to mill around her empty house. For a while she tried to picture where she would put furniture, but soon her mind was buzzing with anxiety. She'd never been good at idling. At that moment, she decided she would never buy a house this big. It made her feel small.

Since they were renting, and Tilly had a very healthy savings account, she'd decided to sell her old car and buy a new one once they'd arrived in New Mexico. *No time like the present*, she thought, picking up her phone to schedule an Uber.

Three hours later, she was the owner of a brand new Toyota Avalon Hybrid in some sort of amber color that seemed like it would be easy to spot in the sea of silver and white cars she saw cruising the streets. While waiting, she'd called Esperanza House—home of the local SANE program—and set up an appointment to discuss openings. She drove her car to the bank nearest her house, opened up a new bank account, and then headed to the DMV to get a New Mexico license.

By the time she arrived home, she was feeling pretty accomplished. The porch lights were on, and Jim's car was parked in one half of the garage. She pulled in beside him, closed the garage door, and headed inside.

"Welcome home!" Jim said brightly. "Did you get a car?"

"Yep, want to see?"

He followed her to the garage. "What color is that?"

Tilly laughed. "I know. I'm still not sure if I like it, but it's growing on me."

Jim put his arm around her shoulder. "It's not horrible. I can see some potential there."

"Sheesh, it's just a car," Tilly exclaimed, but she was still smiling. "I opened up a bank account and stopped by the DMV."

"You're way ahead of me. I was at the office the whole time."

"How was it?"

"Boring," he said with a grin. "Just paperwork and orientation. But they're already assigning cases."

"Did your clearance come through?"

"Not yet, and I can't take the lead on any cases until it does.

But it will give me a chance to get to know the other attorneys and see how the office runs."

"Sounds pretty ideal," Tilly said. "You seem happy."

"I am happy," he said. "How are you? I know you got a lot done today, but how are you really?" He was smiling, but Tilly could see the worry in his eyes.

Tilly shrugged. "I'm fine, but antsy. Sitting around the house was driving me crazy, so I called the SANE office and I have a meeting tomorrow."

"That's great. Are you sure you're ready to get back to work? You could take a few weeks off while we get settled."

"I know." Tilly tried to keep the irritation out of her voice. She knew Jim's intentions were good, but she'd never wanted to be kept by him. To rely on him for everything. It felt like turning over too much control of her life. "I think getting back to work and doing something productive will help me feel more settled. Until the movers get here, there's not much for me to do. Anyway, it's a recon meeting."

Jim smiled. "Yeah, but you know they're going to want you."

Tilly smiled. It was true. She was a good nurse. A good SANE. And she knew these programs were always under-staffed, so it wasn't likely they'd turn her away. She'd taught classes at the New Mexico advocacy conference every year, so she'd even met several of the nurses from this region. There were a lot of areas where Tilly felt shaky, but work was not one of them. She had confidence in her abilities and was ready to start feeling useful again.

"Do you want to go out for dinner?" Tilly asked, eager to change the subject.

"Can we order in? I'm still tired from the drive and it was a long day in the office." Jim stretched his arms above his head and yawned dramatically. Tilly noticed that he looked pale. "If you don't mind ordering, I think I want to change into shorts."

A few minutes later Tilly went back to the bedroom and

found Jim laying across the bed, snoring softly. He'd managed to get his shoes and jacket off, but otherwise he was still dressed for work.

CHAPTER 5
KATE

Kate shifted uncomfortably in her seat. She was dressed in slacks for the first time in ages and had arrived early for the networking meeting hosted by the Chamber of Commerce. She was surrounded by faces she didn't know, cementing the fact that she'd made no effort to be part of the community. A fact she hoped to rectify starting today.

She hoped the effort wouldn't kill her. She was having to work to keep her nerves in check as she watched several women making the rounds from table to table. She felt very ordinary by comparison, which was mildly comforting.

"Hello there, I'm Mary Beth from Cross Ridge Realty. Is this your first time?" The woman extending her hand to Kate was the textbook definition of a realtor. She had perfect immobile hair, a glossy smile, and gaudy accent jewelry that was perfectly coordinated with her skirt suit and colorful blouse.

"You're right. I'm a newbie. My name's Kate." The women shook hands and, much to Kate's relief Mary Beth flitted to the next table with more exuberant greetings.

"Mind if I join you?" An older woman was standing across from Kate, her hand on the back of the chair, waiting for an invitation to sit. Her gray hair was piled high on her head and each hand showcased huge rings with oversized stones, a look that could only be pulled off stylishly by a woman of her age and class.

"Of course," Kate said with a smile. The woman reminded her of her paternal grandmother, a woman Kate mostly knew through pictures since she'd passed away when Kate was a little girl. "I'm Kate."

"Ruth Flores. So nice to meet you, Kate. Is this your first time joining us?"

"Is it that obvious?" Kate replied nervously.

Ruth smiled. "I'm getting old, but I know a new face when I see one. Though yours is awfully familiar. Is your family local?"

"Yes. My father was Frank Medina. He passed away a few months ago."

Ruth placed a hand to her chest. "Oh my gracious, yes. You're Frank and Addie's daughter."

"You knew my mother?" The stab of pain that Kate got whenever she spoke about her father was replaced by surprise and delight.

"Your father and my late husband worked together at the bank. We used to see Frank and Addie all the time. Your mother was such a lovely woman. I was so sorry to hear of her passing. And your father. . . well, it nearly broke my heart."

Ruth's eyes glistened. Kate tried to picture her face at Frank's funeral, but she felt sure she'd never met Ruth before. And hearing her mother's name was a rare occurrence. True, Frank Medina had been very involved in the community, but despite meeting a lot of his friends and colleagues none of them ever mentioned her mother.

Kate was grateful that the program started shortly thereafter. She needed a few minutes to regain her composure. She'd gotten so used to her dad being the center of her world, it wasn't often that she thought about her mother in context of the town. She sort of separated the two in her mind—Frank, the consummate community member and her mother Addie, a born mother. Despite her misgivings about getting involved, Kate was suddenly very glad she'd come.

———

After the presentation, conversations popped up at each of the tables. Ruth and Kate had been joined by two women from a local bank. For a few minutes, they made small talk.

"So what do you do?" one of the women asked Kate.

"I'm a licensed psychologist. I'm opening up a new practice and I'm hoping to get more involved in the community."

"Oh, you should look into the Health Council," the other woman said. "My husband works for the county counseling center. He's always saying they need new blood." She chuckled. "Actually he said fresh meat, but you get the picture."

Kate laughed, but she instantly disliked the woman. Well, no one said you had to make friends with everyone, she reminded herself. "Is your husband a counselor?"

"No. He's the financial officer. They take turns attending health council meetings, I think. Sounds like it might be right up your alley." She was trying to be helpful, Kate could tell, but it was clear that she had no real interest in Kate's work. Or her husband's by the sound of it.

Luckily, another woman popped over to the table and whisked the two bankers away, leaving Kate and Ruth alone. "They're a little much," Ruth said, smiling conspiratorially at Kate. "But they're nice girls."

It was the sort of thing you'd expect to hear from an older woman, and Kate couldn't help but love the motherly tone Ruth took even though she was talking about colleagues.

"I never asked what you do, Ruth," Kate said.

"Well, I'm mostly retired these days, but I've been involved in this group for so long I couldn't imagine not being here. Before my husband passed, we were both very active in the Chamber and Rotary. A whole group of us—your mother and father included. We did everything together. Oh my, he loved being right in the thick of things and I guess I do too, because here I am."

Kate smiled. "Sounds familiar. I remember attending banquets with my dad when I was younger. It always took forever to say hello to all his friends, and that never changed. I remember the last time I took him out to lunch. Same thing. By the time he got to our table, I had already ordered."

"Why didn't you ever come with him when you moved back? I know he still attended some of those meetings. At least for a while."

"Oh. Well, I wasn't involved in the business world at that point. I worked at the high school."

"That's right. I remember Frank telling me you were working there. He used to joke about the transition from working with criminals to teenagers being an easy one."

Kate nearly snorted. "That sounds like something he would say. Actually it was a pretty low-key job, right up until the end." Kate's voice trailed off.

Ruth reached across the table and patted her hand. "Yes, that terrible business with the young girl who died. Not the kind of thing that usually happens around here."

Kate couldn't help but think how far from the truth that actually was.

CHAPTER 6
TILLY

Tilly pulled into the parking lot and sat for a moment. Esperanza House was located on the hospital campus, and though the area was quiet in front of this particular building she saw lots of people scurrying around the campus. She took a final sip of coffee and headed in.

"May I help you?" the receptionist asked as Tilly approached her station. The woman appeared to be in her fifties, with graying hair braided down her shoulder. She sat behind a plexiglass barrier and had stopped tapping away on her keyboard as soon as Tilly walked in the room. The lobby was small but cozy, with chairs and benches spread about.

A few patients waited. The organization offered counseling and crisis intervention, in addition to sexual assault and domestic assault exams. Two doors, one on either side of the reception area, led to rooms beyond. It was impossible to judge the size of the building from the lobby, but Tilly was happy to see cipher locks on both of those doors.

Security was always an issue in offices like these.

"I'm here to see Marie," Tilly said, stepping forward to sign in on the visitor sheet the receptionist had passed across the counter.

"I'll let her know you're here. Can I get you some water or coffee?"

"No, I'm fine. Thank you."

Tilly sat down on a nearby chair. She didn't have to wait long. The door opened, and a woman with frosted blond hair appeared. "Tilly?"

Tilly hopped up and followed her through the door. "That's me. Thank you for seeing me so quickly."

"My pleasure," Marie said. Her face held lines created by years of working with victims. Years of worry and stress, but Tilly knew there were also smiles and laughter. It was the nature of the job. She opened the door to an office and ushered Tilly inside. Tilly took a seat and looked around the office while Marie got settled.

"What brings you to Las Cruces?" Marie asked, cutting right to the chase.

"Alamogordo is my hometown and my sister lives there, so I wanted to be a little closer. And my boyfriend got a job with the US Attorney's Office." She reached into her bag and passed Marie her résumé. "I've been a nurse practitioner for nearly 20 years, and a forensic nurse for almost that long. I think we might have met at last year's conference."

"I remember you," Marie said. " I attended your class on documentation. It was wonderful. When you called yesterday, I thought I'd won the lottery."

Tilly laughed, her cheeks getting pink. "Well, I don't know about that, but I am definitely interested in joining the team. I'm licensed in New Mexico. Do you have nurses on staff here or are exams done on a contract basis?"

"Both," Marie said. "Right now we're looking for a new clinical coordinator, and having an NP in that position would be amazing. May I ask what your plans are?"

Marie's eyes shone with intensity. Tilly knew that look well. These types of services were largely grant-funded, and supporting victim services was not always high priority for government officials holding the purse strings. She'd done her fair share of lobbying when major bills like the Violence Against Women Act came up for renewal, knowing that those funds would never be enough but that they were absolutely critical nonetheless.

"I'm open," Tilly replied. "What's the position look like?"

"Regular hours for the most part. Chart review, training, work with patients. We do have a pretty solid team of coordinators so you'd be part of that team, but your focus would be on a clinic as a whole not just the SANE side. You'd also be on call rotation, but only one week a month."

"You must have a lot of nurses."

"We're well-staffed at the moment, but you know how that goes," Marie said with a weary smile. "That might change from time to time. Pay isn't great, but you do get a full benefits package through the hospital. Use of the fitness center. Et cetera."

"Sounds perfect. When do I start?"

————

Tilly was impressed by how fast this new program moved. After meeting with Marie, she spent the rest of the morning filling out paperwork with the hospital's HR department. By the time she headed back to the clinic, she had a badge in hand and was cleared to start work immediately. She was happier than she'd been in weeks—full of purpose.

But as she approached the entrance to her new workplace, she heard raised voices inside. For a moment she paused, wondering if she should avoid whatever drama was unraveling or maybe call the police. Before she could decide the door swung open, and a man in a suit stormed out, nearly knocking Tilly down. He reached out and grabbed her arm roughly, steadying her from where she'd been teetering on the edge of the sidewalk.

"Careful," he said gruffly, shifting the blame to Tilly. He released his grip and stalked away, leaving her on the sidewalk rubbing her arm. She watched him drive away, his face tight with anger, before she walked into the lobby of her building.

Inside, Marie was sitting beside a young nurse. Tilly could see wet spots on the young woman's scrubs where her tears had landed.

"What happened?" Tilly asked as she sat.

Marie smiled wearily. "A cheerful visit from our favorite assistant district attorney."

Tilly nodded knowingly. "Let me guess. The ADA wants to press charges. The victim does not."

The young nurse looked up at Tilly, her eyes red-rimmed. "How did you know?"

Tilly smiled kindly. "I've been a SANE for a long time and have had to deal with my share of irritating attorneys and know-it-all law enforcement officers."

"Meg's only been with us for a few months. This was her first case," Marie said. "Trial by fire is the name of the game here. It's unfortunate that she pulled Bross on her first case, but he's heading up that division at the DA's office. He's here a lot."

"What's the story?"

"The victim changed her mind. It was a domestic call. Marital rape. Meg did the exam, but the victim decided not to press charges."

"Nothing new there," Tilly said. "Can't be the first time the ADA has had that happen."

"That's the problem," Meg said with a sniffle. "Apparently the husband is a repeat offender. Bross wants to make sure he stays locked up for a while, but the rape injuries were more severe than the other visible injuries and he can't access our documentation."

"I'm sure that's frustrating," Tilly said. "But it's not your fault, Meg. You did your job. It's not always easy being in this position."

"Yeah, I know," Meg said. She stood, looking at Marie. "I'm going to finish up my reports and head out." She turned her focus to Tilly and smiled. "Thanks."

CHAPTER 7
KATE

Roman got home from his interview beaming. "I got the job. You're going to be sleeping with a special agent in a few months."

Kate laughed. "Lucky me."

"They called APD for a reference. It would appear that my record is clean. Not even a mention of taking me off the case last year. They talked to Gunnison, but he didn't say anything negative."

Kate frowned. "That makes me nervous."

"Me too," Roman agreed. "Then again, I can see how he might want to avoid scrutiny now that I'm out. If he stays calm, then I look like a lunatic by accusing him. At least until we have proof."

"Play the game," Kate muttered. She had always hated politics, but she wasn't naive enough to think that the criminal justice system wasn't brimming with political agendas. For a moment, she fantasized about being a detective in one of the crime fiction novels she'd loved to read—breaking all the rules but living to see another day. Putting the bad guys behind bars over the course of a four-hundred-page book. Life didn't work that way, but she wished that it did. For all their sakes.

She didn't realize Roman had put his arms around her until he was whispering in her ear. "How was *your* day?" Kate took a deep breath, letting her tension go so that she could be present. "It was good, actually. I went to that networking lunch. Met a few women from the bank. Do you know Ruth Flores?"

Roman pulled her around to face him then rested his forehead against hers. Kate wondered what he was thinking. They were having a pretty casual conversation, but he seemed to need the physical contact. She wondered if he'd even heard her. Finally, after a moment he said, "Just in passing. I've heard her name. Her and her husband. And I'm sure I must have met her before. They were very involved in the community. I think he passed away a few years ago."

"She seemed nice. Reminded me of my abuela. Good memories."

"Aw, I miss her," Roman said. "She used to yell at me about my car being noisy. I think she even threw a spatula at me once."

"That's love. And for the record, your car *was* noisy," Kate chuckled. "She was such a wonderful woman." Kate could feel tears building in her eyes. She turned her head up and kissed Roman. "What do you say we take the night off?"

"You sure? I was going to stain the rest of the outer beams."

Kate smiled. "Yeah, I'm sure. It's been a long week. I could use a little bit of down time before business picks up and I have to be away from home all day." She knew Roman would be away too, but she wasn't ready for details so she shoved the thought away.

As if on cue Rusty came bounding out of the yard, his favorite mangled chew toy in his jaws. Roman picked it up, wincing a little at the dog slobber now coating his hand, and stepped to the door so he could throw the toy. "I think Rusty missed me."

"Looks like it," Kate said. They walked back into the atrium so that Rusty could get a little play time in. The scene was so domestic and tranquil, it almost made Kate laugh out loud. Things were moving forward again. Kate could feel a knot of stress in her stomach, but a part of her was relieved. She'd never been good at sitting with her own thoughts and feelings, so having something to do was what she'd been looking for.

———

Everything happened too fast.

Kate put her best foot forward, helping Roman pack up the things he would need for nearly five months of training and field work across the country. She didn't shed a tear, but at night the panic came in waves and then he was gone. She thought she'd have more time to adjust to the idea, but like so many things in Kate's life she had to jump in head first and hope she stayed afloat.

Thankfully, Tilly and Jim were already getting settled in Las Cruces and Tilly was planning on spending the weekends with Kate for a while. When Kate spoke to Tilly, she was nearly bowled over by the intense emotional hurricane her sister seemed to be living in.

"But you're okay?' Kate asked for the hundredth time, knowing she sounded like a broken record.

Tilly sighed dramatically. Kate could picture her face on the other end of the line. She waited for another snow job, but instead Tilly said, "I don't know."

Kate waited.

"I'm glad I'll be going back to work right away, because settling into the new house is making me jumpy and irritable. I can see Jim tiptoeing around me and that makes me even angrier."

"What's he doing that's upsetting you?" Kate asked.

"That's just it," Tilly replied, and Kate could hear the weariness in her voice. "Nothing. He's his usual cheerful self. We've both been tired from the move. He was asleep last night before I came to bed. It's me, Kate. I swear, there's something wrong with me. Maybe I'm not programmed right for domestic happiness."

Kate laughed, but she sympathized. Despite coming from a seemingly happy home, both sisters had had trouble with relationships as adults. Roman was Kate's first long-term relationship, and Tilly had barely made time for dating until she met Jim. From what Tilly had said the relationship was a product of Jim's persistence, though anyone could see they loved each other.

"We'll talk about it more when you get here tomorrow. You sure you're up for being here in town?"

"Well, it wouldn't be my first choice, but it can't be much worse than puttering around the house. The movers came, but now it's a maze of boxes and I don't have it in me to tackle them yet."

"Not exactly a ringing endorsement, but I get it. Do you want me to come help you unpack?"

"Nah, let's binge on *Forensic Files* and eat a lot of Mexican food. I'll see you bright and early."

Kate could tell that Tilly was trying, but there was so much underlying pain and fear behind her words. Kate wondered if this move was going to be the first step in Tilly's undoing. She tried to distract herself with thoughts of her sister, but as soon as Kate started turning out lights and getting ready for bed her anxiety picked up.

Despite having no close neighbors, the desert surrounding her home was not a quiet place. Coyotes howled in the distance. The breeze rattled against the window screens, and the leaves of creosote and mesquite bushes scratched at the adobe walls. Beams of light from the occasional passing car, and sometimes smaller points like flashlights, pierced the night. In the dark, shadows moved across the walls and ceilings of Kate's bedroom reminding her that while she was isolated, she was not alone.

CHAPTER 8
TILLY

Tilly's first few days in the office were relatively quiet. She was accustomed to shared spaces, so finding out that she'd have her own small office was like a dream come true. By the end of the week, she'd read through so many case files her eyes were beginning to glaze over.

There weren't many surprises, which was depressing. Sexual assault, domestic violence, child abuse—these crimes happened everywhere and the stories were sadly familiar. On paper the stories started to blur together, painting an unflattering picture of humanity. Tilly was looking forward to working directly with patients and the nurses in the clinic. Having that personal contact helped Tilly stay grounded. She never wanted to be one of those people who became desensitized by all the violence. Instead she worked on achieving a proper balance, compartmentalizing when necessary but allowing herself to feel all the emotions that went with the job.

"Knock, knock!"

Tilly looked up and found an unfamiliar face at her office door. "Can I help you?"

"I wanted to stop by and welcome you onboard. I'm Brynn Hartford." Tilly stood to shake hands.

"You're the clinic psychologist?"

"Social worker actually, but I specialize in trauma counseling. I'm only here a few days a week so when I saw your door was open I figured I'd pop by and introduce myself. How're you settling in? Marie told me a little bit about your background. I'm excited you're on the team."

Tilly smiled. "Thank you. I'm glad you stopped by. I've been reading files and I'm going cross-eyed. I need a break."

"I have an hour before my next appointment. Would you like to grab some coffee from the cafeteria? It's actually pretty decent."

"Absolutely," Tilly said. She grabbed her bag and followed Brynn, closing the door behind her.

The women made small talk as they walked to the hospital, mostly about Tilly's move and what brought her to Las Cruces. Brynn listened attentively but didn't add much to the conversation until they took a seat with their beverages.

"So, your sister is the psychologist who was involved in that case in Alamogordo last fall?"

Tilly sat up straighter. "You heard about that?"

Brynn smiled sheepishly. "When you started talking about Kate, I realized I've heard about you before. Don't panic," she said. Tilly's discomfort must have been obvious. "I spend enough time with law enforcement that I hear stories and Alamogordo is not that far away. There's a lot of cross-talk. I believe that you met my friend Angie Lopez last fall? She's with the State Police."

Tilly began to relax. "Yes, I did. How is she, by the way? I haven't heard anything about her for a while."

"She's doing well. I heard your sister was consulting for the department for a while."

Tilly wasn't sure how much Brynn knew about Angie's

relationship with Roman, or Kate's role in their lack of relationship, and she didn't want to be the one to bring it up. "She was. Now, Kate is opening up a private practice in Alamogordo."

"That's great. Angie described her as tenacious. Probably just what that town needs."

"Not a fan?" Tilly asked.

Brynn laughed. "It's fine. Just a little off the beaten path. I always feel like I've gone back in time when I visit."

"I know the feeling," Tilly said with a sigh. "I'm heading over again this weekend. My sister's boy...er, friend, is out of town for a while so I'm keeping her company."

"I heard. FBI training?"

Tilly raised her eyebrows. "Angie's keeping tabs?"

"Listen," Brynn said, her expression serious. "Angie is one of my best friends. I've known Roman forever. I'm aware of everything that went down last fall, at least from Angie's perspective, but I'm not interested in interfering or taking sides. I was being honest when I said how thrilled I am that you're working here now, and I wanted to be the one to tell you about our mutual connections because it's important to me that we build trust. I'll be working with a lot of the victims you see and I want us to have a strong relationship. Our previous clinical coordinator never warmed up to me and I'm hoping we can start off on a good foot."

Tilly studied her colleague for a moment. "Fair enough. It's a small world after all. We'd better get back to the clinic."

Brynn gave Tilly an overview of her work and process as they headed back to the office. As she listened, Tilly made a mental note to keep details about her sister's life to herself.

———

"Roman's doing well, then?" Tilly asked as Kate flitted around the kitchen, maniacally making lunch. Tilly could feel the anxiety emanating from her.

"Like a kid in a candy store," Kate answered with a laugh that sounded a little strained. Tilly got up from where she was sitting and put her hand on Kate's arm.

"Stop right there," she said, pulling Kate over to the bar and forcibly sitting her on a stool. "I'm glad Roman is living his dream, but let's not wait too long to address the obvious."

Kate sighed. "I feel like I'm running on adrenaline. More likely caffeine. I haven't been sleeping well, so I may have over-compensated this morning."

Tilly sat down next to Kate and leaned back on the counter. "Understandable. You and Roman have been attached at the hip for months. Anyone would come a little unglued."

"I know. But I'm also so damned mad at myself for acting this way. I lived alone my whole adult life. Now I'm a total basket case and he's only been gone a little over a week."

"Man, I hope you don't hold me to those lofty expectations. It's okay to be human, Kate. You're not doing it wrong. You can give yourself a minute to feel annoyed that Roman is so far away or lonely or whatever it is that's happening in there." Tilly gestured to Kate's gut. "Isn't that what you told me when I was freaking out about Jim? And now look at us."

Kate laughed. "Yeah, you two were alarmingly adorable last weekend. I'm surprised he let you out of the house this weekend."

"Sister sleepovers are non-negotiable," Tilly said. "Besides, they threw him right into the middle of a big case so he's working this weekend."

"Poor guy," Kate murmured, but Tilly could see that her mind was drifting.

"Have you gotten any new clients?" Tilly asked.

Kate's eyes brightened. "I have. Just two for now, but I've only been open for a few weeks so it's a good start."

"Anything interesting?" Tilly asked.

"You know I'm not going to tell you about them," Kate said, then added, "But no, nothing out of the ordinary. I have mixed feelings. I'm a little disappointed that my office isn't flooded with trauma-survivors, and also thankful that I get to ease my way into this." Kate reached over and plucked a cucumber slice off the veggie tray she'd been working on. "I'm not sure how I'd handle it all right now anyway, given that I'm going all psycho." She popped the cucumber into her mouth.

Tilly slid the tray closer to them. "It'll happen when it happens. Word of your exploits have been heard as far away as my new office in Las Cruces, so I'm sure you have a bit of a reputation here in town."

"My exploits?" Kate said with a chuckle. "You sound like one of those books we used to read til they fell apart." Tilly and Kate had traded crime fiction novels back and forth, immersing themselves in the latest Christopher Pike or R.L. Stine thriller in middle school and moving on to John Grisham and Patricia Cornwell mysteries. It wasn't a surprise that both sisters had gone into criminal justice in some capacity.

"My colleague Brynn is a friend of Angie's." Tilly hadn't been sure she wanted to broach the topic with Kate, but she still felt a little strange about how that information had come out. "I guess Angie told her about the Gabby Greene case and every-thing that happened last fall."

"Everything?"

"I don't know," Tilly said with a sigh. "I didn't ask. For what it's worth, she seemed genuinely interested in your work and not the least bit catty. She also wanted me to know about her connection with Angie so it wouldn't interfere in our working together."

"Well, that's something," Kate said. "I hate the idea that they're talking about me, but I suppose I deserve it."

"Hey," Tilly said, giving Kate's arm a squeeze. "She'll be okay. And you're right about one thing, Kate. You deserve to be happy and so does Roman. Things are exactly as they should be." Kate smiled, but Tilly could see that she didn't believe her.

CHAPTER 9
KATE

After Tilly's visit, Kate calmed down a bit. She returned to work on Monday determined not to let Roman's absence or her paranoia occupy too much space in her day. Unfortunately she didn't have enough clients yet to fill the time, so her mind kept drifting. She worked all morning at organizing her filing system and administrative work, and had decided to call it a day when there was a knock at the outer office door.

"Sorry, that wasn't supposed to be locked," she said as she opened the door to a middle-aged woman in jeans and a graphic t-shirt. She looked vaguely familiar. "How can I help you?" She led the way into her waiting area, taking a seat in one of the chairs and gesturing for the woman to do the same.

"I'm Delia Cordova. Is it okay that I dropped by?"

Kate smiled. "It's fine. There will be a sign on my office door if I'm in session, but otherwise my office is open. What can I do for you, Delia?"

"You do counseling, right?" Delia asked, fidgeting in her seat.

"That's correct. I'm a licensed psychologist. Do you want to set up an appointment with me?"

"Yes. Actually, I'm on my lunch break right now. Is this a good time? I work at the high school."

"Of course. In fact, I don't have any appointments this afternoon. Would you like to start today? We can at least work through intake."

Delia nodded, and Kate directed her toward her office. She walked behind her desk and reached for a clipboard on the shelf behind her. She handed the board to Delia, along with a pen. "I'll need you to fill this out, but before you get started can you tell me a bit about what you're wanting to work on with me?"

"Well," Delia started, then paused. "I'm having some trouble sleeping."

Kate waited, but when it was clear that Delia wasn't going to say anything more Kate dove in. "Tell me about that. Trouble sleeping can have a variety of causes, some of them medical. Let's determine whether I'm the right person to help you or if you need to see a doctor."

"Oh, I've seen the doctor. She gave me some sleeping pills, but I don't like to take them. They make me too groggy and I have to be at work early. Anyway, the real problem is that my mind won't slow down at night."

"What are you thinking about when you're trying to fall asleep?"

"Everything. Anything. I've tried drinking tea, taking melatonin, meditation—sometimes I'm able to fall asleep but . . . I have nightmares."

"Nightmares? Do you remember them when you wake up?"

"Always. And then I can't get back to sleep. Sometimes I feel like I can't breathe."

"You may be having panic attacks," Kate said, picturing her own middle-of-the-night struggles. Her first night alone she had a bad attack—the worst she could remember. It took a lot to get back to sleep, and she was annoyed that she'd become so reliant on Roman's presence to help ease her panic. "Can you tell me a little bit about the nightmares? Do you know what's causing them?"

Delia tugged at a stray piece of hair that had fallen into her face. "Yes, ma'am. I've had them since I was a teenager."

"Did something happen to you when you were a teenager?" Kate braced for what she knew was coming.

"Yes. I was raped."

———

After Delia left her office, Kate locked the door and headed home. She'd worked with many trauma victims in the prison system, but wasn't accustomed anymore to the exhaustion that followed a trauma disclosure. Delia's story had fanned a spark of anxiety in Kate. Not that the woman had divulged many details. Before they could dive deep into Delia's issues, Kate had her work on the intake paperwork and then set up an appointment for the following week. She needed time to read over Delia's notes and formulate a plan.

Rusty met her at the gate, tail wagging furiously.

"How did it go?" she asked him, squatting down to give him some love. Rusty seemed to be handling Roman's absence better than Kate. Of course, she suspected that he was just as eager for Roman's return. Either way, the days spent alone didn't seem to be fazing him much. He was always happy to see Kate, but after the initial burst of energy wore off he mellowed out and found a place to curl up.

Kate made her way into the house with Rusty at her heels. She filled up his bowl with kibble and freshened his water. Luckily the hacienda had a nice big courtyard, so Kate didn't have to coop him up in the house during the day. Most evenings, Kate and Roman retired to the patio after dinner. For the first few nights Kate had avoided that routine, sure it would make her miss Roman more. But Tilly had convinced her she needed to quit living like a widow and resume her normal activities. After all, Roman wasn't dead.

She made an early dinner and then took her laptop and notebook out to her favorite lounge chair. She'd been meaning to sift through articles on the legalities of safe houses, but her mind kept drifting back to Delia. The woman was in her late thirties, and she was an Alamogordo native. Kate hadn't wanted to open Pandora's box until their first official session, but she was pretty sure that Delia's story would sound much like Tilly's. Or maybe not. She had to remind herself that not every case of sexual assault would be linked to the trafficking ring.

She was waiting for her evening call with Roman, hoping to bounce some ideas off of him. Things were starting to happen, and the fact that she was alone weighed heavily. She may have been agonizing over her lack of progress in uncovering the trafficking ring for months, but if Delia's visit was the first step in finding answers she wasn't sure she was ready. She was mulling this over when her phone rang.

"Hey babe," Roman said when she answered. He was out of breath.

"Calling me from the treadmill?" she asked, knowing that Roman hit the gym immediately after his training ended for the day. He was on the east coast, but it was still pretty early for a call.

"No. Sorry, I ran up the stairs to my apartment. Give me a second."

Kate laughed. "You didn't have to call me the instant you got home."

"What, are you complaining?" Roman teased, but she could hear something strained in his tone.

"Is everything all right?"

"Yeah," he said with a long sigh. "I just miss you."

Kate felt an achy pang in her chest. "Me too." She felt her eyes growing misty and decided to head her tears off at the pass. "How was your day?" Usually this question resulted in an hour of Roman telling her, in intricate detail, about his schedule —starting from the moment he woke up. Some days Kate found it endearing. Some days she wanted to hang up on him after the first ten minutes. Her emotions were all over the place.

But this time, the question was met with silence.

"Roman?" Kate was beginning to worry.

"I'm here," he said. Kate waited another beat. "It was a long day. We're starting to get past the basics and get into the realities of FBI work. It's a big adjustment after working at APD."

"You need some rest," Kate said. "You've been hitting it hard since you got there. Why don't we keep this call short so you can get some sleep."

The silence that followed had Kate's heart hammering in her chest.

"Yeah, okay. I'll talk to you tomorrow," he said. The sadness in his voice made Kate pause.

"Unless you want to talk?"

"No, it's all right. You're probably right. I need some down time. I love you."

"Love you, too," Kate said. Roman disconnected the call immediately. The click was like a shot to her heart.

CHAPTER 10
TILLY

Tilly wasn't looking for a fight. At least she didn't feel like she'd been trying to start one, but it was pretty clear that Jim saw things differently.

"So let's talk about it," Jim said, his face red with frustration. "Obviously, something happened today. We agreed we wouldn't keep secrets from one another, remember?"

"That doesn't mean I have to tell you every single thing about me or my day."

"True," he said calmly. "But when you bite my head off the minute I walk in the door, I think I'm at least entitled to know why I'm being attacked."

Tilly gritted her teeth. "I didn't attack you. I just asked why you were home so late tonight. We had plans." True, Jim had texted her earlier and told her he'd be late. True, she'd told him it was fine. But that was before Daniel Bross walked into the clinic. He wasn't even her problem, but she was still fuming when she arrived home and Jim was an easy target.

It wasn't fair.

And the fact that she'd had two shots of whiskey before he walked in the door wasn't helping her be reasonable.

"Don't," Jim said, holding up a hand. "We've already been around in circles over this. I absolutely understand that you're upset about dinner tonight, but the way you're acting right now is completely out of proportion with the crime."

Tilly snorted. "Don't be so dramatic, Mr. US Attorney. No crime has been committed, sir. But I'm not happy about being so low on your priority list these days."

Jim flinched.

Since the move, both Tilly and Jim had been adjusting to new jobs. New schedules. New responsibilities. And Tilly had spent every weekend in Alamogordo with Kate. Tilly knew she was being mean. She couldn't even pinpoint why she'd lost her cool so thoroughly. She was used to dealing with the bad attitudes and behavior of law enforcement and the other professionals she crossed paths with in her job. Bross's comments hadn't even been aimed at her, but she'd felt them like a direct hit to her gut.

The ADA was still raising hell about his case and Tilly had intervened, not because it was any of her business but because she knew how it felt to be low-man on the totem pole. Meg, the SANE nurse she'd met on her first day, was young, naive, and not likely to stick around if the abuse continued. Tilly hated to see a good nurse beaten down that way, especially when they were all supposed to be on the same team. Unlike any previous experiences she'd had Bross had backed down quickly, which left Tilly feeling even more rattled.

"Come on, Tilly. Please tell me what happened." Jim's voice had grown quiet and she could see from his expression that he'd cooled down enough to give up the fight. Most of the time, Jim's calm nature was comforting to Tilly. Today, it made the ground she stood on feel shaky.

"I'll be back." Tilly slung her purse over her shoulder and opened the front door.

"Tilly, wait," Jim said, but she closed the door without looking back.

———

A group of cowboys sat at a corner table, laughing louder with every round they ordered. Tilly made her way to the opposite end of the bar, careful to avoid eye contact, but the catcalls came anyway. She'd been buzzing with angry energy all the way over and now she clenched her fists, holding back a completely reckless urge to get into a fight.

Of course, once she'd taken a seat at the bar and ordered a drink, Tilly felt foolish. She'd been ignoring the mounting anxiety she felt by throwing herself into work and telling herself she had to be strong for Kate. Normally, she was good at keeping her emotions in check. It had been a while since she let them boil over, and she felt bad for being mean to Jim.

It wasn't his fault.

Since crossing the state line, she'd felt the threads of her life —the ones that kept her tethered to who she was now, the life she'd made for herself—unravel one by one. For nearly two decades, she'd convinced herself that she was okay. That she'd put the past behind her.

There had been little hints at unrest over the years. When her mother died and she'd decided not to go home for the funeral. And every single time she saw her father and sister after. Those visits never went smoothly, and she always felt a little out of control right after. Usually she worked harder, took more calls, fought harder for those around her. Allowing her own trauma to fade to the background.

"Another?" The bartender was smiling at her, making her wonder how long he'd been standing there while she spaced out.

Despite feeling a little off-kilter, Tilly smiled back and

nodded. "I think I can handle one more." The bartender thunked another shot glass next to the first and filled it. "Enjoy."

As she raised the glass to her lips, she felt the brush of fabric against her arm as someone sat on the stool beside her. She wasn't sure why she expected it to be Jim, but she was startled when she saw who had taken the seat.

"Modelo, please." The man was dressed in jeans and a t-shirt —a far cry from the suit he'd been wearing the last time she saw him. Her stomach soured.

"Hello, Mr. Bross." She gave him what she hoped was a glare, but her face felt too relaxed from the alcohol to know how effective it might have been.

He looked at her, his expression neutral, and for a moment she wondered if he even recognized her. They hadn't been formally introduced, even when she'd lashed out at him earlier that day.

"I'm sorry about the way I acted this afternoon," he said. Tilly had steeled herself for an argument, so his apology caught her completely off guard. "This case is getting to me. I shouldn't have taken my frustration out on Megan."

"No, you shouldn't have." Tilly's anger had cooled a bit, but she was in no rush to let him off the hook. The pained look on his face finally pierced the wall of anger Tilly had been hiding behind all evening.

"You're absolutely right. I'm Dan, by the way." He'd left the path clear for her to introduce herself, but turned back to his beer.

"I'm Tilly Medina, the new clinical coordinator at Mesa."

He looked over at her again, his expression unreadable. "I'm sorry to have made such a terrible first impression."

"It was a second impression, actually," Tilly said. Then, seeing the quizzical look on his face, she added, "You nearly threw me off the curb my first day on the job. After making Meg cry." For a split second she felt vindication, but the feeling faded fast. Here he was apologizing, and she was determined to make him feel small. Apparently, Jim wasn't going to be the only recipient of Tilly's hostility.

He thought for a moment, then frowned. "Right," he said, exhaling. He finished his drink, put a twenty on the bar, and said, "Thanks, John." The bartender nodded. "Have a good evening, Ms. Medina."

As he walked away, Tilly's face burned with shame.

CHAPTER 11
KATE

"You and Jim made up, right?"

Tilly had just finished filling Kate in on her night, and Kate was worried. She'd expected the move to be hard on Tilly, but the thought of her sister storming out to a bar on the heels of an argument was troubling. Kate had thrown out several wine bottles they'd polished off over the weekend.

"Yes. Jim never stays mad at me for long, and I did apologize. I don't know what's wrong with me."

"Yes, you do," Kate said gently. She'd already suggested that Tilly seek some help during this transition, and she didn't want to push. Especially given how long it had taken her to address her own issues. She waited uneasily through the silence that followed.

Tilly laughed. "You're right, I do. Self-awareness is half the battle, eh? I'll be fine. Enough about me. How're you?"

Kate was seated in her office with about a half-hour til her first official session with Delia Cordova. She was feeling nervous, which was not a feeling she was used to in her work. It was the one place she usually felt completely confident. But this appointment felt like a beginning, and Kate knew she was making too much of it. She needed to calm down and remember her priorities.

"I'm good. I have a new client coming in at noon."

"That's great. I'm glad people are coming in."

Kate picked up on Tilly's implication.

"I know. Me, too." When she'd decided to open her practice, Kate knew there was a distinct possibility that her reputation with the powers that be would make it impossible to do business. It had been so easy to assume that everyone in town was part of the problem, but she was relieved to be proven wrong. "Slow but steady. I have appointments every day this week, and another lunch with that women's group."

"Better you than me," Tilly said with a chuckle. "I'd be bored to tears. Give me a multidisciplinary team with adversarial police officers any day."

"I didn't think I'd like it," Kate said. "But the women are nice, and it's a good chance to get my name out there without having to run into anyone I'm not ready to see." Kate knew at least a handful of businessmen who were involved in trafficking teenage girls in town. She wasn't sure she'd be able to hold her tongue if she ran into any of them. "Anyway, I'd better let you go so I can get ready for my client."

"I'll see you this weekend," Tilly said before disconnecting.

Kate sat back, thinking about her sister. Tilly had been dealing with hard-to-handle attorneys her whole career. It was hard to picture Tilly losing her cool with one this early in the game. Granted, Kate and Tilly's relationship have been strained for a long time, so it was only recently that Kate started hearing the details of Tilly's professional life. Maybe this was something that happened all the time. And then there was the fight with Jim.

Something was up with her sister, and Kate wished she had more time to figure it out but she turned her attention to her client.

Delia appeared at Kate's door right on time.

———

Delia shifted awkwardly in her seat as Kate situated herself in her chair. The call with Tilly had thrown her off, and so she was a little bit disorganized. And while she hated to make her client anxious, it was always interesting to see how they handled the quiet.

"Thank you for seeing me," Delia whispered.

"Thank you for choosing me," Kate said, hoping to instill a sense of agency in her very timid client. Though she was around Kate's age Delia's face was care-worn, giving her a much older feel. It was the look of a person who'd seen more than their fair share of sorrow.

Tilly had that look. Kate probably did too.

"Can you tell me a little bit more about the concerns that brought you to me?"

Kate waited while Delia gathered her thoughts.

"Like I said, I've been having trouble sleeping. My mind won't quiet down, and then I wake up feeling so groggy."

"Have you talked to your primary care physician to rule out a sleep disorder?"

Delia nodded. "He did one of those test thingies where you sleep with that, um, that tube up your nose."

"No sleep apnea?"

"Nothing. He recommended taking melatonin, and that helps a little with falling asleep, but then I wake up over and over. The sleeping pills were worse. I'd fall asleep, but then I'd get stuck in my nightmares. Like I couldn't wake up."

"Okay, let's go back to the time before you fall asleep. Is there a particular thought keeping you awake?"

Delia's face turned ashen.

"A memory."

"Of being raped?"

"Yes." Delia was so still and quiet, it took everything in Kate's power to wait her out rather than trying to fill the gap. Finally, Delia let out a soft sigh.

"When I was in high school, I was raped by multiple men." Delia paused, as if every word cost her something and she wanted to make sure she chose them carefully. "I've been able to put it behind me, mostly. I'm not sure why these memories are showing up now."

"You mentioned that your niece is in high school. Are you two close?"

"Yes. Very." Delia's face wilted. "We have been."

"Did something happen?"

"I don't know. Maybe." Delia cast nervous glances over her shoulder but didn't continue. The hairs on the back of Kate's neck stood on end, but she wasn't here to investigate anything other than Delia's troubles.

"Is your niece about the same age as you were when the assaults happened?"

"Yes."

"It's very common for trauma victims to begin to have flashbacks and painful memories when loved ones reach a comparable age. Parents often experience this with their children, and since you and your niece have a close relationship it's not unusual for you to be having the same sort of reaction. Especially since you work around kids that age."

The look of relief on Delia's face was transformative, lifting years away from her features. "Thank God," she said, and Kate's desire to ask about Delia's niece almost pushed her to cross a line. She waited for Delia to say more, but the conversation that followed was mostly superficial. Under normal circumstances Kate would value this time as a crucial part of building rapport, but her mind reeled from the possibilities. She'd never found it this difficult to keep her mind on her job.

Kate finished her session with Delia, scheduling her for another to work on anxiety-reducing techniques. After closing the office door Kate retreated to her desk, sinking into the cushion while resting her face in her hands.

She'd been wound so tightly during the session. At the mention of Delia's niece, Kate's blood pressure spiked. Delia hadn't been specific about her own assaults, but her story paralleled those of other trafficking victims. Was it possible to find a link to the case this quickly?

The moment that thought formed, real anxiety began to set in. Her stomach roiled. Had Delia come to set her up? Or worse, was the abuse so rampant that nearly everyone had a tie to it?

It was hard to decide what was more likely when all paths led to something awful, and Kate fought to calm her panic. She'd only been in practice for a few weeks, and already she was struggling to keep herself rooted in patient care.

Over the past few months, she'd fooled herself into thinking that because she couldn't see the abuse happening, things were quiet. That somehow the abuse had been paused. She knew that was a lie. A delusion. People knew where to find her. She was being watched. Was Delia really looking for help?

Kate felt like there were very few people she could trust. She couldn't allow herself to suspect her clients, but she would have to be careful—hiding behind her professionalism while she tried to make sense of everything.

CHAPTER 12
TILLY

Tilly's first case was a doozy. Yvette Delgado, a Mexican national working in Las Cruces, had been raped after having drinks with her coworkers. The group had been together at the door of the restaurant when the victim had returned to use the restroom before driving home to Ciudad Juarez.

She'd been approached at her car, held at knifepoint, and assaulted.

The exam itself had been easy. Yvette was collected, despite being tearful. She was able to recount every detail of the incident clearly and there were very few injuries to record, making the exam go quickly.

The assailant had not worn a condom, and Tilly was sure that the DNA evidence would be plentiful.

As a Mexican citizen assaulted on United States soil, the jurisdictional implications were new to Tilly. Though she supposed it wasn't impossible to have victims who were non-citizens elsewhere, the chances here near the border increased exponentially. She made a note to learn about victim services for non-residents.

The hardest part of the exam, as was often the case, had

more to do with the investigating officers than it did with the crime or the victim.

Sexual assault calls usually went directly to a detective but in this case, the first responder was a seasoned veteran who should have known better and still proceeded to harass the victim. It wasn't the first time Tilly had seen police officers unable to keep their biases to themselves. When Yvette handed the officer her work visa, any semblance of compassion had walked right out the door.

Luckily, after the initial shock had worn off, Yvette had regained her composure enough to give a detailed version of events, including the officer's behavior. Tilly was pretty sure she would be reporting him to his superior and she hoped that his reprimand included some sensitivity training.

Tilly had been called in to work the case around 8 o'clock the previous evening, but she was still in the office at six the next morning. Detective Gardner, who'd been assigned to the case, had asked that the victim stay in the country until they had a chance to brief the DA's office. Given the way Yvette had been treated, Tilly wasn't going to leave until she was sure the woman was safely on her way home.

Tilly groaned when ADA Bross walked into the clinic.

"Good morning, Ms. Medina," he said as he entered, his expression completely unreadable.

"Morning," Tilly replied, trying not to give anything away. She was still a little rattled from their brief but confusing encounter at the bar a few nights ago and she didn't quite know how to treat him. "You're here for last night's case?"

"Yes. Is the victim still here?"

"She is. Let me go get Detective Gardner."

Once Tilly had delivered Bross to Gardner, she returned to the exam room where Yvette was sitting, sipping a cup of coffee.The shadows under her eyes were so dark it looked like she might've been punched, but Tilly knew she hadn't.

"The ADA is here, so it shouldn't be much longer. How're you holding up?"

"I'm okay," the woman said, inhaling deeply. "I'm ready to go home, take a shower, and sleep. I'm calling in sick the rest of the week."

"Good plan," Tilly said. "Make sure to call the advocate if you need anything. We have some great counselors here on staff, and also available via televisit. Sometimes it takes a few days to process what's happened, and then you might need someone to talk to."

"Thank you," Yvette said. "You've been so helpful. I can't believe this is what you do for a living. It must be so depressing."

Tilly smiled. "It can be. But it also feels good to know that I can help someone like you. I know how it feels."

The woman looked up at Tilly. "I have three sisters, and they've also been raped at some point. One by a boyfriend. One by a man who knew our parents. And the youngest at a school party. My family is no stranger to pain."

Tilly's heart clenched tight at this admission. Yvette's words were flat, as if the inevitable had happened and she wasn't the least bit surprised. Tilly tried to imagine living your life knowing that someday you'd be attacked. Knowing it as a certainty.

It took her back to her own past, though the repeated assaults she'd endured had been organized and part of something that Tilly had been unable to stop.

Was it really any different?

Sure, this woman's attacker had been a stranger and the assault had been a random bit of back luck. Wrong place at the wrong time. She hadn't been stalked, groomed, and then subjected to repeated torture. But still, Tilly wondered if there had been some relief at seeing your worst fears manifested.

For Tilly, once she understood that there was no way out,

the anticipation leading up to her assaults had been worse than the actual acts themselves. Some of the men had been kind to her. She knew what they were doing to her was absolutely vile, but in a way she'd appreciated the ones who treated her humanely.

She wondered if Yvette would now be able to move on with her life. She would never forget, but she'd discover that she could live through it and thrive. Maybe having her sisters as role models would speed up the process.

Tilly hoped so.

CHAPTER 13
KATE

Kate lay on her side, staring at the empty space in her bed. It had been almost three weeks since Roman left for training, and she felt his absence so profoundly she wondered how she was going to make it through the next four months. Rusty snored in his bed beside her, the only comfort she had on these lonely nights.

She was thankful she'd moved out of her father's house and into the hacienda. Its sturdy brick walls made her feel safe. She'd finally gotten used to all the desert sounds. It was still early autumn, but the summer heat hadn't completely gone away. Kate slept with the windows open.

The master bedroom was on the first floor, which might have been a source of stress for Kate; she still remembered the flaming mass thrown through her window in the fall, but the builder had outfitted all the windows with decorative wrought iron bars. Tilly said it reminded her of a prison, but Kate loved that no one could access her without a lot of effort. Between those bars and the desert foliage surrounding the house, it was more like a fortress. The security cameras she and Roman had installed around the property didn't hurt either.

She wasn't anxious about being alone, not like she'd been at the beginning. Rather, what had her on edge increasingly at night was how much she'd come to rely on Roman's presence. At first she'd fought against those feelings, reminding herself that she and Roman had a solid, healthy relationship and it was normal to miss him when he was gone.

But as the days passed, her longing had formed hard edges. In the past year, she'd had to face a lot of truths about herself and the decisions she'd made in her adult life, pushing people away and using her career as a barrier between herself and the people who cared for her. Her reasons for moving home had been largely selfish, and though she'd cared for her father until his death, she knew that what had kept her in her hometown hadn't been her father. It was fear.

Despite living alone her whole adult life—an independent and self-sufficient professional—she'd allowed a trauma to send her running home. True, she was hurt—both physically and psychologically—but she'd refused to deal with her trauma head-on. Even though it was her choice, she'd resented returning home to live with her father. She'd allowed her attacker to change the course of her life; something she'd often counseled clients to rally against. Hiding behind the walls of her childhood home had provided both a refuge and an excuse to ignore her own hypocrisy.

Then, she reconnected with Roman.

She'd fallen in love. She'd rediscovered her purpose. She'd gotten her fight back.

But old habits are hard to break, and she was having a hard time separating her own growth from Roman's place in her life. She worried that Roman was the only thing holding her together and that her current anxious state was a sign of dependence.

The feeling was eating her alive, keeping her awake at night

when she should be resting. Tying her stomach in knots whenever she had a few minutes to consider her situation.

It had to stop, but she wasn't sure how to make that happen.
At first, the anger she felt at being left alone fortified her. She
even flirted with the idea of a clean break, using Roman's
absence to justify going back to her old habit of avoidance and
isolation. She'd made the mistake of voicing that idea out loud
to Tilly. Thankfully her sister wouldn't hear of it, refusing to
relent until Kate acknowledged her self-sabotage and promised
to work on it.

Unfortunately, at night, Kate was alone with her thoughts,
and her sounding board was nearly two-thousand miles away
and feeling more distant every day.

———

By the light of day, Kate felt ridiculous for her nighttime
worries. She got ready for work and then took Rusty out for a
walk in the desert. It was still cool, but she kept a sharp eye out
for snakes just in case. As kids, she and Tilly had gone walking
in the desert and had run across their fair share of rattlesnakes.
She remembered the thrill, but as an adult she recognized the
danger.

As they came back around toward her house, Kate noticed a
trail of dust in the distance. The properties north of her house
were surrounded by rows of pecan or pistachio trees. Or they
were fenced-off horse ranches. South of her house was nothing
but desert for miles, with a deep arroyo snaking its way across
the valley and up to the foot of the mountains. Kate often spied
trucks and other farm vehicles driving amid the trees as the
workers tended their land, but vehicles on the road to her
house were infrequent. Especially one moving fast enough to
kick up that much dust.

She'd taken Rusty off-road, so she was quite sure that she wouldn't be noticed, but when the dust cloud subsided near her house she instinctively crouched, ducking behind creosote bushes as she crept closer. Rusty's tail slowed its wag as he picked up on Kate's tension. An old beat-up pickup truck was parked about 20 feet away from her front gate. Its owner, a lanky man dressed in dirty jeans, a tattered t-shirt and a baseball cap, was running his hands along the wrought-iron of her front gate.

Rusty caught sight of their visitor and let out a series of ear-splitting barks, intended to run off the intruder. And it worked. Kate hadn't yet emerged from her cover, but Rusty's warning got the man moving. He sprinted to his truck and backed away at top speed, raising another huge cloud of dust as he retreated down the road. By the time the dust cleared, the truck was gone.

Nevertheless, Kate approached with caution. Rusty stuck close to her side, but she let him have a longer lead on his leash when they reached the front door. He sniffed around, but soon his tail was wagging again. Kate took that as a sign that it was safe enough to go inside. As soon as she was clear of the door, she shut the gate and locked herself in tightly. She still had some time before she had to go into town, and she wanted to examine her camera footage.

The man's face would have been clearly visible on camera, except that he'd pulled a bandana up over his nose.

She studied his face, but couldn't discern any distinguishing features. He may not have known where the cameras were, but he'd been prepared for their existence.

Good, Kate thought. *At least they know I'm watching them, too.* The experience should have frightened her, but instead she felt exhilarated. She knew they'd eventually come looking for her and now they had. She thought about the nights she'd seen lights dancing in the desert and wondered how long they'd been out there.

It was aggravating thinking of her enemies as a nameless "they" but a chain of events had been set in motion the moment Kate decided to stay and fight the abuse she'd seen. Now, the pieces were in play. It was her turn to make a move.

CHAPTER 14
TILLY

"The US Attorney's office is handling the prosecution," ADA Bross said to the group. Tilly was attending her first multi-disciplinary meeting. "But we're pretty sure this offender is the same one who grabbed that girl outside of the Village Inn a few months ago. Same MO. Same basic description. Hopefully we'll be able to hand that case over as well."

Tilly watched Bross as he spoke. His whole demeanor was an impenetrable wall. His expression gave nothing away, and he seemed almost formal in the way that he presented his department update. The only things that belied another side to his story were his eyes. There was fire there, and sadness.

"Tilly?" Marie whispered, poking Tilly's arm. She'd been so immersed in her study that she's lost track of the conversation.

Tilly's cheeks flushed. "I'm so sorry. What was the question?"

"Dan was asking about the bruising you documented."

Tilly had gone over this several times already, but she made eye contact with Dan while she answered. "The bruising where her sternum hit the car was the only visible injury. I took a series of photos with scales. They'll be in the file."

"Did the bruises seem new?"

"Yes, they were barely visible at the start of the exam, but by the next morning they were beginning to darken. I took photos at both points during the exam."

"Thank you," Dan said, giving Tilly a meaningful look that she couldn't begin to dissect. He might have been trying to be kind. He might have been simply being polite. But whatever it was she couldn't read him at all, and it put her on edge.

"It's my job," she said with more of a bite than she'd intended. Marie raised her eyebrows in Tilly's direction, but the conversation had already moved on.

After the meeting, Marie and Tilly walked back to the parking lot.

"Is everything okay?" Marie asked as they climbed into her car. They'd carpooled to the meeting, and now Marie seemed intent on using Tilly's captivity to get some answers.

Tilly sighed. "Yeah, sorry. I didn't mean to drift off in there."

"It didn't look like drifting off to me. You looked like you were boring holes into Dan's face. Is there something I should know?"

"No. I'm trying to figure him out. He comes off as a complete SOB at times, and then ice-cold at others. From what I can tell, he's competent at his job, but I can't get a read on him. Have you known him long?"

"Yes, a long time. He's been with the DA's office longer than I've been here. And he's always been this way, though it got a lot worse after his wife died."

"Oh," Tilly said, feeling guilty for having formed such a quick opinion of him. "How long ago was that?"

"Three or four years. It's been a while. He has a teenage daughter and I'm sure it's a lot to try and juggle." Marie smiled. "That being said, at times he goes above and beyond at being miserable to work with. But, he wins. Best conviction rate in town on SA and DV cases."

STUMBLE & FALL   75

Tilly shook her head. "Hard to imagine. He has such a hard exterior. How is he with the victims?" Tilly hadn't been present when he'd interviewed Yvette, since the DA's advocate had been with her.

"That's the reason I forgive him a lot for his sour attitude. He's brilliant with the victims. I've never heard a single complaint."

"Hmm," Tilly murmured, even more perplexed than she'd been before.

"Looks like your office landed one of my cases," Tilly said to Jim over dinner. Things had settled back into a routine, and it seemed like all the animosity of the prior week was water under the bridge. Jim's easygoing nature was one of things that Tilly had first fallen in love with. Sometimes it annoyed her, especially when she was feeling confrontational, but his willingness to let things go paved the way for a mostly tranquil home life.

"Indeed. I wish I was assigned to it. I've done a fair number of interstate cases, but nothing international. Not that there's much difference since the crime happened on US soil. Living this close to the border is going to be interesting."

"Who got it?" Tilly asked. Jim had been talking about a few of his colleagues but she knew the office was big.

"Walters in Violent Crimes. He's apparently got a great track record for prosecuting these kinds of cases."

"Have you met him?"

"You'll probably meet him before I do. They keep us pretty busy and there's not a lot of crossover unless the cases are related."

"Well, I hope he's not a jerk. This may very well be the first case down here where I have to testify. It'll be nice to have a slam dunk on the first go."

"Did they catch the perp?" Jim asked.

"Not yet, but they think he may be a repeat offender. So I imagine the DNA will be invaluable once they get him. He wasn't careful."

Jim frowned. "God, sometimes I wish there was a way to wish all this violence out of the world."

"I know," Tilly answered quietly, but something about the sentiment made her feel uneasy. Both she and Jim worked in fields that exposed them to some of the worst things that one human can do to another. Tilly often wished she could ease the suffering of her patients, and occasionally she wished for vengeance, but she accepted that the problem was a hard one not easily solved. And though she abhorred the violence, she did love the work. She loved giving her patients hope. She loved being part of the team that sought justice for victims.

Would she eradicate violence if she could? Sure. But she wondered what she'd do with her life in that case. It seemed that her entire identity had been forged by violence, and she wondered if she'd be able to find purpose without it.

CHAPTER 15
KATE

Kate's second session with Delia was less stressful. They worked on breathing and grounding techniques, which was just as helpful for Kate as it was for Delia. She'd kept her mind squarely in the present and was pleased that she was feeling more in control of her emotions.

Afterward, Kate was updating her patient files when the door to her office swung open. A teenage girl rushed in, slamming the door behind her as if she was shutting out a pursuer on her heels.

Kate jumped up behind her desk. "Oh my God. Are you all right?" she asked as she approached the girl, looking for any obvious injuries. Kate's heart was threatening to explode. She could see that the teen was shaking as she opened her mouth to speak. But where she'd been expecting a desperate cry for help, she was instead surprised by the girl's question.

"Are you Ms. Medina?" Her breath came out in puffs. Her face was bright red.

"Is someone after you?" Kate asked, locking her office door before directing her visitor to a chair.

"You're Ms. Medina, right?"

"I am." Kate handed her a bottle of water from the mini-fridge she kept behind her desk. When the girl had had a few minutes to slow her breathing, Kate asked, "What's your name?"

"Linnie. Short for Melinda."

"You look like you've been running."

"I have," Linnie said, checking back over her shoulder. "I lost them a few blocks ago, but I didn't know if they'd figure out where I was headed."

"They who? And why are you here?" Kate was trying not to rush the girl, but she was picking up on the girl's fear. Her brain was screaming danger and keeping herself calm was becoming more of a struggle with each passing moment.

"Is it true you have a place I can stay?"

Now Kate was on high-alert. "Who told you that?"

"Is it true?" Linnie asked again, more insistent this time. Almost angry.

"It depends," Kate hedged. "You need to tell me how you found me."

"Leah, Mandy's little sister." At the name, Kate sat up straight. "She told me to find you."

"Who are you running from, Linnie?"

"She said you would help me. That you would know what was happening. Can we go? I just want to go." Linnie was rocking back and forth in her chair. Her eyes were starting to fill with tears, all the bravado she'd had upon entering lost to the wave of fear now emanating freely from her.

Kate logged out of her computer, picked up her purse, and said "Let's go."

Linnie hadn't spoken a word since leaving Kate's office, and by the time they left the city limits Kate was resigned to waiting until they reached her house to get answers. She didn't have to wait long. As soon as the lock clicked on the courtyard gate, Linnie spilled her story.

"I'm a senior this year. I got into Texas Tech. I'm so close to getting out of here. I can't believe this is happening."

"Slow down. Start from the beginning," Kate said, leading Linnie into her living room after setting the alarms. Until she got to the bottom of this, she wasn't taking any chances.

"Mandy and I were in Lit together last year. We weren't that close, but when she started freaking out after that dinner, I asked her if she was okay."

Kate remembered that time. Mandy had been a student Kate worked with at the high school and Mandy's mother had been dating Benny Parks, the man convicted of killing one of Mandy's classmates. Kate also knew that he'd been responsible for beating Mandy to within an inch of her life, as well as trafficking her to the same group Kate was trying to unmask. Kate needed to know what Linnie knew but she treaded carefully, her sense of danger fully triggered.

"Mandy told me what happened with her mom's boyfriend and those other men." Linnie frowned. "At first, I didn't believe her. But then I was out at the bus stop one day after school and I saw one of them pick her up. She looked so scared, but she went with the man. I don't know who he was but I remember his car."

"Did that man come after you, too?" Kate asked, picturing Linnie's mad dash into her office.

"No. At least I don't think so." Kate's hopes fell. "But a man I didn't recognize came up to me after school today. He was hitting on me, but he was old." Linnie shivered in disgust. "I told him to get lost but then he started to follow me all slowly, like in one of those horror movies. So I ran."

"How did you know to come to my office?"

Linnie looked at Kate in surprise. "Everyone knows you, Ms. Medina. We remember you from school and I knew that you helped Mandy."

"But I only opened my office a few weeks ago. How did you

know where to find me?" Kate's heart was thrashing in her chest.

"Everybody knows where to find you."

———

The rest of Linnie's story was simple enough. A troubled foster kid, she'd found a forever home with her adoptive parents in middle school and had done a complete one-eighty in school. Getting into a good college was a major milestone, one that Linnie had worked hard for. To get there, she'd put in a lot of hours volunteering and interning around town.

"Last week, we had an awards ceremony for one of the programs I volunteer at. I got to talk about my life and how I got into the school I wanted. It was pretty great," Linnie said, smiling. But the smile turned into a puzzled frown. "Afterwards, this guy came up to me. I think he works for the city government."

There it was. The connection. Kate had to resist drawing lines that didn't exist until she heard more.

"He was nice. He congratulated me, and wanted to know more about my family. At first it was nice to talk to him. He seemed really interested. But then it seemed kind of weird. He kept asking me what I liked to do after school and what my favorite restaurants were, kind of like he was flirting. Which made me super uncomfortable, so I told him I had to go speak with one of my teachers and then I high-tailed it out of there."

"Was he the one who approached you today?"

Linnie shook her head. "No. I didn't recognize this guy at all. He started flirting and I gave him the brush-off, but then he mentioned something about my volunteer job. He sounded like that guy from the award ceremony. They talked the same, you know?" She shivered in the telling. "Then he started following me. I cut across the field and then ran."

"Can you describe him to me?"

"I don't know. He looked like most of the old guys you see around. He had a lot of gray in his hair. No beard or anything. He didn't have a lot of wrinkles so I don't know. It seemed like he might be older than my mom. She's almost fifty."

"Okay, listen Linnie. You can stay with me, but you should let your parents know where you are. Can you talk to them about what happened?"

Linnie shifted nervously. "I don't know."

"What aren't you telling me?"

Linnie's eyes shone with fresh tears. "I used to lie a lot. Mostly before, when I was with my foster parents. But sometimes I lie to my parents now, and I don't even know why."

"You're afraid they won't believe you?" Kate could see how hard it was for Linnie to admit this. And she knew that it was common for kids with traumatic backgrounds to lie as a means to getting attention or self-sabotage.

"Wouldn't you be?"

Kate sighed. "Let's get you somewhere safe and then we'll talk about what to do next." Linnie's visit was a reminder that not only were there predators out there, but that their chosen victims often carried a lot of baggage.

CHAPTER 16
TILLY

It didn't take long before Tilly got into a routine. She spent part of her week reviewing reports and doing administrative work for the clinic. The other part she spent working directly with patients. There were a number of assault cases each week, and while Tilly caught some of those she also did a lot of follow-up care for survivors—documenting new injuries or changes in medical condition so that their files would be as detailed as possible.

Unlike working with assault victims, the ongoing cases gave Tilly a chance to get to know her patients—a luxury she'd never been afforded in previous positions. It was both heartbreaking and rewarding in ways that she had never imagined.

Tilly walked into the exam room to find her current patient, Alvina, hugging herself with tears spilling down her cheeks. This was Alvina's second visit. The first visit had been very routine. Alvina's boyfriend was an abusive alcoholic. A few months ago, the police had been called to respond to a domestic situation in Alvina's apartment. They'd broken up the fight and sent Alvina's boyfriend to jail for the night, but she refused to press charges and they'd had to let him go.

Thankfully, the advocate had talked Alvina into receiving both medical and psychological care at the clinic.

"What happened?" Tilly asked, shutting the door behind her and taking a seat beside the sobbing woman. "Are you hurt?"

"No," Alvina replied miserably between sobs. "I think I'm pregnant."

"Did you take a test at home?"

"No," Alvina replied. "I didn't want him to find out. Can you test me here?"

"Of course."

A few minutes later, the test confirmed Alvina's fears.

"What do you want to do?" Tilly asked, rubbing Alvina's arm as the woman worked her way through another round of tears.

"There's nothing I can do," Alvina whispered. Her voice had grown hoarse from crying. "I'm stuck."

"No, you're not stuck. You have choices, Alvina. This is your life and it's a big decision."

Alvina laughed darkly. "Oh sure, you think he's bad now. How do you think he'd react to me having an abortion? He might actually kill me." Her hand traveled to her abdomen. "Not that I would, you know? I mean, it's a sin."

Tilly sighed. "He wouldn't have to know," she said, but she already knew she was fighting a losing battle. Alvina's boyfriend forbade her from using birth control, and she hadn't been willing to risk taking it behind his back. Her ending up pregnant was his end game, and it looked like he was going to win. Alvina's beliefs would seal the deal.

"Well, if you're going to keep the baby, you'll need to get prenatal care. I can prescribe vitamins now, and then you should make an appointment with the women's clinic here on campus.

"Maybe he'll stop hitting me, you know, to protect the baby. Who knows? Maybe he'll stop drinking." Alvina's tone was dripping with sarcasm, but there was enough hope to make Tilly wince.

"Just focus on taking care of you and the baby," Tilly replied, unable to support Alvina's fantasy but wishing with every fiber of her being that she could.

When she returned to her office, she put her face in her hands and gave herself a moment to feel the burden of this new patient. To be angry for her situation and for the baby who would be brought into a hostile world. Tilly hoped the abuse didn't extend to the child, but she knew the odds weren't in its favor.

"Hard day?" A familiar voice jolted Tilly from her thoughts. Bross was standing in her doorway, his face as stern as ever. She was nearly bowled over by a wave of exhaustion at having to deal with Bross when her heart was already so heavy.

"No worse than usual," she replied. "What can I do for you?"

He walked into her office, standing behind a visitor chair. "This is going to be harder than I thought," he said, earning a quizzical look from Tilly. "I was hoping we could call a truce."

"We're not at war," Tilly replied, but it felt a little disingenuous.

"Technically, no, I suppose, but since we'll likely be working together on a number of cases. I want to pave the way for a productive working relationship."

"We're both professionals. I don't see why that would be a problem."

"True," he replied. "And yet I seem to have earned myself a reputation with you already. Usually it takes a few months for my charm to truly have an effect." Only the slight upward tilt of his lips gave Tilly any hint that he was trying to be funny. Or least trying to lighten the mood. When she didn't say anything, he continued.

"Anway, I won't take up too much of your time." He was

shifting awkwardly behind the chair. Tilly probably should have offered him a seat, but she was in no mood to prolong the visit despite her growing curiosity. On the other hand, she was beginning to feel like her own coldness toward this man was way out of proportion.

"I appreciate you stopping by," she said, hoping for a more conciliatory tone.

He nodded left without saying anything else, once again leaving Tilly feeling like an asshole.

———

"Why does he bother you so much?" Jim asked. In a moment of irritation, Tilly had mentioned her ongoing issues with Dan Bross. She should have known that he'd try to help her reason it out.

"I don't know," she huffed, throwing her hands up for dramatic effect. She wasn't in the mood to be reasonable, mostly because she truly didn't know the answer and that only frustrated her more. "I mean, I've only been working at the clinic a few weeks and he's already been a jerk to one of our nurses more than once. Did I tell you he made her cry?"

"You did." Jim smiled. "But it sounds like he's trying to repent."

"Ha!" Tilly scoffed. "He doesn't want me to think he's a jerk."

"From what you've said, he doesn't strike me as the kind of guy who'd care what you thought of him. You think he's not being genuine?" Jim asked. He leaned back into the couch, closing his eyes. Tilly tucked herself up under his arm. She could feel the color in her cheeks, and was relieved that she didn't have to look Jim in the face.

"No, it's not that." She waited for Jim to hop in with another argument, but his breathing had slowed and soon he was snoring softly. She glanced at her watch. It wasn't even 9 o'clock. He's been worn out all week, but he'd never actually fallen asleep in the middle of a conversation. She scooted out from under his arm, shaking him gently.

"Looks like it's time for bed," she said, hauling him up off the couch and to the bedroom.

"Sorry Til," he said with a yawn. "What were we talking about?"

She smiled. "Nothing." By the time she'd finished putting on her nightgown and brushing her teeth, he was asleep again.

For a while, she was restless. Lying beside Jim was a comfort and allowed her to explore the more upsetting and troubling thoughts she had in a safe space.

She thought about Dan Bross, but she was no closer to understanding her reluctance to give him a second chance. She was tired of feeling stressed over the situation and decided that, starting tomorrow, she would treat him like any other person she worked closely with—with detached professionalism. No need for further hostility.

Feeling satisfied with that decision, Tilly moved on to thoughts of Jim. She wondered how long it would take before things settled down at home. She'd done a bit of unpacking, but there were still boxes here and there. Most nights he was exhausted and she knew that the US Attorney's Office was pushing him hard. She hoped he'd find a balance, and that maybe that would translate to their relationship. The way things were going, Tilly felt more disconnected from Jim than she had in all the years they'd lived in Colorado.

As she fell asleep, she found herself wondering again if this was the beginning of the end of the stable life she thought she'd built for herself.

CHAPTER 17
KATE

After getting Linnie settled in one of the upstairs rooms, Kate called Roman. He answered on the first ring.

"Is this a bad time?" she asked at the sound of his labored breathing.

"No, just got back from the gym. I was unlocking the door when the phone rang. Nearly dropped it, I was so excited to see your name on my screen."

Kate felt a twinge of guilt. "You always seem to beat me to it." They both knew that wasn't entirely true, but Roman didn't press her on it.

"So tell me about your day," he said. He must have sensed that her call had a purpose, and she was grateful for the opening. It made her feel a little bit less of a jerk for being such a lousy listener lately.

"It was weird. There's a girl staying with me, at least for tonight."

"Who?" She could hear the distrust in his voice, and she knew if the shoe was on the other foot she'd be just as concerned.

"It's a high school girl. Her name is Linnie. She came into my office today."

"Did they…" he started.

"No, but they tried. Or at least, that seems to be where things were headed. But that's not the weird part. When I asked her how she found me, she said everyone knows where to find me. It was creepy."

"And you decided to bring her home with you?" Roman asked, unable to hide the annoyance in his voice. Kate knew he worried, so she took a breath and tried to keep herself from rising to the bait.

"We had a conversation before I agreed to let her stay with me. Her explanation was interesting." Kate paused, speaking more to herself than him. "I have to keep reminding myself that I'm not invisible anymore."

"What are you talking about?"

"Linnie said that Mandy's little sister Leah told her about me." Images of Mandy's face covered in bruises and swelling took Kate's mind to a very dark place. She wondered if Roman saw the same things. For a moment, they were both silent.

"I guess it's not surprising that Mandy told Leah what happened. It's probably a good thing. It'll help keep her safe," Roman finally said. The line went quiet for a moment. "So, tell me more about Linnie."

Kate took Roman through everything that had happened that day from the time Linnie barged into her office. "She was definitely scared. And she doesn't want to go home or back to school."

"You'll have to be careful, Kate. Does her mother know where she is? If her parents report her as a runaway, you could be charged with harboring."

"I know." Kate sighed. "She told her mother she was staying over at a friend's house tonight. We'll have to figure out a better plan for tomorrow. Linnie thinks her mom will understand why she needs to stay away, but she's fairly certain her father is going to go ballistic. She can't stay here, but I won't make her leave."

Roman grumbled something unintelligible and Kate wondered if she was about to get a lecture, but he seemed to change his mind. "Just be careful."

"I can take care of myself." She instantly regretted the words as they flew out of her mouth.

After an awkward pause, Roman said, "I know you can. I don't want to lose you, Kate." He chuckled. "You're not the only one with control issues, you know."

The irritation Kate had been feeling dissipated. She was being unfair to Roman, taking out her own anxiety and doubt out on him. As much as she'd struggled with him being away, she knew it had to be so hard for Roman. He was working toward a goal that would give him an opportunity to continue doing the work he loved. But he was a long way from home, and he knew the dangers Kate faced as well as she did.

She wasn't the only one who'd been assaulted and injured during the course of the murder investigation where they'd discovered the existence of the trafficking ring.

The moment she'd received that phone call from the hospital saying that Roman had been attacked and the terror she'd felt as she rushed to his side replayed in her mind now. He was her best friend and the love of her life. She didn't want to lose him either. Especially by her own hand.

"I'm sorry, Roman. I'm struggling," she said, though she was sure he already knew. He knew her better than anyone else. "I love you."

"My heart belongs to you, Kate," Roman said, and even after they hung up Kate could still hear the unspoken message: Please don't break it again.

———

Kate worked into the night searching the internet for pictures from the ceremony Linnie had mentioned. When that failed, she started bookmarking pages featuring city staff at civic functions, hoping that Linnie would be able to identify the man who tried to pick her up.

It infuriated Kate, how brazen these men were. How must it look? An older gentleman tailing a teenage girl down the street. Openly coming on to her at a public event.

From what Tilly had told her, the recruiting tactics of the organization had changed over the years. Kate wasn't sure which was worse; to have your teenage boyfriend hand you over to his father like a piece of meat, or to be stalked by men in positions of authority as you walked home from school.

Kate walked upstairs to check on Linnie. The girl tossed fitfully in her bed, her hair forming a messy mop that hid her face. Closing the door quietly behind her Kate walked around the upper floor checking window latches. She stopped to peer out each window, searching for movement but the desert was eerily quiet.

She wasn't a fool.

Kate was not looking to invite danger into her home, but with Linnie sleeping nearby she found the unwavering darkness around her unnerving. She'd never been comfortable with the unknown and, unfortunately, she was surrounded by it. No matter how terrifying a situation might be, an unseen threat was worse.

Leaving the office with Linnie, Kate had looked over her shoulder and in her rearview mirror so often that she'd barely paid attention to the traffic on the road or the girl sitting beside her. The task of keeping Linnie safe—of keeping any of these girls safe—was going to be insurmountable if Kate couldn't conquer her anxiety.

Fear was normal. Incapacitating anxiety was not.

Back in her room Kate picked up her tablet and logged in to her security system, checking her cameras and ensuring that all the alarms were armed. It was her nightly ritual, but now that she had someone else in the house it was a necessity. Reassured, she settled into bed for her own fitful night of sleep.

CHAPTER 18
TILLY

"Are we still on this weekend?" Tilly asked Kate. Since Tilly started working their phone calls had become more sporadic and it was Thursday before Tilly realized they hadn't talked since the previous weekend.

"Yes, but I have a girl staying with me so things are a little different around here."

Tilly's back stiffened. "Fill me in."

Kate went through the events of the week. Linnie was still staying with Kate. She'd created a story about a friend whose family was out of town. Linnie told her mom that she'd volunteered to stay with the girl for the week. It took some convincing, but finally her mom had gone along with it.

"Has she been going to school?"

"Yeah, I've been dropping her off at a friend's house. Safety in numbers. She hasn't seen the guy or his car anywhere around her, so either they lost interest or they're waiting her out. Either way, I'm glad she has a place to stay."

"You're not worried?"

Kate laughed. "Of course I am. I'm a nervous wreck, but this is what I wanted, right? A safe house where these girls could come to get away from bad men. Even if it means inviting danger to my door. I knew this would happen if I stayed in Alamogordo so I'm determined not to let my nerves keep me from doing what I need to do." Kate paused. "But I also don't want to bring you into the middle of it. So, full disclosure seemed like the right choice."

"Much appreciated, but you know I don't spook that easily." Tilly said it with as much bravado as she could muster, but her heart was thrumming a little bit faster than before. "I'll see you Saturday."

Tilly got off the phone and turned her attention again to the report she'd been writing. It was nearing the end of the month, and one of Tilly's least exciting jobs was to prepare the data report for the hospital. She'd been pulling together information from various sources all week, and was finally putting the finishing touches on her report. Since the last clinical coordinator had left, the reports had become a hodgepodge, pieced together in whatever fashion got it out the door fastest. Tilly had reformatted so it didn't look like Frankenstein's monster. Certainly not her most exciting work, but she did believe in putting a professional front on everything that she did.

"Knock, knock." Brynn was standing at the door. They'd spoken only briefly since their awkward coffee date, and she still felt a little uneasy.

"Hi, Brynn."

"I'm meeting Angie for drinks after work. Want to join us?"

Tilly's automatic reaction was to politely decline, but her gut told her otherwise. If she had any hope of forming a relationship with Brynn, she would come face to face with Angie sooner or later. "Sure. You don't think I'll make it awkward, do you?"

Brynn laughed. "Nah. It'll be nice to forge some common ground together, eh? Do you want to meet us there or ride over with me?"

"I'll drive so I can head home after. Let me call Jim and let him know."

"Great. Happy hour starts in half an hour, so we'll see you there."

Tilly finished up her report, closed down her computer, and texted Jim a quick note telling him she wouldn't be home for dinner. He'd been working fairly late, and she knew it was just as easy for them each to grab a quick bite as for her to try and coordinate a meal when neither one of them would be home right away. In his usual easy going fashion Jim texted back an upbeat "Have fun" and before she knew it she was out the door.

They were meeting at a Mexican restaurant not far from Tilly's house. When she arrived, Brynn and Angie were sipping margaritas. The salt on the rims of their glasses was thick and chunky. Tilly's mouth started to water.

"Well, I was going to be good and have a glass of wine, but now?" Tilly said, taking the seat across from Angie.

"Trust me, you won't regret it. Best margaritas on the planet," Angie said. "It's so good to see you, Tilly."

"You, too. Your hair looks great, by the way," Tilly said with a smile. Last time she'd seen the detective, she'd had an edgy asymmetrical cut that, paired with the dramatic makeup she always wore, made her striking. She'd softened a bit. Her hair was brushing the tops of her shoulders, and it seemed to Tilly that her hard edges had been filed down.

"Thanks. I think I had a little bit of a mid-life crisis since the last time you saw me," Angie said. Tilly stiffened. Angie seemed to notice. "I know Brynn already cleared the air with you, and now I'm hoping to do the same thing because I want us to have a fresh start. So, here goes. My breakup with Roman was hard. Not gonna lie. I'd been planning on marrying that man, and I think we were close to it when Kate came back into the picture. I was hurt and angry. And the minute that case ended, I disconnected."

"Understandable," Tilly said, nursing her own margarita. The conversation was uncomfortable, but she'd been expecting some kind of confrontation so she decided the best thing was to let Angie get it off her chest.

"Anway, when Brynn told me you took the job at the clinic here, I wanted to see if we could be friends. I will completely understand if it's too weird, but I promise you I have no hard feelings toward Kate or Roman. Just give me a little bit of time to readjust to having them brought up in conversation." Angie looked hopeful, and Tilly really did like her, so she figured why not.

"Here's to starting over," Tilly said, raising her glass. The three women clinked their glasses, and the rest of the evening rushed by. Angie and Brynn talked about the ins and outs of the departments Tilly would now be interacting with. Tilly told stories of her final cases in Colorado and the police detective she hoped she'd never have to see again.

"We've got a few of those here too," Brynn said, rolling her eyes. "Usually men and they all think they have some sixth sense that allows them to sniff out crime without having to actually investigate."

"Thankfully, most of our SA and DV detectives have been well-trained. They're not always as compassionate as they could be, but they try," Angie added. Then, changing topics, she asked, "How was the move? Are you all settled in?"

Tilly sighed. "Still unpacking, and since we're renting I'm finding it hard to get motivated to finish the job."

"Are you looking for something to buy?"

"Not yet," Tilly said. "We signed a year lease, so the decision is tabled at the moment. We're both still adjusting to our jobs, so not sure where we want to end up yet."

"Your boyfriend is an attorney, right?" Brynn asked.

"Yes, he's working for the US Attorney's office. Mostly fraud and commerce cases so far, but he wants to work on violent crimes eventually. That's what he did with the DA's office back home."

"What's he like?" Angie asked.

"Jim?" Tilly laughed. "He's an open book. What you see is what you get. He's pretty athletic. Very easy going. Always the first to concede to end an argument." Tilly's description sounded uninspiring, so she added, "He's passionate about helping victims. It's one of the things that brought us together."

Angie smiled. "Yeah, I can't see you with someone who didn't have that same kind of fight."

Tilly nodded, but something about Angie's words tugged at her heart. She knew Jim's passion for his work was genuine, but it was academic—not forged in grief and trauma like Tilly's. For the first time, she realized how much that bothered her.

CHAPTER 19
KATE

When Tilly arrived Saturday morning, the shadows under her eyes were cause for concern. They settled into the kitchen with some coffee.

"Where's your boarder?" Tilly asked, shifting her gaze upward.

"Sleeping. She's definitely a teenager," Kate said with a smile. "You remember when Mom used to come in around noon on Saturdays and yank our covers off?"

"I do indeed," Tilly laughed. "I'd put on an oversized hoodie and pull my knees inside so I could stay in bed."

"Clever," Kate said. "So, what's going on with you, Til? You look tired."

"Thanks a lot," Tilly said, but she sighed. "I'm having a hard time sleeping. Too much to think about."

"Work?"

"Not really." Tilly took a slow sip of her coffee, and Kate wondered if she was going to continue without being prodded. Thankfully, she did. "I'm not happy."

"I can see that," Kate said gently. "What's happening?"

"Honestly, I don't know. Nothing has changed between

Jim and me, but I feel frustrated a lot. Everything is so easy for him. I feel like I'm always struggling and fighting and with Jim things happen. And when they don't happen, he's okay. He moves on. He doesn't hold grudges. He doesn't drag out fights." Tilly closed her eyes, taking a deep breath. "Those are good qualities, right? I should be happy to be with someone who is easy to be with. It doesn't have to be difficult, right?"

Kate took Tilly's hand. "You don't have to be happy just because you ought to be, Tilly. You can't force it."

"I know," Tilly said miserably. "But we moved all the way down here because of me. Jim gave up his whole life…"

"Let's stop right there," Kate said. "Jim didn't *give up* anything. He made a choice. We're all adults and have to own up to the consequences of our actions, intended or otherwise. There's never a guarantee that things are going to work out."

"Jim deserves to be happy," Tilly offered meekly.

"The implication there is that you don't. That's where you're going wrong, Sis. You both deserve to be happy. We all do." Kate felt another pang of regret over all the selfish feelings she'd been having lately. Dispensing advice was always easier than following it.

"What's wrong with me, then? Dad always used to say I looked for fights. Why am I still doing that?"

"I don't know," Kate said. "But give yourself time. You've only been here a month. You're already back at work. Transitions are rough."

Tilly's face brightened. "Speaking of . . . Guess who I had drinks with the other night?"

Kate knew the answer before Tilly said it. "How's Angie doing?"

"She seems good. Both she and Brynn, the social worker I work with, have now reached out and 'cleared the air'. It's both awkward and interesting. I've always liked Angie, so I'm glad

STUMBLE & FALL   99

I'm getting a chance to know her outside all of this." Tilly
gestured around her, making Kate blush.

"Roman says she's still avoiding him," Kate said.

"I don't think that's going to stop for a while. She said the
breakup was pretty hard. I get the feeling she might be
punishing him a bit."

"I thought that might be the case," Kate said. "Well, at least
she'd chosen a non-violent means of making her point. I
suppose it could have been worse." Kate had been trying to
make a joke, but it landed flat. Both Kate and Tilly had experi-
enced enough violence in their lives to know how very true that
statement was.

Tilly sighed. "I started seeing patients for follow-up visits.
I'm glad I can have a bigger impact on their lives, but you know
how these situations are. I feel so helpless sometimes."

"All you can do is give them the best care you can on that
given day," Kate said. In their fields, you walked a fine line
sometimes between wanting to protect victims and not wanting
to step all over their autonomy.

"How's our special agent in training?" Tilly asked, changing
the subject. She'd always liked Roman, though she often treated
him like a sibling who wouldn't go away.

"He's doing well," Kate said. "Working out a lot. We talk
most nights and he usually sounds completely exhausted, but
happy."

"Speaking of giving yourself time to adjust, how are
you?" Tilly gave Kate a knowing grin.

"Having Linnie here has been helpful. I didn't realize how
lonely I'd been. She's barely around, but knowing she's here
makes me feel needed." Kate had cared for her father up until
his death, and she was still processing a lot of grief and emptiness. She and Tilly had lost both parents in the span of five
years. "I didn't realize how much I enjoyed taking care of Dad.
Having Linnie here reminds me how nice it is." She paused,

then blurted, "And I don't want to be so damned reliant on Roman."

"Wanting to be with Roman doesn't mean you're not capable," Tilly said, reversing their roles. One of Kate's favorite things about having her sister back in her life was having a sounding board for all her crazy, selfish thoughts. She knew she could tell Tilly anything.

"I know. I tell myself the same thing every day, but it's harder to convince my feelings to follow suit. Those first two weeks just about undid me."

"But things are better now?"

Kate wanted to give a definitive yes, but the truth was she wasn't sure. Things felt tentative. She missed Roman as much as ever, but she was distracted by her house guest and the revelations that came with her "More or less. I'm sure the next four months are going to be hard on so many levels, but it'll all work itself out. That's how life is, right?"

Tilly nodded and smiled. Both sisters sat back and sipped their coffee in silence for a while, knowing the conversation hadn't been laid to rest forever but needing some space from it.

———

Later that night, after Tilly had gone to bed, Kate sat alone in her room looking through an old scrapbook. While her father lay dying in a hospital bed someone had trashed his house, destroying many of Kate's most treasured family mementos. She'd managed to save several scrapbooks, but she'd been too busy to look through them. Or she'd kept herself too busy. As she flipped through the pages, she felt tears forming.

Page after page of happy family photos. She and Tilly as babies. Pictures of family vacations to see Kate's grandparents. A trip to Disneyland that Tilly was too small to remember and Kate only had vague memories of.

This particular book ended at Kate's eleventh birthday. Looking at the pictures—knowing what would happen to Tilly a few years later—a spark of anger ignited in Kate's core. Anger at the men who'd abused her sister, throwing their happy family into a perpetual state of turmoil. Anger at her parents for failing to protect them.

Then there was shame.

It felt unfair to judge her parents harshly, especially her mother, for a situation that they had no idea how to navigate. Kate had watched her mother and sister tear each other down night after night, and though she still harbored resentment for the unrest it caused in their lives, she could imagine how confused Tilly's outbursts must have made her mother.

Most of all she felt a deep abiding sadness that her mother and father never got a chance to have a relationship with Tilly. Their father Frank forgave Tilly everything, knowing that he should have done more to help her but the silence between them was a wall that neither could scale. The guilt followed him to his grave.

In Kate's haste to get on with her life, she'd also missed out on the opportunity to connect with her parents as an adult. She was grateful for those years when she'd with her father, but even then the void left by her mother's death was ever present; often keeping father and daughter at arm's length, emotionally.

Kate thought about Roman and the family she'd only recently started to imagine building. Though she'd never dreamed of being a mother the way many of her friends had, her perspective was beginning to change. And that terrified her.

She thought about Linnie. About Mandy and her sister. About Gabby Greene and Tilly and all the other girls who'd had their lives torn apart by violence and abuse. How could she even consider bringing children into a world like this?

As if on cue, a flash of light moved across her bedroom wall. Kate picked up her phone, walked upstairs, and looked out the window in time to see a car driving slowly down the road. It didn't stop at her house, but as the driver approached her property the headlights went out. Kate stood frozen at the window, listening intently as the vehicle passed. She gripped her phone, ready to call 911 but the driver had turned around. And as they passed by her house again, she could see taillights heading back to the highway.

CHAPTER 20
TILLY

Tilly slept well for the first time in a week. In fact, she only slept well at Kate's house, which she found very confusing considering it meant being very close to all the trauma and memories that haunted her. Jim handled her absences with grace, but she wondered if he was counting the days until Kate didn't need Tilly so much or Roman got home, whichever came first.

Sunday morning Kate suggested they go to town for brunch, and Tilly surprised herself by agreeing. Linnie had decided to spend the day at home, so they dropped her off and headed to the restaurant.

"I like her," Tilly declared when Linnie was safely in her house. "She reminds me of me. Before."

"She's pretty spunky. As soon as she got settled, she perked right up. I hope she's safe at home."

"You're worried about how her father might react?" Tilly asked.

"I'm trying not to worry. I can't keep looking at every man in town as a potential threat. It's eating me alive. And besides, everything she's said about her father leads me to believe he's more of the overprotective type than the sexual predator type."

They made their way to a booth near the back of the restaurant. Tilly scanned as they went, looking for any familiar faces, but the crowd was light and seemed mostly composed of families. Not that that precluded them from wrong-doing.

"I see what you mean," Tilly said as they took their seats.

"What?"

"I can't help but look at everyone and wonder, you know?"

Over breakfast, Tilly shifted topics to Daniel Bross. She gave Kate a rundown on their encounters, starting with his mistreatment of the young SANE nurse and up to his recent olive branch offering. "I looked up some of his cases. His track record is impressive but I can't for the life of me figure out how to not feel all off-kilter around him. He runs so hot and cold."

Kate laughed. "Sounds familiar." She winked at Tilly, which caused Tilly's cheeks to flame.

"I'm not mercurial," she insisted, but even she didn't buy it. Especially the way she'd been feeling toward Jim lately. "Okay, fine. You may be right. Maybe that's why he rubs me the wrong way. Too much alike."

"Sounds like you're surrounded by extremes. Jim on the upbeat side. The ADA on the intense side. I can see how that would make you feel unbalanced. Especially since you're also right in the middle of this huge life transition."

"Yeah, I guess," Tilly said grudgingly. She tried not to be annoyed when Kate turned therapist on her. Or was it big sister? Either way, Tilly always felt the need to argue. To assert her individuality. It wasn't far off from their teenage years, which was depressing. They'd lost so much time and yet they were still reliving so many old patterns.

"Enough shop talk. What do you want to do today before I head back?" Tilly said, finishing her last bite of eggs and then pushing her plate away.

"Farmers market?" Kate said. "There's a cute one up the mountain with art and other non-food knick-knacks."

"Done. And maybe a hike? We could do the trestle trail."

Kate smiled. "Rusty would love that. Let's take him with us. He hasn't been out on the town in ages."

Tilly picked up the check and they were on their way. As they pulled out of the parking lot, Tilly noticed a man in a police uniform staring at them. He was standing at the door of the restaurant and it was clear that he was watching them.

"Do you know him?" Tilly said, nodding toward the door. Kate looked up, and the man retreated back into the restaurant.

"Maybe. He looked familiar, but so does everyone else around here. I've only met a few of Roman's friends from the department, but there aren't a lot of people he's willing to trust right now so he hasn't kept in touch."

"Understandable," Tilly replied with a sigh. Being back home always made her feel haunted, the ghosts of her past unwilling to let her be. "Well, let's pick up the pup and head to the mountains. I've got to walk off all those potatoes."

———

Tilly enjoyed the market. She and Kate split some kettle corn, and Tilly found some pieces of art for her new house. They loaded their purchases in the trunk and drove to the trestle trailhead. Rusty was nearly beside himself with joy as they made their way down the steep path to the first view point. It was near lunchtime and all the early morning hikers had already come and gone so the trail was quiet.

As they walked, Tilly's thoughts wandered. Her father had brought her and Kate hiking on this trail when they were girls. They'd come up after breakfast, walk to the old trestle, have a picnic lunch, and return home to a big dinner. While they were gone, Tilly's mom invited her friends over for coffee and to have some "alone time". As they got older, Kate sometimes stayed home to work on school projects or see her friends, but

Tilly had loved those times even more, when it was just her and her father. They'd walk a little slower, taking time to explore.

"You still with me?" Kate asked, making Tilly jump. Rusty had stopped to sniff the underbrush and Kate was standing close to Tilly.

"Just thinking about being up here with Dad."

"Yeah, I miss those days," Kate said. Rusty started tugging at the leash, so the women began walking again. "I remember that time you guys came home and you'd fallen off a rock. Your leg was all bloody. Mom was freaking out, but Dad carried you in and cleaned you up, calm as can be. Said you'd been so brave."

"And he went out and brought us ice cream." Tilly smiled. On her own she tended to gravitate toward the dark parts of her past, but with Kate it was easier to welcome the happy parts in. "I still have a scar. It hurt so bad, but Dad always knew how to make us feel better."

"You were limping around and he said you could stay home from school on Monday, but you were all packed up and ready to go."

"I hated missing school. Not because I liked going—I just hated having to make up work."

Tilly paused as they neared a fallen tree across the path. A cloud passed overhead, shrouding the forest in an uneasy shade. A memory of another day flashed through Tilly's mind. Jacob Copeland walking ahead, holding out a hand to help her over a fallen tree. He looked down at her and all teenage Tilly saw was that dazzling smile. Like a punch to her gut, Tilly was brought to her knees by the overwhelming feeling of loss. It was only a few weeks after that day hike that Jacob had thrown Tilly to the wolves—taking her virginity and then handing her over to his father and all the men who would use and torment her, ripping her world apart.

"Til, are you all right?" Kate was kneeling beside her. Rusty planted himself beside her and nudged her chest, licking at her arm.

"Yeah. Just give me a minute." Tilly felt a tear sliding down her face. She reached out and scratched Rusty behind the ear and she slowed her breathing. It was ironic Kate was prone to panic attacks but here she was, her hand on Tilly's back. The strong one. Tilly sat back, thankful that it hadn't been raining lately as she settled against a tree, bringing her knees up to her chest. Kate sat beside her, her face etched with concern.

"I'm okay," Tilly reassured her sister. "I'm having a lot more anxiety right now."

"What were you thinking about? Still Dad?"

"Jacob Copeland," Tilly replied, noting the look of disgust on Kate's face. Tilly had finally told Kate about the abuse she'd suffered as part of the trafficking situation Kate was determined to take down. The confession had opened the door for their reconciliation, but once opened it wasn't easily shut. "I ran across a picture of him while we were packing up our house. He keeps popping into my head now, and it's like having the wind knocked out of me."

"I'm sorry, Tilly." Kate reached out to take Tilly's hand. "It must be torture coming up to see me. Maybe I should start coming to you. I could bring Rusty." The dog's ears pricked up at the mention of his name.

Tilly smiled. "No, I need to face these demons. I've always thought of myself as being strong, but when Dad died I realized how I've let those bastards take away so much more of my life than those years in high school. I'm angry. I know I made the decision to stay away, but I also feel like these guys chased me away from my family."

"I can relate. That's how I felt after leaving my job at the prison."

"I know. And that's probably the reason I feel like I can talk to you about it. Jim was there when I found the photo and it was a disaster. I know he wanted me to tell him more, but I can't bring myself to go into those details with him. It's not just about the assaults. It's the betrayal, you know? I remember the girl that came up here with her new boyfriend, all full of hope and possibilities. She never even had a chance, and I wonder how my life would have been different."

"Maybe we shouldn't have come up here," Kate said.

Tilly squeezed Kate's hand. "No, we definitely should. I've spent enough time avoiding. It's actually a relief to feel angry. I need to figure out where to put that anger."

CHAPTER 21
KATE

Just before Tilly headed home, Kate got a call from Linnie.

"I'm staying home tonight," Linnie declared. She sounded upbeat, not a hint of the worry from their first days together. "I talked with my mom, and she's going to do my school pick-up and drop-off for a while, so I think I'll be okay."

"That's good, Linnie. Keep in touch," Kate said, hanging up reluctantly. What more could she say?

"No more house guest?" Tilly asked.

"No, but it's good news. Her mom is stepping up and making sure she stays safe." Kate sighed. "Linnie was never a good match for the safe house. But it was nice to have her around and to have a relatively low-drama introduction to what it might be like."

"Do you want me to stay another night? I can drive straight to work tomorrow."

Kate smiled. "I'll be all right, Tilly. Rusty's got my back, and I have four appointments tomorrow. A full day for me. It'll fly by."

Tilly gave Kate a hug then left. Kate headed upstairs to clean Linnie's room. Linnie had stripped the bed and left her towels in a pile, like she'd known she wouldn't be coming back. Kate frowned. She wanted to believe the story Linnie had told her, but there was something off. The girl's fear on that first day seemed genuine, and yet the turnaround was so fast. If her parents could protect her, why hadn't she gone to them in the first place?

Once again, she found herself wondering why Linnie had chosen her. And why now?

Kate's cell phone chirped, an indication that someone was at the door. Rusty had been curled up, snoring away, but at the sound of the door he jumped up and barked ferociously. Kate's heart hammered in her chest. She wasn't expecting anyone, and couldn't think of anyone who would show up at her house unannounced.

Roman had installed a camera at the door so that Kate would know exactly who she was about to see before she opened it. She'd loved the idea at the time, and even more so now that people were starting to come around, invited or otherwise. Kate pulled up the app while she walked. When she saw who it was, she quickened her pace.

"Ruth?" Kate said, opening the door and unlocking the gate. "Goodness, what are you doing all the way out here?"

"I saw you at the market this morning, but you were with someone so I thought I'd wait and stop by this afternoon on my way home. Is this a bad time?"

"No, come on in," Kate said, trying to remove the shakiness from her voice. The last time she'd seen Ruth she'd told her a little bit about where she was living. Anyone in the area would have known the house from the description, but she was unaccustomed to guests. When she was young, people dropped by her house to see her parents all the time. But given the circumstances, she was pretty sure she'd never want that for herself.

That's what the cameras and alarms are for, she reminded herself. Then she looked at the older woman standing beside her and felt ashamed. Ruth was dressed in the polyester pants and striped shirt combo that seemed to be the weekend uniform for women of a certain age. Kate chided herself for being so paranoid. If she was going to be a part of the community, she was going to have to get used to interacting with people socially. She'd have to set some boundaries.

"Can I get you something to drink? I can make some iced tea."

"Oh, no, dear. I wanted to drop in and see if you'd like to have lunch this week. Wednesday or Thursday?"

"Sure. I have a client Wednesday at lunch but Thursday would work. You came all the way out here to ask me that?" Kate asked, unable to hide her skeptical tone.

Ruth laughed. "Well, no actually I was terribly curious about the hacienda. I've never been inside."

"Not even when it was built?" Kate asked, astonished. The family who'd built the house had given tours before they moved in. That's how Kate had seen the house when she was a little girl. "I thought everyone had been in here."

"Afraid not, dear. I do remember when it was built, but we weren't friendly with the family so I suppose we didn't get an invitation. Though I hear a lot of people did."

"Yes ma'am. My mother brought me to see it when it was brand new. I remember running down the walkways with Tilly."

"How is your sister?" Ruth asked. Kate had led Ruth into the sitting room, and they were now seated across from each other. Ruth was looking around the room intently. Kate thought she probably should have offered a tour—that's what her mother would have done—but she'd been in the middle of cleaning when the doorbell rang and didn't want to explain her house guest to Ruth.

"She's doing very well, thank you. She got a job in Las

Cruces a few weeks ago, so she's been busy. That was her you saw with me this morning."

"She's still a beauty," Ruth said.

"Oh. Did you meet her, too? I mean when we were younger?"

Ruth looked away from Kate, clearing her throat. "I must have." She coughed quietly into her elbow. "You know, I think I could use a glass of water after all. Would you mind, dear?"

"Not at all," Kate said, fetching a glass for her guest. Ruth took several small sips and then stood abruptly.

"I must be on my way. I have a few errands to run this afternoon, and I'm a terrible dawdler on the weekends."

She put her glass on the coffee table and turned to the door. Kate followed her, feeling bewildered by the visit. "I'll see you Thursday then?" Ruth asked as she opened the door.

"Absolutely. Why don't I call you from the office and we'll figure out the details."

"Sounds good. Thanks for letting me interrupt your afternoon."

"It was my pleasure," Kate said goodbye, locking the gate and setting the alarms as Ruth drove away. She'd had enough excitement for one day.

————

Kate finished up in the room Linnie had slept in, moving all the bedding and towels into the hall. She went into the next room, the one Tilly usually stayed in, and began stripping the bed. As she walked around the edge of the bed, her foot hit something hard and she heard a clink like glass hitting metal.

Reaching under the bed skirt, Kate felt around until her fingers hit the object in question. She thought maybe a water glass had fallen from the bedside table, but what she felt was more the size of a perfume bottle. Maybe smaller. As she pulled

STUMBLE & FALL   113

her hand from under the fabric of the skirt, she felt a rush of dread.

In her hand was an empty vodka bottle—one of the ones you found on airplanes and in hotel minibars. Kate sat down on the bed to think. She'd been relieved when Tilly declined a drink at dinner, having polished off a whole bottle herself the previous weekend. Self-medicating wasn't unusual in trauma victims and Kate realized she didn't know much about how Tilly had learned to cope with hers.

She hoped she was overreacting.

CHAPTER 22
TILLY

When Tilly got home, Jim was sacked out on the couch. He had the television on reruns of *Leave it to Beaver*. She put down her bag and snuggled in beside him, pulling the blanket over her.

"Hey, beautiful," he said groggily, wrapping an arm around her. "I didn't hear you come in."

"You were snoozing peacefully. I didn't want to wake you," Tilly said, relishing the feel of his chest under her cheek. It reminded her of the early days of their relationship, when she would come home from a case and fall into bed. Without waking up, Jim's body seemed to curl itself around her. It was the most lovely feeling. It felt like safety and love and all the things she'd never thought she'd have in her life.

"Did you work late?" she asked.

"Not really. I didn't sleep well last night, and I was sitting watching TV. Could barely keep my eyes open, so I laid down for a few minutes." He checked his watch and groaned. "That was three hours ago. I'm turning into an old man."

"Wow, you must have been exhausted. I've never seen you take a three-hour nap. In fact, you don't usually nap at all."

"Probably worn out from all the work," he replied, but even now his eyes were drooping.

"Are you feeling sick?" Tilly asked, propping herself up on an elbow so she could look at his face. He looked a little bit pale.

"I'm fine," Jim murmured. "Just drowsy. Lie back down."

Reluctantly, she did. A few minutes later, Jim was snoring lightly again. Tilly had gotten rest at Kate's and wasn't in the mood to stay put. She eased herself off the couch, trying not to disturb Jim any more than she had to. He barely seemed to notice. She pressed her lips against his forehead, but he didn't feel feverish.

Resolved not to worry, Tilly unpacked her bag and started a load of laundry, which consisted mostly of scrubs. Jim did his own laundry. She'd never been able to convince him that she could wash all their clothes together, and now she'd grown accustomed to only having to do her laundry once a week. She still wasn't convinced that Jim was feeling well, so she put together some chicken soup for dinner, pouring herself a glass of wine and humming as she cooked.

"Yum," Jim said, nearly making her jump. He'd wandered into the kitchen, but she'd been lost in thought and he'd managed to sneak up on her. "Sorry, babe. Didn't mean to scare you."

Tilly laughed. "I guess I should have picked up on the lack of snoring."

"You said my snoring was cute," Jim argued playfully. He wrapped his arms around her waist while she stirred the pot. "Mmm. You smell good." He pressed his face into her hair. Then he stiffened. "Ugh, now I know why I don't nap. My back is killing me."

"Nothing wrong with napping," Tilly replied. "But couches weren't made to be beds. Want me to rub your back?"

"After dinner," he said. "Is it ready? I'm starving."

"What did you have for lunch?"

"Nothing. Or breakfast for that matter. I think I pretty much slept today. Guess I needed some rest."

Tilly turned off the burner and turned to face Jim. "Are you sure you're feeling all right?"

"Ask me when I didn't just wake up from a back-breaking day of doing nothing. Or at least, after I've had a chance to stretch."

"Go sit down and I'll bring you a bowl."

Jim obeyed cheerfully, and he moaned with pleasure as he inhaled the soup. His enthusiasm was infectious and Tilly felt all her tension melting away. When she wasn't second-guessing and overthinking everything about her life, she was reminded why she and Jim had made it this long. It was simply impossible to be in a bad mood with such a cheerful person. Where Tilly was cynical Jim was optimistic, always willing to see the good in people. His outlook balanced Tilly out perfectly. This move had put a strain on their rhythm, and while Tilly might have doubts a few things were certain. Jim loved her. And she loved him right back double.

After dinner, Tilly convinced Jim to lie down so she could rub his back.

"How was your visit with Kate?" he asked while she massaged. His muscles felt a little bit tight, but not as bad as she'd thought from the way he was moaning and groaning. Men were big babies about pain.

"Good. She's building up her practice, and she even managed to have a house guest—a teen who might have been in danger of getting picked up by the trafficking organization. Sounds like a false alarm, but I think having a project was important. Roman being gone is hard on her."

"I can imagine," Jim said, sighing. "I get lonely when you're gone for the weekend. I can't imagine what it would be like to know I wouldn't see you for five months. Feels like a lifetime."

She laid down beside him so they were facing each other. "I know Kate is anxious to bring down these bastards, but I worry she's going to put herself in more danger than she acknowledges."

Jim wrinkled his brow. "She's planning on opening a safe house for abuse victims. There's an inherent danger in that. I'm sure she knows."

Tilly was immediately on the defensive. "You don't know Kate. She seems to think she's invincible," she said, then shuddered. "You should have seen her when that creep broke into her house. I will never get the image of her unconscious on the floor out of my head. And that only made her more determined."

"Not a pretty picture," Jim said. "But Kate can handle herself. And they put in all that security around her house. As long as she's careful…"

Tilly sat up. "Seriously? You're telling me you wouldn't worry if I were in that situation? Living alone out in the middle of nowhere in a town where at least some of the people have tried to hurt me and maybe still want to?"

Jim propped himself up on his elbow. "I'm not saying that. I'm just saying that Kate knows what she's getting herself into. She's a grown woman, Tilly. We all work in fields that expose us to risk. It's a fact of life. Do you know how many times you've left to take a case and I've laid in bed wondering if you were safe? I worry about everything from having one of the assailants lash out at you to you driving at three in the morning on icy roads."

The fire Tilly had felt began to fade. "Yeah, I know," she said reluctantly. "I'm just not used to worrying about her. Sometimes I think it was easier when I kept myself separate. But I also know I couldn't live without her now if I tried."

"I get it. But try not to take on her stress, too. You've got enough on your plate already."

A while later, Tilly opened up a book in bed. Jim was fast asleep again, snoring lightly beside her. Kate was right. Tilly ran hot and cold, her moods shifting so suddenly they threatened to knock her over. Before moving to New Mexico, before her father had died, Tilly and Jim had been rock-solid. But none of Tilly's secrets had been uncovered at that point. He didn't know her at all back then.

Maybe Tilly was too broken for a guy like Jim.

CHAPTER 23
KATE

Kate met Ruth for lunch Thursday afternoon.

"I had forgotten that house was so huge," Ruth commented. "What made you decide to buy it?"

Kate paused. Though she accepted the fact that people would know the safe house existed, she wasn't ready to have that part of her life known. Especially with Roman being gone for so long. She felt conflicted. Ruth had shown her nothing but kindness, but she still wasn't sure she wanted to open up.

"I've always loved that house, and when I saw it on the realtor site I fell in love with the idea of living there." Kate smiled. "I know it's kind of crazy."

"It's such a big space," Ruth continued without missing a beat. "Is it just you?"

Kate shifted uncomfortably in her seat. When she answered, it was a bit too slow. "For now." An awkward silence followed, in which Kate wondered again why she was being so obtuse and difficult. Ruth was engaging her in casual conversation, the kind she'd be subjected to a hundred times as she got to know people in town. Why was she so on edge? She decided to change the subject.

"What about you, Ruth? Do your children live nearby?"

Ruth smiled sadly. "My husband and I never had any children, so I'm on my own now that he's passed. Bless his soul."

"I'm sorry. I shouldn't have assumed."

Ruth waved away her apology. "It's not a problem, dear. I've had a full life, and a good career. My employees are like my children."

"I'm not sure I've ever asked what you do," Kate said, realizing that she knew very little about Ruth. "Do you work at the bank?"

"Ah, no. I do love to chat with the girls at our women's lunches, but my connection to the bank was through my husband. Now I'm a mostly retired consultant."

"Oh. What kind of consulting?"

Ruth grinned. "Recruitment. I'm a headhunter of sorts" she said. "But I try to spend most of my time volunteering or having lunch. My days of hard work are definitely over."

The rest of the meal was spent talking about Ruth's volunteer project, a smoking cessation program that she'd been working on for several years. As they spoke, Kate studied the lines on Ruth's face—the ones that her carefully applied makeup couldn't hide. Kate could see evidence of stress and sadness around Ruth's eyes, and it brought her own grief to the surface. When they said their goodbyes, Kate found herself wishing her mother and father were still alive.

Back at her office, Kate got back to the project she'd begun earlier in the week. She signed in to her computer and pulled up the city website. The list of staff was long—everyone from cashiers to maintenance to administration. Kate had started a list, beginning with the Copelands, Benny and Allen Parks, and a few other businessmen she'd spotted in photos together. Now she was adding anyone from the city staff who might be a possible culprit. Without any solid evidence she decided to work her way through local government and as many businessmen as she could, familiarizing herself with their bios and community work.

It was like finding a needle in a haystack, but it made her feel like she was doing something tangible to try and track these men down. She'd gone through some photos with Linnie, but the girl wasn't entirely sure who she'd spoken with. So Kate was left with many possibilities and no real answers.

Kate sighed. When she'd finished with the city website she opened a new tab and began a search for Joseph Moore, a name she didn't recognize but possibly one of Linnie's stalkers.

Joseph Moore was a vice president of one of the local credit unions. He was not an Alamogordo native, but Kate found pictures of him all over the internet—participating in ribbon cuttings and networking events. When she ran across a picture of Moore shaking hands with Benny Parker, who was currently serving a life sentence for the murder of high school student Gabby Greene, she paused. Benny Parks had been tied to so many other businessmen in town, it wasn't enough of a connection to mean anything. But the look on Joseph Moore's face was strange. Benny Parks smiled at the camera, his expression smug. Moore, on the other hand, looked conflicted. He was smiling, but the expression looked forced—the smile didn't reach his eyes. And if Kate were a betting woman, she'd say he looked scared.

She searched until she found a date with the photo. Seven years had passed since the event. Kate saved the photo on her desktop and then wrote down the facts she'd managed to gather about Joseph Moore, noting his connection with Benny Parks.

But the next man on the list, Gerald Foster, didn't seem to have any connection to Benny at all. He'd only been in town a few years, taking the long-vacant position as head of Parks & Rec with the City of Alamogordo. He didn't appear to partici-pate in any of the civic organizations that the Parks men frequented, and other than his bio on the city website Kate couldn't find much about him.

She was lost in thought when there was a knock at her door.

"It's open," she said. She didn't have any more clients on the schedule that day, but dropping by seemed to be as popular as picking up a phone. Several of Kate's newest clients had come from drop-ins and her light schedule meant that she usually had time to do intake on the spot.

Unfortunately, the man who walked in wasn't new. Kate planted her feet solidly on the floor and looked him in the eye.

"You need to leave, Mr. Parks," she said, her voice pure steel and dripping with hate.

Allen Parks made no move to close the door behind him or to move further into her office. Instead, he stood where he was and smiled. Kate remembered the last time she'd been this close to Parks—outside the jail where his nephew was being held as he awaited his trial. He'd gotten right in her face and told her to leave town. It was the moment she finally realized she would never quit until she saw this man behind bars.

The longer he stood at her door, the more furious she became.

"I'm not going to tell you again," she said more forcefully. "I will call the police."

"Now why would you want to do something like that, Kate, when I came here to talk." Parks kept his smile in place despite Kate's hostility.

"Why would you think I would want to talk to you?" Kate growled.

"Oh, I don't think you want to, but you still *need* to hear what I have to say." Parks' emphasis on the word need put Kate on edge. He was still standing at her door, but the way he commanded the space it felt like he owned it. She could see how Benny had grown up with such an overinflated sense of entitlement, and for a second she almost felt sorry for him.

"All right. Tell me what you came here for and then get out."

"Tsk. Tsk. Such poor manners. Your father must have forgotten to teach you respect for your elders."

Kate's blood began to boil, her heart racing. Allen Parks was baiting her, and it was going to take every ounce of self-control to keep her cool. She sat back in her chair and crossed her arms, refusing to speak another word.

Parks frowned, showing the first sign that Kate wasn't the only one on edge. "Fine, Kate. Right to business." He took one step closer and narrowed his gaze. "I know what you're doing Kate. Didn't I warn you to stay out of this?'

"You did. And if I'm being honest, it had the opposite effect." Kate stood and walked toward Parks, causing him to take a step back. She was determined to keep control of the conversation. "You listen to me, you bastard. I won't rest until every one of you monsters is locked up."

For a brief moment Parks' confidence faltered, but then the moment was gone and the smile returned. He stepped up to Kate—standing close enough that she could feel the heat of his body. She wanted to back away but couldn't let him gain any ground, so she held hers.

His breath was hot against her face, the subtle scent of cinnamon gum or breath spray nearly making her gag. "Don't say I didn't warn you." Neither of them moved for a solid two minutes. Finally Parks sighed and walked out the door, shutting it behind him. When she heard the outer doors close Kate sprinted from her office to the restroom where she threw up.

CHAPTER 24
TILLY

As she sifted through a stack of handwritten reports on her desk, Tilly allowed herself to miss her old clinic a tiny bit. They'd upgraded to a fully computerized reporting system several years back, and it saved so much time. A lot of smaller offices had no choice but to use paper—with budgets so limited an upgrade was not at all feasible. Some offices stuck to paper when their coordinators or directors weren't tech-savvy enough to put trust in digital records. Thankfully most places were choosing to digitize their records which made statistical analysis and information recovery infinitely more accessible.

Unfortunately, Tilly's new job was largely paper. As clinical coordinator, she was going to find a way to change that as a matter of self-preservation. She'd already created a new document template for her monthly reports, and once she got a few months into the job she'd be working from her own digital files. Next step was getting all the nurses using electronic charts.

Her desk phone rang.

"Hi Tilly. The hospital is on the phone." The receptionist transferred the call.

"Ms. Medina?"

"That's me. How can I help you?"

"I have you down as the emergency contact for James Schmidt." Tilly had been organizing her files, but she stopped short. She dropped the stack of files back onto her desk and tried to breathe, though it felt like all the oxygen had been sucked out the room.

"Is he okay?" Tilly's voice trembled.

"He's had a cardiac incident, ma'am. We need you to come to the ED now if you can."

"I'll be right there."

Tilly grabbed her purse, locked up her files, and nearly sprinted out the door of the clinic without a word to anyone. She thought about how tired Jim had been. He'd assured her that he was fine, but hadn't she known it wasn't true? All her instincts had told her something was wrong. Was it a heart attack?

Tilly's mind raced faster than her feet as she jogged across campus. When she arrived at the Emergency Department registration desk, she was out of breath. She identified herself.

"He's in surgery," the nurse told her. "Do you know where the surgical waiting room is?"

"No, but I'll find it."

"I'll let them know you're coming." The nurse picked up the phone as Tilly turned away.

———

Tilly started at the wall, focusing on her breathing as the surgical nurse spoke to her in a hushed tone.

"His office called the ambulance when they found him. He mentioned to his secretary that he thought he might be coming down with a cold. She noticed him rubbing his chest and thought it was odd so she went to check on him a little while later. Maybe 20 minutes. She found him behind his desk, unconscious."

Without looking up, Tilly asked. "Heart attack?"

"Unfortunately, no. It looks like an aortic aneurysm. We're seeing a lot of internal bleeding. I will let you know what we find as soon as I can."

"Thank you," Tilly said. She heard the nurse leave and as soon as the door shut she allowed herself to fall apart. Internal bleeding meant some kind of rupture, and though she had never encountered Jim's particular condition in her practice she knew that the situation was critical. She cried until her scrub top was soaked, and she felt exhaustion and emptiness take over.

Then she began to strategize.

When Jim came home he would probably need constant care, at least for a while. She was new on the job at Esperanza House, but she hoped they would let her stay home and stay off the call rotation for a while. She'd already received a text from Marie and had given her a top-level rundown on the situation. She needed to call Kate, should have done so from the start, but she'd waited for an update, hoping to have better news.

She picked up her phone.

"What's wrong?" Kate asked as soon as Tilly said hello. Tilly gave her the briefest summary of the events of the day, which was enough to convince Kate to come to Las Cruces. When Tilly hung up she slumped back in her chair, allowing a wave of fatigue to settle around her. It would likely be hours before she got more news, so she resigned herself to a long wait. She almost picked up her phone to research more on aortic aneurysm but she knew it would only make her more anxious.

Kate appeared an hour later, having dropped her bag and Rusty at Tilly's house. And it wasn't until that moment that Tilly fully considered the reality of the situation. Kate wasn't here to visit for an hour or two. She was prepared to stay overnight which meant that this ordeal would not be ending anytime soon.

"How is he?" Kate asked.

"No idea. It's only been an hour, so I . . ." Tilly was interrupted by the nurse walking back into the waiting room, followed by the surgeon. Tilly grabbed Kate's hand, bracing for bad news. "It's not good," she said to no one in particular.

The surgeon sat across from her, clasping his hands in front of him. "I'm sorry."

———

Hours later, Tilly couldn't remember the exact words the surgeon had spoken to her. But she would never forget the moment she knew that Jim was dead.

Somehow Kate had gotten her home and transferred her to her bed where she now lay, staring at the ceiling, wondering how the world could be so cruel. Her sadness was so deep that she could not access it. All she could do was lie still and stare, eyes wide open, her heart a void.

"I brought you some tea," Kate said, making her way to Tilly's bedside table and placing a mug on the coaster. She sat gently on the edge of bed. Her eyes were red rimmed and puffy. Tilly felt a stab of sympathy, but she was too numb to offer any comfort. She couldn't even muster the energy to thank Kate for the tea. Instead she sat up shakily against the headboard, picked up the mug, and took a sip.

"Not sure if you're ready to talk about this, but I called Jim's parents and let them know what happened. They're flying in tonight." Kate took Tilly's free hand. "I canceled my appointments for the rest of the week and called your office and spoke with Marie. She sends her condolences and said not to worry about anything. She said she'll check in with you next week."

Kate looked away as she took a deep, steadying breath. "I'm sorry if I overstepped."

"Thank you," Tilly whispered. "I really appreciate you being here Kate." She set the mug carefully on the table. "I think I just need to sleep a while."

Kate smiled sadly. "Call me if you need me. Anything you need." She left the room, closing the door quietly behind her. Tilly laid back down, pulling her blanket over her head. She angled her body away from Jim's side of the bed, not yet ready to face the new reality of her life. Thankfully exhaustion, or maybe shock, pulled her under.

CHAPTER 25
KATE

Kate kept the house quiet while Tilly slept. She sat on Tilly's couch and made phone calls, Rusty at her feet providing comfort. The hospital had asked whether she wanted them to notify Jim's parents, but Kate had declined the offer. She knew the next few hours and days would be the hardest his parents—and her sister—had ever had to endure. She wanted to honor Jim's memory by being there for the people who loved him.

She also knew that Tilly was in shock, and was in no condition to talk with anyone. Kate had watched the blood drain from Tilly's face as the doctor explained what had happened. The aortic aneurysm that ruptured causing internal bleeding. The time that had elapsed while Jim lay on his office floor—precious moments that may have saved him.

Kate had spoken with Jim's mother briefly, but the woman's grief had soon overtaken her. She passed the phone to Jim's father. After some heavy silence, Jim's father explained that there was a history of heart conditions in Jim's family. His voice broke as he explained how his brother and two uncles had died young. Tilly had never mentioned this, and Kate wondered if her sister even knew.

After hanging up and checking on Tilly, Kate readied the spare room for Jim's parents. The bed was brand new. The sheets were still in their packaging. As she looked around, Kate's heart filled with sorrow over the end of her sister's new beginning.

As she finished making the bed, her cell phone vibrated in her pocket.

"Is everything okay?" Roman said when she answered. The fear is his voice was nearly her undoing.

"I'm at Tilly's. Jim was taken to the hospital today. He had an aortic aneurysm."

"Oh God. Is he all right?"

"He didn't make it." Kate barely got the words out before tears began spilling down her cheeks.

"I'll fly home," Roman said, his voice barely more than a whisper.

Kate wanted Roman with her more than anything, but her pragmatic side kicked in. "You should wait, Roman. Jim's parents are flying in tonight and Tilly's practically catatonic. As much as I want you here, I'm not sure what you could do."

"I would be there for you," Roman protested. "I don't have to do anything except be with you."

Kate sighed. "I know, but how would that impact your training?"

"I don't know," he replied miserably. "I suppose I would have to make it up."

"Then stay for now. I'll be helping to make arrangements for the next few days. Rusty and I will be here at Tilly's house for at least the next few days. I'll let you know as soon as the funeral is planned."

"I don't like it."

"What's to like?" Kate said with a small smile. "I miss you."

"Me too," Roman said. "I can't believe this is happening." He paused for a moment. "When I saw that you called in the middle of the day, I was so scared. I thought something might have happened to you. I'm sad for Tilly and for Jim. He was too damned young. Every day away makes me feel a little bit more uneasy."

"I know the feeling. But I think we're both where we need to be right now. Tilly is going to need me. And I don't want you to be gone any longer than you have to be."

"Please stay safe," he said. Soon they said their goodbyes and Kate went back to her vigil.

———

"Still doesn't feel real," Tilly said. She and Kate were sitting on the couch. The house was mostly dark. Jim's parents had retired early after a long day of funeral arrangements and going through Jim's things. As soon as they'd arrived, Jim's parents enfolded Tilly in a protective bubble. There were so many tears, but also laughter. Most of all a pervasive sense of disbelief. Kate was grateful that Tilly had come out of her shell a bit, allowing herself to grieve openly.

"I know. Roman's going to fly to Denver late Friday and then back to Virginia on Sunday. Do you think we should get an Airbnb and invite Jim's parents to stay with us?"

"I'd rather find a hotel," Tilly said with a sigh. "By the weekend I'm going to need somewhere to hide out."

Kate understood that need better than anyone.

"And then," Tilly continued, "I think I'd like to come stay with you for a few days. If you don't mind."

Kate wrapped an arm around her sister's shoulder. "Of course." They sat in silence for a few more minutes. Tilly sat so still that Kate wondered if she was starting to fall asleep, but when she began to speak her voice was clear and alert.

"I brought this on myself, you know. I'd been questioning

our relationship. Wondering if I was too damaged to be with a man like Jim."

"Oh, Tilly."

"I know what you're going to say," Tilly said, stopping Kate mid-thought. "I'm not saying it's my fault that he's gone. It's also not that I think I don't deserve love." She took Kate's hand and finally looked at her. Her eyes were still red and she looked so weary. Kate's heart ached for her sister. She wanted to reassure her. To tell her everything would be okay. But it was clear that Tilly was not finished, so Kate kept quiet.

"You know, Jim and I never talked about marriage. We were together nearly four years, living together for three of those, and we never talked about what came next. When we decided to move here, it wasn't a next step. It was just another thing to do."

"So what are you saying?"

Tilly sighed. "I'm babbling. I feel sad, but not sad enough I think. Not the way I should feel. Jim deserved better."

Both sisters jumped at the sound of Jim's mother entering the room. "Jim knew how much you loved him." As the older woman made her way to the couch, Kate wondered how much of their conversation had been overheard. She almost expected Jim's mother to feel angry at Tilly's words, but it was clear from the woman's expression that there was nothing further from the truth.

"Ellen, I'm so sorry . . ." Tilly started, but Jim's mother held up her hand

"You don't have to apologize to me, Tilly. Jim has told me a little bit about your story over the years. You're too young to have seen this much tragedy in your life. Jim knew exactly who you are and he loved you."

A tear slid down Tilly's cheek.

"Did Jim ever tell you why he became an attorney? And why he worked on the types of cases he did?" Ellen asked.

"He wanted to help people find justice," Tilly answered. Kate was surprised by how rehearsed that answer was. She wondered if that's really all Tilly knew about Jim's motivations.

"When his sister was in college, she was raped by a boy she was seeing," Ellen said. From the look on her face, it was clear that Tilly had not heard this story. "She was never the same, and Jim felt so helpless. Sometimes I think his whole career was a type of self-imposed penance for not being able to do more for her."

"He never told me," she whispered.

Kate held her breath, her heart beginning to race. Neither Jim nor Tilly had ever mentioned a sister, and Kate couldn't help but notice the way Ellen spoke about her daughter in the past tense.

"He told me once that he didn't want to burden you. And I told him on more than one occasion that he was making a mistake by not sharing it with you." Ellen sighed. Her eyes were puffy and red, and she rubbed her hands together nervously. "I'm telling you now because I want you to know that, despite outward appearances, Jim made mistakes like the rest of us. He wasn't a saint. He wasn't perfect. And he never wondered for one second about whether or not you were good enough for him, so I hope you won't spend any more time thinking that might have been the case."

Ellen rose, turning toward the spare bedroom. She smiled at Tilly.

"Thank you," Tilly said quietly.

When the door clicked closed, Kate asked Tilly, "Are you okay?" Kate was still feeling the effects of the strange encounter, and she couldn't imagine Tilly being all right, but Tilly nodded.

"I think I am," she said. "I wonder how many things I never knew about Jim's life. I guess I wasn't the only one keeping secrets in our relationship." Tilly yawned. "I'm going to bed. I think I might actually get some sleep tonight."

Kate gave her sister a hug, but she didn't go straight to bed. Instead, she cuddled on the couch with Rusty at her feet, wondering if you could ever know anyone at all.

———

With Jim's parents doing the heavy lifting, the funeral arrangements went smoothly. Kate watched Tilly do the most basic tasks in a haze, as if grief had completely clouded her mind. And every night after Tilly went to bed, Kate kicked herself for all the time she'd wasted with Roman. She and Tilly both knew how quickly the rug could be pulled out from under your feet. With Tilly's grief so near the surface, it was hard not to reflect on how little time they all had.

Friday morning, Kate and Tilly dropped Rusty off at the hacienda on their way north to Colorado. Kate kept the music going so Tilly wouldn't feel like she had to talk, but Tilly was asleep before they'd made it to Albuquerque. Kate didn't wake her until they arrived at their hotel in Colorado Springs.

"Time to wake up." She shook Tilly's shoulder gently until her sister finally opened her eyes. Tilly looked around with a confused expression. Then Kate's words seemed to make sense.

"I'm sorry, Kate. I slept the whole way," Tilly said sourly.

"You needed it," Kate said. She got out of the car and started pulling their bags out of the trunk. They checked-in to their adjoining rooms. Roman was due in a few hours, and Jim's parents had come the night before. They'd agreed to meet for dinner, and Kate knew that Tilly was dreading every moment to come.

Thinking she might need a snack before dinner, Kate knocked on Tilly's door and then let herself in when her sister didn't answer. Tilly was sprawled out on her bed, snoring softly.

For the next few hours, Kate watched TV and counted down

the minutes until Roman arrived. When she heard someone opening the door, she nearly knocked him down in her haste to be near him. He swept her up into his arms and buried his face in her hair. They stayed that way a long time.

There was so much to say but the reason for their reunion was so laden with sadness, neither she nor Roman seemed eager to speak.

"How's Tilly?" Roman finally said. He untangled himself from Kate's embrace and led her over to the bed, leaving his overnight bag where he'd dropped it against the door. He sat down and Kate joined him, resting her head on his shoulder.

"She's sleeping," Kate said. "She slept most of the way up here. I'd be more worried, but honestly, when she's up she looks like a zombie."

Roman swallowed hard and Kate could see tears glistening in his eyes. "I can't imagine how she's feeling right now."

Kate squeezed his hand. "I love you, Roman."

He smiled. "I know. I love you, too."

The service was absolutely beautiful. The funeral home was overflowing with Jim's friends and former coworkers. Even a few of his new colleagues had made the trip to Colorado to pay their respects. Though Tilly's eulogy touched on their relationship and all of the good work that Jim had done while she'd known him, the raw sorrow in her voice nearly broke Kate's heart.

"I can't wrap my brain around this yet," she said, her voice growing quieter as she neared the end of her speech. She leaned into the microphone. "I know that I'll always be grateful for the time I was given with Jim. He was truly one of the best people I've ever known."

Tilly returned to her seat beside Kate, her shoulders shaking as she cried silently. The service ended, and Tilly joined Jim's parents at the back of the room in a receiving line. After what felt like an interminable amount of time, the room cleared. As soon as the last person left the room Tilly's shoulders visibly dropped. Kate rushed over, wrapping her arms around her sister. She reached into her purse and pulled out her keys, handing them to Roman who was standing nearby.

"Let's go back to the hotel," Kate said, taking Tilly's arm and leading her out to the waiting car.

"What about Jim's parents?" Tilly asked wearily.

"We'll see them tomorrow. Right now let's get you to bed."

CHAPTER 26
TILLY

Tilly pressed her cheek against the car window. Kate had insisted on driving back from Colorado, so Tilly had a lot of time to think. It had only been a little over a month since she and Jim had made this trip together. She'd been wary, but also hopeful. As the landscape sped by, Tilly felt more and more untethered. The idea of living in New Mexico, alone—it was hard to imagine how she'd gotten to this place in her life. And yet here she was.

In the days after Jim's death, his mother had filled her in on the hereditary heart disease that had run rampant in Jim's family, taking several family members so young—two before their 35th birthday. Jim's mother Ellen, though distraught, accepted her son's death with the grace of a woman who'd been through it more times than she'd like to count. There were tearful hugs as Jim's parents headed to the airport. Tilly knew she'd most likely never see or hear from them again, and she was both sad and relieved by that fact.

"We're here," Kate said softly, waking Tilly from her trance. She'd probably been sleeping, but it felt more like being hypnotized. Her mind was foggy and she felt weary deep in her bones. All she wanted to do was sleep.

They'd pulled up in front of Kate's house, and a very excited Rusty was barking behind the gate. After nearly being bowled over by Kate's furry friend, Tilly made her way up to one of Kate's spare rooms and threw herself face first onto the mattress. She heard Kate walking up to her door.

"Brought you some water," Kate said, walking across the room and setting a glass beside the bed.

"Where's the mutt?" Tilly groaned.

Kate laughed. "The excitement was too much for him. He's already conked out on his bed in the living room."

"We should all be so lucky."

"I don't know. You seem to be on your way there. Do you want me to bring you anything?"

Tilly shook her head, her face still buried in a pillow.

"Get some sleep," Kate said. She shut the door, leaving Tilly in darkness. Tilly barely managed to crawl under the covers before she fell asleep.

————

The next 48 hours passed in a haze of grief and exhaustion. Hard as she tried, Tilly couldn't stay motivated enough to stay upright. She watched as the voicemails and texts amassed on her phone, but she couldn't find the energy to respond. She knew she'd eventually have to return to the world of the living, but the idea of having to start over formed a knot in her chest that weighed her down. She couldn't even think about Jim without being overcome by grief.

Kate went back to work, and Tilly could see that her sister was growing more and more concerned, but thankfully Kate didn't push her to get out of bed.

Jim would have. He would have cheered her up, or if he

couldn't he would have nagged her out of her depression. Every time she imagined his face in her mind, she felt the rock in her chest grow harder and colder. She had too much time to think. Too much time on her own. By the end of the second day, she was more or less sure her sanity was nearly gone and she hoisted herself out of bed and into the shower.

After getting dressed, she went to the kitchen and began cooking an elaborate meal. Rusty danced at her feet, elated that he had a daytime playmate. When Kate got home, the shock on her face made Tilly laugh out loud.

"What? Didn't Roman ever make you dinner?" Tilly's attempt at playful sarcasm felt hollow, but she was determined to fake it until it began to feel real. At least for this one day.

Kate put her purse down on the table beside the door and walked over to the kitchen table, bending to pet Rusty every few steps as he hopped along beside her.

"That smells amazing," Kate said.

"Really? Because you look like you're approaching something that's going to eat you." Tilly struggled for humor, hoping that Kate would quit looking at her like she was so fragile. Hoping that if Kate stopped looking at her that way, she'd stop feeling it.

Kate seemed to take the cue. "Can I help with anything?"

"It's pretty much done. Want to set the table?"

For a few minutes, the room was quiet as Tilly served up their dinner and Kate poured glasses of iced tea. They ate in silence for a while, until Tilly couldn't take it anymore.

"How was your day?" she asked Kate.

"Good. My schedule isn't that full yet, so I didn't miss much. Tomorrow is the women's luncheon but I'll skip that and head home early."

"Why?"

Kate looked away. "I hate to leave you alone so much."

Tilly closed her eyes. In the blink of an eye, she'd gone from the hardass sister to the one needing support. She hated being coddled by Kate, but was afraid to be on her own. And she knew that Kate meant well. In fact, the love her sister was showing her was both welcome and painful. Tilly couldn't help but think of all the years she'd held Kate at arms length. It felt wrong to take so much affection from her sister. She didn't deserve it.

"I think I'm going to head home tomorrow actually."

Too quickly, Kate asked, "Do you want me to come with you?"

Tilly's mind screamed yes, but she managed a reassuring smile. "I think I'd like to see how I'm feeling when I get there. I need a little bit of normalcy, in so far as that's possible. I need to see if I'm going to be able to stay in that house. Probably not. It's too big for me. It was too big for us." She knew she was rambling and she could see the alarm on Kate's face. She forced herself to take a deep breath. "I appreciate you letting me stay with you, Kate. I'm not sure if I'll be okay over there, but I won't know until I go. But I know where to find you and I'm not afraid to come running back here if I can't handle it."

Kate seemed to be choosing her words carefully. "Okay, I'll work on getting back to normal too. But I'll have my cell phone on all day. Please promise you'll call me even if you just want to say hi. If you go dark, I'm going to come looking for you."

Tilly laughed. "Understood. Now eat. I didn't slave over the stove all afternoon for you to let the food get cold."

The rest of the evening the sisters maintained a level of small talk that didn't entirely hide the layer of tension that was a constant companion. Tilly asked Kate about the women's luncheon, pleased with herself when Kate decided to go ahead and attend. But all she wanted to do was go back to bed. She held out as long as she could.

"Sorry, Kate. My eyes are drooping. I've got to get some sleep." Kate's hug lasted a little longer than usual and Tilly leaned in to her sister, knowing that the next few days were going to feel incredibly empty. She hoped that getting back to work would provide enough structure to get her through.

————

The first thing Tilly did when she got home was to move all of her things into the spare room Kate had slept in. The drive to Las Cruces had given her way too much time to think, and the bedroom she'd shared with Jim felt haunted. She wondered if she'd ever be able to sleep there.

She spent a few hours cleaning and relegating all of Jim's belongings to their bedroom, closing the door behind her. She poured herself a glass of wine and sat on the couch, a stack of unopened mail in front of her on the coffee table. She'd separated out the bills and junk mail, but the pile of cards that remained was formidable. She began opening them mechanically, glancing at signatures but avoiding the messages that had been written. A few people had written longer missives, which Tilly felt sure were meant to comfort her but knew they wouldn't. After opening the last card, she used a rubber band to bind the stack together and threw them on top of the dresser in her old bedroom.

Tilly had every intention of trying to sleep in bed like a normal person, but when the time came she couldn't bring herself to do it. She pulled a fluffy blanket off the bed and got settled on the couch. She turned the TV on. The house was too quiet. She stared blankly at the screen, grateful for the noise and light, but unable to focus. She leaned back against the cushion, hoping that sleep would take her. But as she finally dozed off, her mind wandered back to the day she'd come home from Kate's and found Jim sleeping on the couch. All her instincts had told her something was wrong, but she'd allowed Jim to convince her he was fine.

A wave of anger passed through her. For all his talk of being open and honest, Jim had been keeping secrets from her and presenting an upbeat side to everything. Tilly's life had been so riddled with grief and disappointment that she'd allowed herself to be shielded from the truth. And now Jim was gone and she was alone. Tilly finished off the bottle of wine before she was finally able to sleep.

CHAPTER 27
KATE

Kate went to work, knowing that Tilly would be gone when she got home. Taking a cue from her sister, Kate decided that she needed to stop sulking and get back to normal. She'd spent the time that Roman had been gone feeling a mixture of loneliness and frustration that had begun to turn toxic in her system. Then Jim died, and Kate realized how ridiculous she'd been. Roman would come home. Their relationship was good, and if Kate didn't completely sabotage it he would come home for good and they would resume their life together.

The same could not be said for Tilly and Jim.

She thought about her parents. For the first few weeks after her mother died, Kate's father had wandered the house like a ghost. Tilly's behavior was so similar it had pulled Kate back into that sad time. She hoped Tilly would be able to find her way past the grief.

Kate headed to her luncheon with a sense of purpose. She was relieved to see Ruth already sitting at their usual table.

"Hey, stranger," Ruth said, standing to give Kate a quick hug.

"How was last week's meeting?" Kate asked, taking a seat across from her.

"Interesting. The owner of the new fitness center gave a presentation on women's health." Ruth took a sip of her coffee. "Of course, she wanted us all to join. I saved you one of the free vouchers she gave out." Ruth rummaged around in her massive purse, her rings knocking against the metal clasps with a soft ding. She found what she was looking for and handed it to Kate. "So, where were you last week?"

Kate sighed. "My sister's boyfriend died suddenly. He had a heart condition. I spent most of last week in Las Cruces and then we drove up to Colorado for the memorial. That's where most of his friends are."

"That's terrible, Kate. Is your sister doing all right?"

"As well as can be expected, I suppose."

"Your family has been through so much," Ruth said. She put a hand on Kate's "I'm so sorry for your loss. Please give my condolences to your sister."

"Thank you," Kate said. She liberated her hand from Ruth's to pick up her coffee cup. Part of getting back normal was not thinking or talking about Jim's death all the time. Kate wanted to be present. "What's today's program about?"

Before Ruth could answer, several women approached their table, greeting Ruth. Kate was thankful for the interruption. She shook hands with each woman as Ruth introduced them, making mental notes about any details they shared. One woman hung back, introducing herself to Kate since Ruth was deep in conversation with her colleagues. Kathleen was an administrator at the hospital. She handed Kate her business card.

"Mind if I join you?" Kathleen asked.

"Not at all," Kate replied as Kathleen took the seat beside her. Ruth was still engaged in conversation with another of the women who'd approached, so Kate focused on Kathleen. "How long have you been with the hospital?"

"Only a few years," Kathleen said. "My husband was stationed at the Air Force base. We love the area, so when he was discharged we stayed here. What about you? You're running a psychology practice here in town?"

"Just opened it. I'm still building up my clientele. I'm doing family counseling, but I'm especially interested in treating adolescents. I worked as a high school psychologist for about five years and I think I could be of use."

"That sounds wonderful. Actually I've been meaning to look for a therapist for my daughter. She's a very anxious fourteen-year-old. Seems like things have gotten worse lately. She's finished up eighth grade, and I think the idea of starting high school is overwhelming."

"I'd love to talk with her. Give me a call and we'll get something scheduled."

The event organizer started tapping on the microphone to call everyone to attention. Kate turned and noticed Ruth looking at her with a strange expression, almost a frown. "Ruth? Is everything all right?"

"Fine, dear," Ruth replied, but Kate suddenly felt very uncomfortable. She was relieved when the organizer started speaking. The presentation went by quickly and afterwards, during social time, Ruth was very quiet. Kate tried engaging her in conversation, but all Ruth offered were one and two-word replies. Finally she excused herself leaving Kate feeling as if she'd done something wrong.

———

Kate arrived home to a very disgruntled dog and an empty house. She took Rusty on a long walk down the road, letting him sniff and mark to his heart's delight. She knew how much he'd been missing Roman and now he was back to being alone at home during the day. When they returned home, Rusty snarfed down his dinner and then laid down for a nap. He snored lightly while Kate cooked herself dinner.

After dinner, Kate texted with Tilly. She resisted the urge to call her sister, knowing that there was a fine line between being concerned and being overbearing. No amount of nagging or coaxing would get Tilly through her grieving process any faster, and while they'd grown so much closer since their father died Kate still felt that her connection with her sister was a bit tenuous. She needed to focus on her own life and let Tilly go through this trauma in whatever way she needed to.

Kate turned off the lights and headed to bed early to do some reading. She was a few chapters in when her phone rang.

"Hi, beautiful." Roman's voice was her undoing. Tears started rolling down Kate's cheeks even as she smiled

"Hi sweetie."

"Are you okay?" Roman asked, on high-alert. Kate laughed.

"Yes, sorry. Tilly went back home today and I was, quote, getting back to normal. Apparently I'm not quite there yet."

"Understandable. Seeing you for twenty-four hours was definitely not enough. I got back here and all I want to do is come home again."

Kate's heart swelled. "I know the feeling, but I think you're where you need to be. And I've got my hands full trying to get this business up and running. I got a new client today."

"That's great. How's Tilly doing?"

"She's struggling, but she wants to get back to work."

"She sounds like you."

"I know." Kate smiled. "I started to argue, but realized she's pretty much doing exactly what I would be doing. So I'm trying to give her some space."

The line was silent for a moment. "I still can't believe Jim is gone." Roman sounded weary. "I keep thinking about how short life is. How many dangers lurk out there that we can't see." Kate had been thinking the same things for weeks. At first, those thoughts had made her resentful of Roman's absence. She'd been lonely, but also a little bit jealous. The work she was doing to start up her new business felt insignificant next to what Roman was working on.

"Jim's dad lost two brothers to the same heart issue. Seems to run on the male side of that family. I feel so bad for them all." Kate had always been wary of the unknown, and the suddenness of Jim's death made her very anxious. "You'd better be taking care of yourself."

Roman chuckled. "I am, boss. No refined sugar and I'm getting plenty of sleep."

"Sure," Kate chided. "I bet you have a bag of Doritos in your hand right now."

"Never," Roman said, but she could hear the crinkle of a bag on the other end of the receiver. "Anyway, I wanted to check in. I've got to be up at 4:00 tomorrow morning so I've got to get to sleep. I'll call you tomorrow."

"Love you," Kate said. She heard Roman pull in a breath.

"I love you, too."

After they hung up, she realized why he'd been so shocked. He usually said I love you first.

CHAPTER 28
TILLY

Tilly woke with a pounding headache. She was not prone to hangovers, but as she stumbled into the kitchen for some water she realized she'd downed a whole bottle of wine without eating anything since breakfast. She sipped gingerly at her glass of water until the nausea began to pass. Then she gulped the rest, refilling it and taking it back to the couch.

It was early, still dark outside. Tilly was due to the office at eight. Actually, no one was expecting Tilly at the office this week, but she planned on showing up right on time. Maybe if she acted like nothing was wrong with her, it would eventually be true. The hard knot under her ribs throbbed as a fresh wave of sadness and grief poured over her, taking her breath away.

She plopped down on the couch, rubbing her chest. After everything she'd been through, she wondered if this latest tragedy would be the thing that finally did her in. How ironic would it be to die of a heart attack mere days after Jim.

Tilly knew she was catastrophizing. She took some slow deep breaths and the knot began to loosen slightly. Enough that she could breathe properly again. Hoping to distract herself, she turned on the television. A local reporter stood in front of a park entrance, a streamer of caution tape behind her. It was dark, but the camera lights showed a flurry of movement behind the reporter.

Police responded to a call about a naked woman roaming the park. When they arrived on the scene, it became clear that the woman was a victim of violent crime. Though her identity has not been released, I am told that a woman in her 20s has been transported by ambulance to the hospital for treatment. Police were able to confirm that the woman was sexually assaulted. As the number of recent assaults increases, the police department is planning a press conference to inform the public about how to stay safe. The conference will begin at 9 AM. Back to you Bob.

The camera image shifted to an anchor behind a desk who shifted to the next news item. Tilly heard him drone on, but her mind was replaying the previous scene. Sexual predation was not generally an isolated incident. Most sexual assault offenders were guilty of multiple assaults, but the term serial rapist was usually reserved for a certain kind of criminal—one who targets adult woman or men and is known to have committed three or more assaults. Like serial killers, serial rapists often had signature behaviors.

With her mind thoroughly distracted from her private pain, she headed to the bathroom to shower. Donning a fresh set of scrubs, Tilly packed her bag and headed to the clinic.

———

"Oh my gosh, Tilly! I didn't know you'd be coming in." Marie opened the door and swept Tilly up in a firm embrace. "You don't have to be here today."

Tilly gave Marie a squeeze. "Yes, I do. I can't spend another minute at home. I need to work and get my mind off things for a bit." Marie nodded, but she followed Tilly to her office. "I saw the news this morning. Did they bring in the victim from the park?"

"Yes, they have her up at the ED. From what I've heard, she was pretty out of it when they brought her in. I've been waiting for a call about going up to do an exam. Tina's off today, so I had planned on doing it myself."

"I can take it," Tilly said, perhaps a little too enthusiastically.

Marie paused. "I don't know. I'm not sure jumping into a case like this is a good idea in your present frame of mind."

"Trust me, the work helps. I've been through enough to know that it's the only thing that helps at times."

It took another minute or two before Marie reluctantly agreed. "All right, but if it gets to be too much, call me. I'll let you know when they call."

Tilly nodded and then busied herself getting caught up on her reports. She'd only been out of the office for a week, but things had begun to pile up on her desk. She'd sorted through the first layer when there was a knock at her door.

"Hey," Brynn said, walking in. "Just checking to see how you're doing. I didn't think you'd be in yet." As the clinic's social worker Brynn had adopted a soothing tone that worked well for patients and victims, but caused Tilly's skin to crawl.

"Hi. No offense, but please, no counseling today. I came in to get my mind off things." Tilly smiled, hoping her words wouldn't damage the budding friendship she had with Brynn.

"I understand," Brynn said. She'd moved into Tilly's office, but made no attempt to sit. Tilly knew she should offer, but she wasn't in the mood to talk. She was counting down the minutes until the hospital called and she could lose herself for a while in a case. "I'm here if you need me, but I won't nag you. In fact, if you hadn't come in I was going to text you. Wondered if you'd like to have dinner with me tonight."

Tilly smiled. "I'd love to. Can I get back to you a little later today? I'm taking a case soon and I want to make sure I'm feeling all right afterward."

"Sure. Let me know."

Tilly continued working until she could finally see the top of her desk and she felt less overwhelmed. It had been two hours. Finally, Marie knocked on her door. "They're ready for you at the hospital. Apparently she came in severely dehydrated and hypothermic. But she's alert now and able to consent to the exam."

"I'll head up there." Tilly picked up her exam bag on the way out the door, turning off the lights behind her.

CHAPTER 29
KATE

Kate had several appointments, including a consultation with Kathleen's daughter, Mira. From Kathleen's description, Mira was a gifted child and suffered from anxiety; two things that often went hand in hand. Gifted kids tended to be perfectionists. Kate remembered being very anxious as a teen, but luckily she'd had Roman. His antics balanced her out, then and now.

But first Kate was meeting with Delia. Delia had been very understanding when Kate canceled their appointment last week, but she was eager to get back to work. Kate was making notes when Delia knocked at the door and then walked into the office. Right away, Kate knew that something was wrong. Delia's eyes were red-rimmed.

"Delia, what's wrong?" Kate ushered the woman over to a chair and handed her a tissue.

"It's my niece, Lucy." Delia blew her nose noisily as a fresh wave of tears streamed down her cheeks.

"Is she all right?" Kate asked, trying to keep the alarm out of her voice.

"I don't know," Delia said. "She hasn't been returning my calls."

"Have you spoken with her mother? Is she safe?"

Delia nodded. "Yes, her mom said she's busy. Her internship at the City has been filling up her hours. She's been getting home late and then doing homework into the night."

Kate began to relax. "Well, she's a teenager. And from what you've said, a very bright one. Maybe she really is too busy to talk right now."

Delia had stopped crying, but she looked at Kate urgently. "Lucy always calls me back, Ms. Medina. Or at least texts."

"Maybe her phone isn't working. But listen, Delia, this is a good opportunity for us to work on your anxiety. You've done your job. You've checked on Lucy to make sure she's safe. Now it's time to let go of that stress you're feeling. Let's work on some grounding."

Kate led Delia through some exercises, but she could tell the woman's heart wasn't in it. As the end of their session approached, Kate tried to give Delia something positive to think about. "I'll see you next week, Delia. In the meantime, I want you to remember that your niece is growing up. She's pursuing her dreams. She might need a little room to breathe. Be patient."

Delia nodded, but as she was leaving the office she turned and said, "I came to you for a reason, Ms. Medina. I hope I can trust you, because I can't wait anymore. Please, ask yourself this. Why is a teenage girl working at the City coming home late every night? The office closes at five."

"What are you telling me, Delia?"

The woman flushed. "Nothing. I have to go." Before Kate could say another word, Delia was gone.

––––––––

Uneasy after her meeting with Delia, Kate had a hard time preparing for her appointment with Mira. Her mind was too caught up in Delia's words and the implications. When Delia first mentioned her niece weeks ago, Kate had jumped to conclusions immediately. It had taken a lot of work on her part to take her patients at face value, without allowing her own suspicions to color her therapy. But if Delia was right, her niece may very well be in danger. Kate's mind was going in circles trying to figure out what to do, so she jumped when there was a knock at her door.

Kathleen peeked around the corner. "Hi, Kate. Are you ready for us?"

Kate smiled. "Yes, come on in." Kathleen's daughter trailed her. The teen's long hair hung over her eye, covering half of her face. She held her hands up defensively in front of her mouth and didn't make eye contact with Kate when she offered them a seat. Kate and Kathleen chatted quietly for a few minutes, while Mira slowly started to look around Kate's office. Finally, Kate decided it was time to make contact.

"I'm very glad to meet you, Mira. Your mom tells me you're having some anxiety."

Mira turned her head timidly toward Kate and this time she met her eyes, giving a barely perceptible nod.

"Well, I am definitely looking forward to working with you on that. I wonder if maybe we send your mom out for coffee, could we have a chat just the two of us?"

Again, the slight nod. Kathleen patted Mira's shoulder. "I'll be back in a little while. Want me to grab you something from Plateau Espresso? It's our favorite."

"I'm good, actually, but thank you." When Kathleen left, Kate gave Mira another minute or two to orient herself to her surroundings. Then she started. "I just moved in a few weeks ago, so I'm not sure this is exactly how I'm going to keep things in here. What do you think, Mira?"

Mira looked around, then turned to Kate. "It's nice. I like the paint color." Mira's voice was soft but confident. She might hide behind her hair and act shy, but Kate could sense a quiet strength in this girl.

"Me, too," she replied. "Would it be all right if I ask you some questions?" Mira nodded more assertively this time. "Tell me a little bit about your school."

It started slowly, but soon Mira was chatting amiably about her friends and the classes she was taking. "Mira, it sounds like things are going pretty well. Can you tell me about what causes you anxiety? What kinds of things stress you out?"

"Normal things," Mira started. "Tests and stuff. And when my friends are fighting."

"I know the feeling. It can be hard not to take sides."

Mira shrugged. "Yeah, I guess."

Kate could see her shutting down again. "Is there anything else, Mira? Maybe something you haven't mentioned to your mom?" Mira's eyes widened, like Kate had seen right through her. Kate smiled reassuringly, "I'm here to help, remember?"

For a moment Kate thought she'd lost Mira, but finally the girl said, "There are these girls."

Kate waited, giving her space to figure out what she wanted to say. Adults often tried to finish teens' sentences. Kate had learned early in her days working at the high school to sit back and let things happen organically.

"They've been hanging around us a lot. And I don't like them."

"Are they in your grade?"

Mira shook her head. "They're ninth-graders. My friend Alicia knows one of them from church. They've been hanging out after school. We used to walk home together, but lately Alicia's been going with them. She's been acting weird."

Again, that sense of foreboding. "What do you mean?"

"I don't know, like, she's never happy anymore. She never smiles or jokes. And she started wearing makeup all the time. Tons of it. My mom would kill me if I wore that much makeup."

Kate smiled. "I can imagine." She was relieved by the innocence permeating Mira's words. Any fear she had that Mira was being victimized was gone, but a new worry had taken its place. She now had two girls in her sights as possible victims of the trafficking ring. And she didn't have access to either one.

"Do you feel more anxious when those girls are around?"

Mira nodded. "I wish they'd go away. I wish Alicia was back to normal."

"I'm sorry you're having to deal with this right now, Mira. I think maybe you and I can work on some ways to cope with your feelings so that you don't always have to feel so anxious. Would that be okay?" Kate wasn't sure Mira needed a lot of counseling, but she didn't want to cut ties until she had a better handle on the situation. And until she was sure Mira wasn't in any danger.

Kathleen appeared a few minutes later holding three coffee cups. "I know you said you didn't want anything, but their coconut cream latte is my all-time favorite. I hope you don't hate coconut." She handed the cup to Kate.

"I love coconut. Thank you," she said, taking a sip. It was delicious. "Mira and I had a good talk. Could you guys come back next week? Maybe around four so we don't make you miss any more school." Mira smiled when Kathleen agreed. "Great. I'll see you next week."

"Will you be at the luncheon next week?" Kathleen asked as they headed to the door. "I can't always make it, but I do try."

"I'll be there," Kate said.

CHAPTER 30
TILLY

When Tilly got to the Emergency Department she saw Dan Bross talking with a group of people including two police officers in uniform. Tilly recognized one of them from her previous case. Bross waved her over.

"This is Tilly Medina," he said, introducing her.

The detective gave her a rundown. "The victim's name is Paige Branson. She's twenty-eight. A graduate student at NMSU. She was in pretty rough shape when they brought her in, but they've tried to get her hydrated and cleaned up without disturbing anything too badly. We wanted to get you in here earlier, but she's only been lucid for a few minutes."

"She knows I'm coming?" Tilly asked.

"Yes, she hasn't said much. We wanted to have you go through things with her first. Our victim advocate, Cara, will be back here in a few minutes if Paige would like her to be present during the exam. Otherwise, she'll be ready to speak with Paige after the exam"

Tilly liked this detective very much. In her experience, the police were often too focused on their investigation to pay much attention to patient care. "All right. I'll go get started. Will you be here? Or did you want me to call when I finish?"

Daniel answered. "I'm going to head back to the office for a bit, but I should be back here in an hour. You have my number?" Tilly nodded. The detective passed her a card as well, then they both left. Tilly checked in with the nurse at registration and headed to the exam room.

The hospital generally referred patients to the clinic as quickly as possible, but for those who needed emergency care they'd dedicated an exam room at the back, away from prying eyes. Tilly hadn't done an exam at the hospital, but she'd been shown the room and knew what to expect. It was always easier to do exams in the clinic where all their equipment and supplies were, but the hospital had done its best to keep the room stocked with everything she might need.

Paige Benson was laying on the hospital bed, still in her street clothes. She looked up at Tilly when she entered, her eyes wide and frightened. "Hi, Paige. I'm Tilly Medina. I'm a forensic nurse and I'm here to do a sexual assault exam." When Paige nodded, Tilly started laying out her kit. She talked as she worked. "We're going to do a lot of talking first, but I want you to know that this exam is for you. If you get uncomfortable or need a break, let me know. I'm in no rush. My job is to gather evidence, but my goal is to make sure you're taken care of. There's also an advocate standing by in case you'd like to have someone here with you."

"I think I'd rather it just be you, if that's okay." Paige's voice was extremely raspy and Tilly could see angry red finger marks on her neck. When she swallowed, her eyes teared.

"Of course," Tilly said. "Did they give you anything to drink?"

"No."

"Okay, let's go ahead and take a couple of swabs inside your cheek and then I can get you something to drink." Paige nodded and Tilly quickly took swabs from inside Paige's mouth, careful to avoid her split lip and the abrasions around her nose. "Do you feel like you can drink some water?" she asked when she'd finished.

"Yes please," Paige said. Tilly grabbed a bottle out of the mini-fridge they kept in the room. She handed the bottle to Paige and then logged in to the exam room computer, booting up the program they used to take medical histories.

"I'm going to start by asking you a lot of questions. We'll start with the easy stuff like your contact information and medical history. Then we'll get into harder stuff. I'll give you a break before we start into the more intimate questions. And, again, if you need to stop, please let me know."

Tilly spent the next hour taking copious notes on Paige's medical and social history. Every once in a while, Paige asked for a break, leaning back in the bed to breathe. "Are you in pain?" Tilly asked.

"A little bit. They said nothing was broken, but I can feel some pain in my groin and on my legs."

"Right now I can give you some ibuprofen. After we're done with the exam, I'll see if they can give you something a little stronger. Cleaning up any abrasions we find may help too. Let's go through what happened, and then we'll get through the physical exam as quickly as we can."

———

The exam ran long.

Paige had been thrown to the ground and had fresh bruises and abrasions on her limbs, chest, and back, all of which had to be documented. She'd fought hard against her attacker. He'd finally strangled her until she lost consciousness. Her memories surrounding the rape were hazy or missing altogether. But the attack had been violent and brutal, leaving physical damage that would take significant time to heal. During the pelvic exam Tilly had to stop frequently, giving Paige time to breathe through the pain.

Tilly worked slowly, talking Paige through each uncomfortable step of the process. Afterward, she handed Paige a pile of clothes—donations that would get Paige through the next stage of her process, going home. Paige's parents lived in Virginia and were en route. Paige's clothes had been taken for evidence, and Tilly knew that being in a hospital gown made most people feel vulnerable. For sexual assault victims, the clinic kept a store of clothes and new underwear. The idea of wearing someone else's clothes was often awkward, but the relief at being out of the gown and fully covered was almost palpable in assault victims. Tilly stepped out so that Paige could get dressed, taking her kit with her.

A strict chain of custody had to be maintained now. Tilly would not let the evidence out of her sight until she signed it over to the investigating detective for processing.

The adrenaline was beginning to wear off and Tilly allowed her shoulders to slump the minute she closed the door. She saw Bross and the detective standing down the hall, and prepared herself for the onslaught. In Colorado she was often accosted by law enforcement as soon as she left the exam room, but the ADA and detective kept their distance. Tilly took full advantage, stepping over to the counter to sort through the kit, making sure everything was in order. She sealed and signed the outer envelope and paper bags, and then made her way over to the detective.

"These are ready," Tilly said, watching as the detective signed below Tilly's signature on the evidence bags.

"Thanks. How's she doing?" the detective asked.

"I asked the ED doc to give her some Vicodin. She's in a lot of pain and I'm concerned about long-term damage from being strangled. She'll need to be monitored at home. Are her parents here yet?"

"They'll be here in about half an hour."

"I'd like to talk with them about her care, if that's okay. The ED discharge paperwork may not address the strangulation issue. The bruising on her neck is going to get really ugly over the next few days and the burst blood vessels in her right eye looks pretty scary. I want to make sure they're prepared."

"Can you stay until they get here?" Bross asked. He'd stayed quiet until that point.

"Yes. I might go grab some coffee from the cafeteria." She needed the caffeine, but she also needed some space to think. She was exhausted and emotionally drained. With her defenses so low, she had to admit that the case had hit her much harder than she thought it would.

CHAPTER 31
TILLY

Tilly was enjoying a second cup of coffee when Dan Bross walked up to her table.

"Do you mind if I sit?"

Tilly waved her hand toward the opposite chair. "Be my guest. Are Paige's parents here?"

"Not yet. ETA 15 minutes, but the advocate is with her now. She'll give us a call when the parents arrive." Daniel sat back in his chair, his brow furrowed. Or maybe not a frown. Maybe his thinking face. Absentmindedly she reached up and rubbed at her own brow, noting the creases. She forced herself to relax. When she looked again at Dan, he was staring at her.

"What is it?" he asked. She wondered if he knew about Jim. Word traveled fast in a small town but they were new here. Just the thought of having to explain her weariness caused her to sigh.

"I've been thinking about Paige. And that last case I did. The parking lot assault?" When Dan didn't respond, she took it as an invitation to continue. "I think it's the same guy."

"Different part of town. Different MO. And the parking lot perp was more restrained."

Tilly felt herself getting defensive, but she could see that Daniel wasn't arguing. He was thinking out loud, just like she was.

"True," she said, "but the victim in the parking lot didn't struggle. She didn't resist, so he didn't have to subdue her. Paige fought hard. She had fiber and dirt under her nails. She has scratches and bruising all over her body And there's DNA everywhere."

"Escalation?"

"Maybe." Tilly said. "The parking lot at the restaurant was a real risk. A stupid one. Anyone could have seen him. The park at night not as much. Paige said she ran there every night. He must have been watching her."

"But our parking lot vic had never eaten at that restaurant before. It wasn't even her idea. It was a fluke."

Tilly sat straighter in her chair. "He could have followed her. She works at the college, right? That might be the connection." After a pause, she muttered, "two victims."

"Three." Dan's voice was barely a whisper and Tilly wasn't sure she'd heard him correctly.

"What did you say?"

"Three victims," he said, his face pale but his eyes alight. "We had a case a few months ago. A woman who worked on campus in the registrar's office. She worked late one night and was assaulted near her building. Her attacker was dressed for winter—coat, gloves, hat, mask. She saw him but couldn't make out any of his features. She froze, and after he was done with her, he took off."

"DNA?" Tilly asked.

"Yes, but not a match for anyone in the system. And we don't have any suspects. No witnesses. No camera footage. When the restaurant assault happened, it was a stretch linking them together. No other ties. Different jobs. Different builds. Different ethnicity."

"Stranger assaults are rare. That's the link. Especially if there are three victims. The DNA will link them. I'm sure of it." Tilly took a breath. "We need to find him."

Daniel's phone chirped. "Paige's parents are here."

———

When Tilly got back to her house in the afternoon, she was bone-tired. She threw her scrubs in the hamper, took a hot shower, and burrowed under her covers. She woke a few hours later feeling completely disoriented. It took her a moment to realize she was sleeping in the spare room, and with that realization came a new wave of grief.

She thought she'd cried herself out, but as she lay in bed, tears soaking through the pillow case, she opened the floodgates. She'd always felt the need to be hard. While she felt a wide range of emotions, anger was often the only one she'd allow other people to see. Jim had changed that about her. He'd been patient with her, slowly chipping away at the wall she'd built between herself and the world.

There had been times when she hated him for it.

It wasn't until she reconnected with Kate that she'd realized how much she had to be grateful for. How much his love and patience had done for her. It made it possible for her to be with her family again. And though that reconnection brought with it a load of unprocessed grief and regret, she'd been freed from her self-imposed emotional prison. He'd shown her that she could be strong without being hard.

Jim's death had left her feeling unmoored, but sitting in the cafeteria with Dan, being invited into his thought process, had reignited her drive. She felt heard in a way she'd never been before. When she'd talked through cases with Jim, it was different. He tried to buffer her from any anger or pain she was feeling. Dan treated her like an equal.

Tilly wiped away the last of her tears and went in search of food. Jim's mom had filled her freezer with homemade frozen dinners and she was grateful. She warmed one up in the microwave, poured herself a glass of wine and settled in on the couch turning the television on. She's made it through a few reruns of *Friends* when Kate called.

"Did you sleep?" Kate asked almost immediately.

Tilly smiled. "Not really. But I had a nap this afternoon, so I'm doing pretty well. I had a case this morning."

"I thought you weren't going back to work until next week," Kate said, concern clear in her voice.

"My brain needed a break," Tilly explained. Most people would have argued that being exposed to trauma and violence was not the sort of break a grieving person needed, but thankfully Kate wasn't most people.

"I can understand that. Just make sure you're taking care of yourself."

After hanging up, Tilly cleaned up the dishes and turned on a movie, hoping it would make her drowsy enough to sleep. But as it got later, her anxiety began to kick in. She relented, pouring herself a second and then third glass of wine. When she was finally able to breathe easily again, she pulled out her laptop and sent a note to the realtor, explaining the situation, and asking if there was any way she could break her lease.

CHAPTER 32
KATE

Kate was restless.

She'd spoken with Tilly and Roman. She'd puttered around her house. Taken Rusty for a walk. All the while her brain churned over all the new bits and pieces of information she'd accumulated over the last few days. Was Delia's niece being trafficked? Were those girls Mira mentioned part of the problem? Each new clue made Kate's skin itch. Just like Tilly she needed something to distract her, so she decided to do something she'd been putting off for a long time.

After their father died Kate and Tilly had gone through his house quickly, boxing up anything that looked personal to go through later, knowing that they might never be able to bring themselves to do it. Those boxes had been sitting in Kate's storage room for over six months and she'd had yet to touch them. A layer of dust had formed causing her to sneeze repeatedly as she moved each box to the living room. Rusty ran around, sniffing each box curiously.

When she finished, she had a dozen boxes spread out in a semi-circle in front of her sofa. Rusty settled on the carpet nearby as she reached for the lid of the first box, meaning to work her way around the circle. As she worked, she made stacks—papers that looked important, things that had belonged to her mother and father, and a pile of things to throw out. Thankfully, the last pile was growing. By the time she'd reached box number seven, she was feeling productive.

This box contained her mother's things. Kate wondered if they'd packed this box, or if they'd moved it exactly as Frank had kept it. Everything seemed dustier here. She pulled out file folders on the top that contained Addie Medina's high school diploma, school assignments, letters she'd written to pen pals as a child. Some things were familiar. When they were young, Kate and Tilly had loved going through Addie's jewelry boxes and mementos. Addie would tell them stories about growing up on a ranch in Southern New Mexico. She'd been studying agriculture when she met Frank and her life changed course.

Kate smiled when she pulled out a stack of pictures of young Frank and Addie. Holding hands. Hanging out with friends. Kate had been close with her parents, but she was definitely her father's daughter. As she'd gotten older, Addie's quiet strength created a steady foundation for their family. Frank was the parent who took them on adventures. Addie was the rock they returned home to. Kate had known so much about her father, but her mother had always been a little bit of a mystery.

Near the bottom of the box, Kate found a bundle wrapped in one of the shawls her grandmother had crocheted. Inside were three journals bound together with a ribbon. The ribbon was fraying at the edges and it came away easily when Kate pulled. The first journal was covered in pictures of pale butterflies. Kate flipped through pages upon pages of her mother's delicate handwriting. The first entry was from 1995, the year Tilly turned fifteen and became almost impossible to live with. Her mother wrote about feeling helpless, wondering what was going on with her youngest daughter. Kate was mentioned too, with Addie comparing her girls, examining her own parenting skills, looking for failures that would explain why things came so easy to Kate and so hard for Tilly.

Mostly, Addie used the space to ask God for patience. It was the sort of journal Kate recommended her clients keep while processing the things they worked on in therapy sessions. Kate wondered if Addie had sought the help of a counselor during their teen years, but she'd been too caught up in her own dreams to pay much attention to how her parents were coping. When Tilly started acting out, Kate had made every effort to avoid the drama and tension that filled their house.

Knowing that Tilly had been preyed upon, that much of her behavior had been fueled by trauma, made Kate's cheeks flush with shame.

Addie had faithfully written in her journal every day. Kate put away the first and went to the second, a continuation with flowers on the cover. More of the same. Turning to the third journal, Kate was surprised to see a shift in dates. The first entry was written nearly a decade after both girls were out of the house.

I'm still in shock.

Seeing those words sent Kate's heart racing. For a moment, she thought about putting the book away without reading. Had her father cheated on her mother? What revelation had been enough to get her mother journaling again? She wasn't sure she wanted to know. But she took a deep breath, and kept reading.

Frank's confession. It's just so unbelievable to me. That he kept this from me all these years. I don't know how I can ever look at him again. It's no wonder our girls never come home. Here I thought we'd built a safe world for them. And then this.

The writing trailed off, but Kate had seen enough. She flipped toward the middle of the journal. The entries were erratic and only some were dated, as though they were written in haste. Her mother's flowery handwriting became intermixed with block lettering, and Kate could see pages where Addie had nearly broken through the page by pressing hard.

She stopped on an entry dated September 2013, less than a year before her mother died.

I talked with Ruth today about my suspicions. She didn't seem to believe it was possible, but I laid out all the facts and I think at the end she agreed with me. At least she didn't try to talk me out of reporting it and I'm thankful, because I'm scared. I've been trying to talk with Tilly but she's good at avoiding my calls. We're all so good at avoiding. Only seeing what we want to see. That's what started the whole thing. Tilly told Frank something bad happened to her, but he wasn't willing to see.

Tonight we're going to talk with Sgt. Gunnison. Frank doesn't like the Chief of Police much, but since he's retiring soon enough we'll talk to Gunnison and hope that he can unravel all the secrets and lies. Frank still thinks he needs to atone, and he probably does, but since his apologies don't seem to make any difference to Tilly I'm not sure he'll ever make it right with her. It breaks my heart.

Whatever happens, this has to stop.

Kate's heart ached. Her mother had found out about Tilly. She'd known about the abuse and she'd been trying, in some way, to expose it. They both had. But they'd never told Kate. Not even after her mother died. She'd lived with her father for five years, and he'd never let on. Or, at least, not explicitly. All those times he'd lamented on Tilly's hard life, asking Kate to be patient. To have sympathy for Tilly, even when Kate so stubbornly refused.

So many secrets and lies.

CHAPTER 33
TILLY

Tilly's desire to get out of the house she'd shared with Jim and into an apartment compelled her. She went to work, searching through listings during her lunch hour and scheduling viewings after work. By Friday, she'd signed a lease on a two-bedroom apartment in a new resort-style development with an attached garage. She sprang the news of her impending move over the phone with Kate who showed up Saturday morning to help her pack.

Tilly had rented a truck and begun disassembling furniture the minute she signed the lease. By dinnertime, they'd moved enough of Tilly's things to get her set up to sleep in the new apartment. Kate promised to come back Sunday to help some more, then returned home to give Rusty some attention.

Tilly felt a little bit indulgent in the new space, which reminded her more of a resort than an apartment complex, but she loved that the units were small, with only two townhomes per lot. She would have neighbors but still have privacy, and the complex had its own indoor pool.

After Kate left, Tilly went to Target and purchased all new bedding. In her house, she'd pushed all memories of Jim into their bedroom. In her new apartment, she was starting fresh but reclaiming her bed. She picked out a comforter that she loved but Jim would have hated. As she returned home, she admonished herself. She was going to have to find a place for Jim—both for her love and her grief—in her life without hiding and avoiding.

Tilly caught a brief glimpse of one of her neighbors as she pulled into her garage. He looked twenty-something and was wearing a suit and tie. She took her purchases upstairs, grateful to have a full size washer and dryer in her space. As she laundered her bedding, she set up the television in her bedroom. It would be a week before the movers could bring over her larger items; the ones she couldn't disassemble herself. Until her couch arrived, her bedroom would be her lounge.

She slept fitfully that night, but when she awoke in the morning, she wasn't as anxious.

Kate showed up around ten with coffee and pastries.

"Wow, you made a lot of progress last night," Kate said, taking a look around. "When do the movers come?"

"Friday," Tilly said. "I spoke with the realtor this morning. They already have a family who'll want to see the house next weekend, so I'll be cleaning after the movers are done here."

"Want me to help? I don't have any appointments on Friday."

Tilly laughed "Are you kidding? Of course! I hate cleaning. Especially move-out cleans. Luckily we weren't there long enough to make much of a mess." All the lightness drained out of the room. Kate crossed over and pulled Tilly into her arms.

"It's okay to be happy and sad all at the same time."

Tilly smiled weakly, a tear sliding down her cheek. "How did you know?"

"Because I felt the same way after Dad died. Every time I made a joke or laughed, I felt guilty."

Tilly looked around. "Well, shall we?" She picked up a

painting and headed over to the hearth. "I think I'll put this one here and the TV over there."

"I'll go unpack the kitchen," Kate said.

Tilly pulled out her phone and put on some music. It didn't take long before the pastries and coffee were consumed, and everything they'd brought over was put away. They made two trips to the house, bringing over more boxes until only the larger pieces of furniture remained. Tilly tried to talk Kate into calling it quits, but Kate insisted that they start cleaning.

"We've got a few hours before sunset, and it'll make Friday go a lot easier," Kate said when Tilly protested. Grudgingly she acknowledged that Kate was probably right and they went about cleaning, closing off rooms as they finished, until everything left was in the living room, waiting to be moved.

They went back to Tilly's apartment and popped a couple of frozen dinners in the microwave, keeping the conversation light. Kate seemed distracted, but when Tilly asked about it she brushed off the question. Finally, the sisters said goodnight.

"Do you want to bring Rusty and stay here next weekend? I paid the pet deposit and he's officially welcome."

Kate laughed. "You didn't have to do that. But yes, we would love to be the first guests in your lovely abode."

―――――

Tilly was almost asleep when a call came in.

"Ms. Medina?"

"Yes?" Tilly said groggily. The speaker's voice was familiar but she couldn't place it.

"This is Jean-Ann. I'm the on-call SANE tonight. I have two cases tonight and I need backup. Are you available?"

Tilly was already out of bed. "Yes ma'am. I can be there in about 15 minutes."

"Thanks. See you soon."

Tilly pulled on a set of scrubs, put her hair in a bun, and headed out the door. It was a little after midnight, and there wasn't much traffic. The breeze was cold, though, and Tilly wished she had put on a jacket. She cranked up the heater on her way, sighing with relief at the warm air blowing on her arms. She arrived at the clinic and let herself in, locking the door behind her.

An older nurse in Mickey Mouse scrubs met her at the front desk. Tilly vaguely recognized her from orientation her first few days. "Thanks for coming." she said, reaching her hand to take Tilly's. "Jean-Ann."

"Tilly. What's the situation?" They walked toward Tilly's office so she could lock up her purse.

"Custody issue for me," Jean-Ann said, giving Tilly a knowing look when she groaned. "I know how you feel, but the little girl is complaining about pain when urinating."

It wasn't uncommon for pediatric cases to come in on Friday and Sunday nights, the most common days for custody transfers from one parent to another. When possible, a forensic interviewer was called in to speak with the reporting parent and the children to decide whether a physical forensic exam was warranted. No one wanted to traumatize a child unnecessarily, even if that child's parents weren't thinking clearly.

"Has the interviewer been in?" Tilly asked

"Brynn is in there now. She'll be out in a few minutes. In the meantime, we have a self-report in room two. Her name is Caitlin Shaw. Sounds like a date rape. She got here a few minutes ago, and I've been sitting with her. She doesn't want to report." There was a soft knock at the door, and Brynn walked in.

"Oh? Hi Tilly." The social worker seemed a little surprised to see her, but she quickly redirected to the task at hand. "The police are on their way. It's going to be awhile."

"I'm going to go get started," Tilly said, leaving the two women behind.

———

Tilly's patient, Caitlin, had been out with the boy she was dating when things went wrong. She seemed to understand that it wasn't her fault and that what he'd done had been wrong, but nothing Tilly could say would convince her to report him. In the end she convinced Caitlin to see a psychologist for follow-up and walked her to her car, watching sadly as she drove away.

It wasn't unusual. For all the work that had been done to provide resources and services for victims of sexual assault, it was still a grueling process. Many victims simply wanted to put the experience behind them. Tilly could relate, though she also understood how futile it could be. She went back inside the clinic to finish up her paperwork and nearly ran into Dan Bross coming down the hallway.

"How's it going in there?" Tilly asked, noting the weariness in his expression. Though he could be gruff and unpleasant, there was also a lingering sadness about the assistant district attorney. She wondered if she looked that way too. It was a hard path they'd chosen. Jim had always tried to be cheerful, especially after work hours, but even he cracked from time to time. It was a hard job.

"It's a mess," he said, running his hand over his forehead with a grimace. "I don't think the mom knew what she was getting herself into. Now CYFD is involved. The kids are exhausted, so the question right now is whether to table this for now. There's no outward sign of abuse, and the girl's not saying much."

Tilly nodded. Not every situation they encountered was clear-cut. "I need to finish up my kit and then I'm heading home. I haven't been to sleep yet. Hope you guys get to wrap things up soon."

Dan nodded once as Tilly turned and walked back into the exam room.She finished the kit, locked it in their storage room, and headed home. Fatigue was taking over, making her stomach roil. When she got home, she fell into bed fully clothed and was asleep in mere minutes.

CHAPTER 34
KATE

Kate had an ethical dilemma and she was determined to figure it out.

She did not want to use her therapy sessions to fish for information. Her clients deserved better than that. These girls deserved her full attention. And yet, when she thought about her upcoming meetings with Delia and Mira, her frustration overwhelmed her. How could she really help without overstepping boundaries that she believed in very deeply? She thought about her brief visit from Linnie, another girl she couldn't reach out to but she wanted so desperately to protect.

Delia had challenged Kate to do more. But how?

For much of her time between sessions on Monday and Tuesday, she searched for ideas. For answers. For anything that would help her take one more step in the right direction, even a small step.

The answer came in the form of a utility bill.

From Delia, she'd learned that Lucy was interning for the City Clerk's office. Utility bills could be paid in person at the city finance office, giving her the excuse she'd been looking for to do some reconnaissance work. At four o'clock on Tuesday, she locked up her office and headed to City Hall. School was out for the day, and with any luck she could fumble her way through making contact with Lucy.

She found a parking spot in the lot and walked into the City Hall building, part of the city administration complex that included the Police Department and the Rec Center. The finance windows were directly in the front doors but Kate made sure to keep her eyes straight ahead, intentionally failing to see those windows. She kept walking until she saw the Clerk's office. She entered the office. A young girl sat at the front desk, filing papers

"Can I help you?"

Kate laughed nervously. "I hope so. I'm trying to figure out where to pay my utility bill."

The girl looked bored, like she answered inane questions like this all day. "You have to go back to the front entrance." She pointed past Kate. "The payment windows are just inside the door."

"Oh, for heaven's sake. I must have walked right by them. Thank you so much for your help . . . er . . . " She looked around, like she was searching for a name plate.

"Vicky," the girl said.

"It must be so exciting to work here," Kate said, trying to keep her enthusiasm from sounding too forced.

"I don't really work here. I'm an intern," Vicky said a flash of irritation. Then her expression changed completely. "Would you like me to show you where you need to go?" she asked Kate, getting up from behind the desk and coming toward Kate, her eyes wide. "Lucy, could you watch the phones? I'll be right back."

A quick "sure" came from somewhere behind Vicky, but Kate couldn't catch sight of the voice's owner. Vicky walked past her, opening the door. "Follow me."

Kate sighed and turned to follow. As she did, a man walked through the door. "Oh hi Vicky," he said cheerfully.

"Hi Mr. Garrett," she said as she led Kate past, but she kept her eyes down.

Kate, on the other hand, caught his gaze and held it. He smiled at her. He was quite handsome, maybe a couple of years older than Kate, and he seemed to radiate confidence. "Sam Garrett," he said, extending a hand. Kate took it. "Kate Medina," she replied, and if he'd heard of her it didn't show. "I'd better catch up. Vicky's showing me the way."

Sam Garrett nodded at Kate as she breezed past him. When she caught up with Vicky, she asked, "Are you all right?"

"I'm fine," Vicky said, but Kate didn't believe it. Everything about Vicky's demeanor screamed fear. She turned in time to see Sam Garrett giving her an appraising look. It made her shudder.

———

When Kate got home, she did some research on Sam Garrett. He'd been the City Planner for about eight years, but was a transplant from Oklahoma. Graduated from the University of Oklahoma with honors. His name appeared on her list, but she hadn't gotten around to looking him up yet. All the press she found seemed to indicate that Garrett was a very capable professional. She couldn't find any personal information on him, and his official biography did not mention a family.

She felt guilty for leaving Vicky, but all attempts to engage the teenager in conversation had been rebuffed. And once she'd delivered Kate to her destination, she turned on her heel and sped back toward the Clerk's office.

When Roman called, she told him about her day.

"Hmm, Sam Garrett," he said. "I know who he is but I'm not

sure I ever spent any time talking to him. Can't even really picture his face."

"He's not a bad-looking guy, but his creepy factor was off the charts."

"He'd certainly be in a perfect position. Lots of access and authority to abuse. And if Chief Gunnison is involved too, that would make a lot of sense."

"Why's that?" Kate asked.

"Again, access. The Chief has police files, that sort of thing. But a City administrator has access to more information on everyone living around here. Garrett's job keeps him busy engaging and interacting with other government officials, community leaders, and business people. It wouldn't be hard for him to move around without raising suspicion. Be careful, Kate."

It didn't seem like a single conversation could go by without him telling her this, and usually it annoyed her. But she was still feeling the effects of that man eyeing her. "I will. By the way, I'll be at Tilly's all weekend."

"The pup going with you?"

"Indeed. I know I need to keep working on things here, but right now I want to make sure Tilly is okay. It's hard to read her right now. She went back to work, and I know she's had some difficult cases so I'm not surprised that she's distracted. I think getting out of her house and into an apartment is going to be a good thing in the long run, but it all happened so fast. I worry about her."

They talked for a few more minutes, then Roman went to bed and Kate went back to the boxes from her father's house. She'd gotten derailed by finding her mother's journals, and though she'd scoured the books over the past few days she hadn't found anything terribly useful. The next box contained pictures. Thousands. Some in photo books, but most in huge intimidating stacks. Kate sipped from a glass of wine while she sifted through. The top of the stack consisted mostly of their family photos. Images of Kate and Tilly with cheesy grins abounded. After a while she gave up on the stack, putting it aside for later. She dug deeper. Near the bottom, she found a thin album with pictures of her mom and dad at civic events. A note at the front of the album thanking Frank for his years of service confirmed that the album was a retirement gift. Kate was a few pages in when she saw a familiar face.

It was some sort of Christmas party with a massive tree in the background. Ruth Flores and Kate's mother Addie Medina were leaning in close, deep in conversation. They each had a martini in hand and their eyes locked conspiratorially with the camera man. Kate smiled. A few pages later, she found another one. Ruth and Addie, arm in arm, at a function in a park. In these photos Kate's father Frank was often nearby, and another man Kate assumed to be Ruth's husband. As Kate flipped through the pages, her smile began to fade. Something bothered her but she couldn't pinpoint the trouble. Frustrated, she closed the book and went to bed.

CHAPTER 35
KATE

Delia was a no-show, and while Kate was disappointed she wasn't surprised. Delia may have been experiencing anxiety, but after her trip to City Hall Kate was sure that Delia's main motivation in seeing Kate was to get her to Lucy. It was exactly what she needed, information, but she had no idea what to do with it. She didn't even know what "it" was. Delia suspected Lucy was in danger, perhaps already being victimized, but other than a few unreturned telephone calls there was no actual evidence. Kate hadn't even managed to catch a glimpse of Lucy and she wouldn't be able to snoop around City Hall without drawing too much attention to herself.

Another dilemma.

There seemed to be plenty of problems but no solutions in sight.

Kate called Delia and left a voicemail, but she didn't expect a return call. Then she tried to refocus on her next two clients. Regardless of her personal agenda her patients deserved her to be present for them and she would not fail them.

After her last client Kate packed up and headed to the library, which was across from City Hall. Carrying a stack of books, she made her way to her car. The library parking lot had been full, so she'd parked across the street in the city lot. She piled the books in the backseat and was about to get in when she saw two people exit the building. It was after hours, and the parking lot was mostly empty. The lights in the parking lot illuminated the taller figure, Sam Garrett, escorting a young woman toward a parked car nearby. Kate watched them closely, and as they walked out from under a light the girl's face was clear for a brief moment. It was Vicky.

Garrett had his hand on her lower back, steering her toward the passenger side. It could have been innocent, but in that moment when Vicky's face was visible Kate had seen desperation and defeat.

Kate didn't pause. She closed the car door loudly, plastered a smile on her face, and walked quickly across the parking lot.

"Vicky!" she yelled, waving cheerfully.

Both Garrett and Vicky looked up, startled. His hand dropped to his side and Kate caught a flash of annoyance on his face before he put on his own fake smile. Kate was thinking fast as she closed the gap between them. She didn't have a plan, and when an idea formed in her mind she wondered if she was about to make a terrible mistake. But her instincts told her that she had to intervene.

As she approached Sam Garrett took a small step back, putting some distance between himself and Vicky. "I can't believe I ran into you today," Kate rambled. "I was hoping we could talk a little bit more about you dog-sitting for me." She looked between them innocently. "I hope I'm not interrupting something."

"No, of course not," Garrett said with a smile. "I was just giving Vicky a ride home. I hate to see a girl her age walking alone at night."

Kate wanted to scream, but she kept her face masked in calm. "That's so nice of you! But would you mind if I spoke with Vicky for a few minutes? Actually," she said, as if the thought had popped into her head, "I could give her a ride and we could talk on the way."

Vicky looked at Garrett and his face flushed. "That would be great. Thank you so much. I'll see you tomorrow Vicky," he said, walking quickly around his car. Kate and Vicky watched him drive away in silence, and were still standing awkwardly in the same spot when Vicky finally spoke.

"Why did you do that?" Her voice was trembling.

"Was I wrong?" Kate asked, cutting to the chase. "Tell me something bad wasn't about to happen and I'll be happy to admit I was wrong."

Vicky looked at her feet. "It was nothing that hasn't happened before."

"I'm sorry," Kate said, her heart breaking for this girl. "I want to help."

"I want to go home," Vicky said. They walked to Kate's car, Vicky gave directions, and they left the parking lot. Kate expected Vicky to shut down, but as soon as they were underway Vicky started talking. "Thank you," she said softly.

"Are you safe at home?" Kate asked.

"Yeah. They don't come around our houses."

Kate's heart raced. "Where do your parents think you are tonight?"

"At the library, studying for a test. My curfew is ten."

They reached Vicky's house. Kate pulled into the driveway and turned to face Vicky. "If you let me, I can help you."

For a moment Vicky looked at Kate with something that looked like hope in her eyes, but the moment was fleeting. Her expression turned to resignation. "No you can't," she said sadly. "If I do what they want, I'll graduate in a few months and get away from here. "

"And that's okay for you?" Kate asked, trying to hide the frustration she felt.

Vicky looked at her. "Of course it's not okay." She sighed. "But the alternative is worse." She slipped out of Kate's car, closing the door softly behind her.

———

Kate had a restless night. She worried about Vicky, and she knew that she'd put herself right in Sam Garrett's line of sight. If he didn't know who she was before, she suspected he was already figuring it out. She picked up coffee on her way into the office Thursday morning and spent the morning making calls about the safe house. It was clear from Vicky's demeanor that the trafficking group was both grooming and managing their victims well. It would be harder than she thought to get them out of harm's way safely.

Just before noon, she headed to the bank for her women's group. She sat near the back as usual and smiled when Ruth arrived, taking a seat across from her.

"How's your sister?" Ruth asked, patting the back of Kate's hand.

"She's doing better. Thanks for asking," Kate responded. "We were reminiscing about Mom and Dad. I had no idea she drank martinis. Is that strange?"

Ruth chuckled. "Why would that be strange? Most adults have had a drink or two in their lives."

"True," Kate said with a smile. "It's nice to think about her in a happy way. Maybe you can tell me about what she was like with you."

"I would love to, dear, but I only saw Frank and Addie a few times a year. I rarely even had a chance to speak with your mother, so I'm not sure I'm the best authority." Ruth's expression changed. "Is anything wrong, dear?"

Kate shook her head. "No, no," she said, shaking away the confusion she felt so that it wouldn't show on her face. She remembered the pictures of her mother and Ruth—the way they leaned in toward one another, faces nearly pressed together. Kate couldn't understand how she'd misjudged their relationship. Or why Ruth didn't remember it the same way. "I'm still a little tired. I didn't sleep very well."

Before Ruth could respond, Kathleen walked to their table. She sat down next to Kate. "Phew, I barely made it today," she said cheerfully, and Kate was so relieved to turn her attention away from Ruth. They chatted for a minute or two before the presentation started. During the talk, Kate's mind wandered. Ruth was much older than her, and though she seemed in good health you never could tell. Frank had been very forgetful as his illness progressed. Was it possible that Ruth was having trouble remembering things?

Kate's grandmother had lived to be ninety-three and her mind was as sharp as a tack the whole time. But Ruth was not Kate's grandmother, despite how much she reminded Kate of her.

"Kate?" Ruth said, tapping her on the shoulder. When Kate looked up, Ruth laughed. "I hope you get some sleep tonight. The presentation is over and I have to leave. Would you like to have brunch with me Sunday?"

"That's so sweet, but unfortunately I can't. I'm helping Tilly move this weekend."

Ruth nodded knowingly. "A rain check then."

As she walked away, Kathleen stepped up next to Kate. "I don't think I've spoken more than two words with her," she said, watching Ruth walk out the door. "I get the feeling she doesn't like me much."

"Really? Why?"

They picked up their coffee cups and headed to the bussing station. "I'm not sure. We served on the hospital banquet committee last year, and she asked me if Mira wanted to wait tables. Earn a little extra money. I said no. I mean, she's only fourteen and, honestly," she leaned in, "between you and me, everyone drinks so much at that event. I don't like the thought of Mira being ogled, you know?"

"Makes sense to me," Kate said. "Doesn't sound like a good environment for any young girls," she added.

"I agree. So after our last banquet, I lobbied to have the caterers bring their own servers. Ruth was not happy. She quit the committee and hasn't had much to say to me since. Seems like a silly thing to get all bent out of shape over."

"Yes, it does," Kate said. "But I suppose it's not uncommon for people to react badly when they don't get their way." Kathleen continued chattering, but Kate's mind was still on Ruth. As much as Kate had been drawn to her, the woman's behavior seemed a bit erratic. Kate wondered if Ruth's mind was more addled than she'd thought.

CHAPTER 36
TILLY

The movers came and went. Kate and Tilly scrubbed surfaces and vacuumed until the house was in better shape than when Tilly and Jim moved in. At the end of the night they loaded Rusty in the car, grabbed fast food and headed back to Tilly's apartment, closing a chapter on Tilly's life. She hadn't been in that house long enough to form any sentimental attachment to the space, and all her memories would be laced with grief.

"That wasn't too bad," Kate said for the hundredth time, but she looked exhausted. It had been a long week for both sisters, and Tilly felt a little bit guilty for making Kate help, though she was insanely grateful for both Kate's help and her company.

"Now, if we can make sense of this mess," Tilly said, pushing her couch across the room. She'd given the movers instructions about where to put things, but once they were in place she changed her mind. She could feel nervous energy coming off her in waves. Maybe the clean-up had been more stressful than she realized.

Kate helped her push the couch into its new, hopefully final resting place. Then they made their way into the spare room. The movers had reassembled the bed, so all Tilly and Kate had to do was put on the bedding and bring in the dresser and bedside tables from the front room. Kate laid Rusty's bed down in the corner and he curled up happily, tired from an exciting day.

Tilly looked at him and smiled. "I should probably get a dog."

Kate flopped onto the bed. "Best thing I ever did. Of course, he loves everyone so he's probably never going to be a good guard dog, but it sure was nice having him around after Dad died." Tilly noticed Kate flinch.

"It's okay, Kate," Tilly said, lying down next to her sister. "You don't have to tiptoe around me. I spent the first few nights locking Jim's memory away. It didn't help. It's just going to take time. Maybe a lot of it."

"Yeah," Kate said with a sigh. "These past few years have been so hard. You know that saying about God not giving us more than we can handle? I try to keep that in mind, but some days it's hard to believe."

Tilly laced her fingers with Kate's and they lay there for a long time, staring at the ceiling fan. Eventually Rusty started snoring, which made both sisters laugh. Tilly got up. "I'm toast. I'm going to bed." When she got to the door, she turned to Kate. "I love you."

Kate smiled, her eyes shimmering with tears. "I love you, too."

———

The next morning, Tilly dropped the keys off with the realtor and then she and Kate went shopping. After lunch and some more unpacking, they took Rusty to a park across town for a walk. They made slow progress; Rusty stopping every few steps to sniff at the ground or sample the grass. The sun was warm and thankfully there was no breeze, so they strolled along, taking it all in.

The walking path ran the perimeter of the park. It was a beautiful day and there were lots of people out enjoying the sunny weather. Tilly was paying more attention to keeping Rusty in line than she was her surroundings, so she was a little bit startled to see Dan Bross walking toward her.

"Hi Tilly," he said as he approached. He was walking with a teenage girl who resembled him so closely there was no mistaking her for anyone other than his daughter. The girl had a chocolatey-brown lab on leash. He and Rusty sniffed at each other, first cautiously then enthusiastically.

"Aw, looks like Brownie has a new friend," the girl said enthusiastically.

"Hi Dan," Tilly said, still processing. It was a little awkward seeing people out of context, and Dan with a daughter and a dog was definitely out of context. "This is my sister Kate. Kate, this is Daniel Bross. He's an assistant district attorney."

Dan reached out a hand to take Kate's. "Dan. Nice to meet you, Kate. This is my daughter, Hannah." The girl smiled, then went back to tending to her dog while the adults suffered through a brief awkward silence.

Kate took Rusty's leash from Tilly. "I'm going to take Rusty to the dog park over there so he can run around a bit."

"Me too," Hannah said, and when Dan nodded she set out behind Kate. They'd chosen this park because it had a nice fenced dog park where they could let Rusty off-leash. Apparently, they weren't alone.

"Do you live around here?" Tilly asked Dan as they followed.

"No. We live out near Mesilla. But Hannah likes to bring Brownie to the dog park here. We don't have much of a back-yard. You?"

"I moved into an apartment complex off of Telshor. My sister is here to help. Rusty is hers and he's been a trooper so we thought he deserved an outing." They were nearing the gate to the dog park. "I may have to get a dog, too. I love having him around."

"Yeah, Brownie was a life-saver after my wife died. Hannah's so much happier when it's not just the two of us."

Tilly tuned to Dan. "I'm sorry."

Dan waved a hand at her. "I'm sorry about your loss. I've been meaning to say something for a while, but I got so sick of all the sympathy and condolences after Jessie died. I didn't want to overwhelm you."

"Thank you," Tilly said, a tear forming in the corner of her eye. She blinked it back. They reached the gate, and Dan held it open for her. Hannah and Kate had taken a seat on a bench nearby, so Tilly and Dan walked over and joined them.

Rusty and Brownie were chasing each other around like old friends. Hannah laughed. Tilly looked over at Dan's daughter. She seemed like such a normal kid. Not a hint of the tragedy she'd endured. Dan, on the other hand, radiated sadness and loss. Tilly had seen it every time she'd interacted with him, even before she knew what he'd gone through. She wondered if she was the same.

CHAPTER 37
KATE

Returning home, Kate's feelings were all over the place. Despite all the sadness, it had been a good weekend. Getting Tilly settled into her new space felt good, and running into her coworker at the park reminded Kate that her sister wasn't all alone. But she felt guilty for not telling Tilly about their mother's journals. She'd had several opportunities over the weekend, but she wasn't sure how Tilly would take the news. And she didn't want to make things any worse for her right now.

"You don't think she can handle it?" Roman asked Sunday night on the phone.

"Shouldn't matter," Kate said, forcing herself to face reality. "I hate the idea of lying to protect her."

"You're not lying, Kate. You're making sure she's okay first."

"Will there ever be a good time to hear this, though?" Kate replied. "Even I can't decide how to feel about it. My mother knew about what happened to Tilly and she never said a word to either of us." Kate had been over every possible reason Addie had kept her investigation to herself and she still couldn't understand. "That reminds me. You remember I told you that Ruth said she didn't know my mother well? It just occurred to me that my mother told Ruth about what happened to Tilly. Why would she tell someone something like that if they weren't close?"

"Maybe Ruth is confused," Roman said, an echo of Kate's earlier thoughts. "Or, and I don't want to fuel your imagination here, but maybe your mom told Ruth and Ruth doesn't want anyone to know." Kate hadn't considered that, but it made sense in a sick kind of way. There were so many people in town protecting the reputations of others. Maybe Ruth hadn't believed Addie and was determined to keep her secrets.

"I hate this!" she groaned. "I need to find something concrete. This speculation is killing me."

"It's frustrating," Roman agreed. "I think that's one reason investigators start to lose focus in their work. No hard evidence and lots of speculation. Before you know it, you start to think the speculation is fact and then you get tunnel vision."

"So what should I do next?"

"Try to be patient. You're doing something positive by seeing clients. And being involved in the community is already leading to new information. Just try to take it one day at a time."

She sighed loudly. "All right, subject change. I'm going to go see a movie with that woman I met last week. Kathleen."

"Tonight?"

"Tomorrow. So I probably won't be able to talk."

She heard Roman sigh. "That's great," he said, but Kate heard the loneliness in his voice. "She sounds interesting. Let me know how it goes."

"Roman?" Kate said, wishing she could reach through the phone and hold him "I love you."

"I love you, too. I'm almost halfway through the program. I'll be home soon enough."

"It's been ages since I've been to a movie without Mira," Kathleen laughed as they exited the theater.

Kate laughed. "Me, too. Well, minus the kids. I never get out. Even when Roman was here, we were too busy trying to get the house ready to live in." They'd gone to dinner and then the movie, getting to know each other. With so much tragedy in her life Kate tried to keep the focus on happy times which mostly revolved around Roman.

"We've only lived here a few years, and it's been hard getting to know people. Everyone is friendly, but most of my socializing is with coworkers and it's always a little weird to hang out with them after hours." Kathleen was an administrator at the hospital, so most of her coworkers were also her employees. Kate could understand the problem. "Tom and I like to take Mira hiking on the weekends, so we spend a lot of time just the three of us."

"My dad used to take my sister and me up to the mountains all the time. My mom wasn't much of an outdoor person, but we loved being up on the trails. Some of my best memories of childhood are tied to those trips."

"Mira's a hard sell," Kathleen said with a sigh. "She's very artistic, but she's never been super excited about our weekend excursions."

"Maybe get her to do some drawings while you're out there?" Kate offered.

"That's a great idea! Why didn't I think of that?" Kathleen said. They'd been walking and had reached Kathleen's SUV. "This is me. Let's do this again sometime soon, okay?" She stepped in and gave Kate a hug.

"Yes, definitely," Kate said with a smile. "I had a great time." She left Kathleen and walked to her own car, musing about the fact that friend first dates were almost as awkward as romantic ones. So much time spent finding common ground. Figuring out which pieces of yourself to share.

When she got to her car, she shivered. She looked up in time to see Kathleen wave as she drove by. The parking lot was full of cars, but there were only a few people milling about. She couldn't shake the feeling that someone was watching her. When she slid behind the wheel she locked her doors immediately, checking the backseat and then feeling horribly foolish for doing so.

It was late, but she was feeling anxious. So she called Tilly, putting the phone on speaker as she pulled out of the parking lot and headed out to the highway.

"How was the movie?" Tilly asked.

"It was pretty good. The latest girl bank robber thing. It was fun." Kate was about seven miles away from her house. It was Monday night and nearly 11:00 so highway traffic was pretty light. A pair of headlights was coming up fast. Kate got over into the right lane to let the driver pass, but her actions were mirrored. "Ugh. I've got some asshole trailing me." This particular stretch of road was a favorite for drag racers. Kate slowed down a bit, hoping the other driver took the hint. She was relieved when they pulled into the left lane and then sped ahead, pulling back into the right lane ahead of her.

"Is everything okay?" Tilly asked.

"Yeah, they passed me. I'm only a couple of miles away from my turn. Just wanted to say hello."

Tilly laughed. "This late? What's going on, Kate?"

Kate sighed. "I was feeling a little freaked out after the movie. I didn't want to drive home alone, you know?" She felt weird admitting this to her sister, but having Tilly on the phone was a comfort. "Shit," she said, realizing that the car in front of her was closer than she'd realized. "Hold on, Til. This guy is slowing down fast."

As she said it, the driver in front slammed on his brakes. Kate swerved to the right, her car careening into the desert.

"Kate? Kate?" Kate's phone had fallen somewhere on the

floor. Tilly was yelling into her receiver and Kate could hear the panic in her voice. She pushed the brake pedal, holding the wheel tightly as the car hit dips in the dirt and creosote bushes. She could see a dark area ahead, and knew that the arroyo was coming up. Her car came to a stop a few feet from the edge. Kate looked around. Her car wasn't more than a hundred feet from the road, but she was far enough off the highway that the lights weren't reaching her.

"Kate?" Tilly's voice was becoming more shrill.

"I'm here," Kate said, rooting around under the passenger seat for her phone. "I'm all right," she said, though she felt panic building. Her instinct would be to close her eyes, do her breathing exercises until she got herself under control, but the darkness around her was terrifying. She couldn't see whether someone was approaching the car. She needed to get out onto the highway.

"Someone ran me off the road," she said, opening the door and stepping out into the dirt. The front end of the car was propped up on a thick tangle of creosote. She stood perfectly still, listening for any footsteps while she surveyed the space around her. Nothing. "My car's stuck in the desert. I'm going to walk to the highway and call 911."

"Are you hurt?" Tilly's voice was shaky.

"Probably a little banged up, but nothing feels broken," Kate said. "I'm okay, Til."

She trudged along, stumbling over rocks and roots. Her panic was rising, but she knew she couldn't stop until she got to the road. To the streetlights. She hoped whoever had done this wasn't waiting for her.

CHAPTER 38
KATE

Kate's car was too far into the desert for a tow truck, so the sheriff's deputy offered to give Kate a ride home. Tilly pulled up right about that time looking frantic.

"Jesus, Tilly. You look terrible," Kate said. Tilly's face was tear-streaked and she'd clearly pulled on whatever clothes were nearby. She was a mess.

Tilly stepped forward to give her a hug, pausing for a moment to make sure Kate wasn't injured. "Yeah, I'm pretty much a nervous wreck. Where's your car?"

Kate nodded over her shoulder. "It's stuck. They're going to have to pull it out tomorrow."

"Can we go home?" Tilly asked. The deputy nodded.

"I'll contact you tomorrow, Ms. Medina," he said, then turned to walk to his car.

Tilly drove Kate home. It was nearly two in the morning, and both women were exhausted, but Kate put on a pot of tea. She needed to talk through things. "The deputy suggested that maybe it was a drunk driver. Someone else called 911. They saw what happened. But they didn't get a plate number."

Tilly sat across the table from Kate. She looked stricken "I remember when Dad called to tell me about Mom. I'd spent so much time telling myself that I was all right without you guys, and then that call came in and I cried so much I felt weak." She looked up at Kate. "Like I died, too."

Kate felt the wind knocked out of her. "Me, too. I'd been so caught up in my own life . . . it had been months since I had a good talk with her. I was still recovering from my assault. Dad called. And it was the only time I ever really wanted to curl up and die. I don't think I've ever felt so helpless." She wrapped her hands around her mug. "I need to tell you about something."

Tilly froze.

"Last week, I started going through the boxes from Dad's house. Finally, I found a bundle of journals Mom had written. Most of them were from when we were in high school." Tilly grimaced, and Kate reached over to pat her hand. "The last journal was different."

"Different how?" Tilly asked. The color had drained from Tilly's face and she looked on the verge of passing out. For a moment, Kate hesitated. Why had she thought this would be the right moment to tell Tilly? But she could see that Tilly wasn't going to let her get away with changing her mind now.

"Did you ever tell Mom about what happened to you?"

"No. I told Dad, and when he shot me down I didn't tell anyone else. Not until Jim."

"She found out, Tilly. She was trying to find out the details. She was investigating, just like me."

Tilly's voice was barely a whisper "She never told me."

"Seems like it took her a long time to work things out. She doesn't mention Dad telling her, so I'm not sure how she found out. But in some of the last entries, she talked about sharing her theories with someone."

"I want to see," Tilly said. Kate retrieved the journal from her bedroom and brought it back to the table, along with the scrapbook she'd found.

"We should probably get some sleep," Kate said. "I don't have any appointments tomorrow. When do you have to be at work?"

"I called in," Tilly said, her fingers tracing the designs on the cover of her mom's journal. "Is it okay if I crash here tonight?"

"Yeah," Kate said wearily. "I'm going to bed. Get some sleep," she said, knowing full well that Tilly wouldn't be getting any rest now until she'd read the journal.

————

"Who is Ruth?" Tilly asked the next morning. "Isn't that the name of the woman you met through your group? Is it the same woman Mom is writing about?"

"I think so. She mentioned knowing Mom and Dad, and then I ran across all these pictures of them together. But I asked her about Mom the other day and she acted like they weren't very close." Kate shrugged. "So maybe it's not her."

Tilly frowned. "Mom's last entry was written a month before she died, which made me wonder. Did you ever see the police report for Mom's accident?"

"No, why would I?" Kate asked, but as soon as the words were out of her mouth she knew exactly where Tilly was going. "You don't think it was an accident?"

"I don't know what to think," Tilly said. "We both know what those people are capable of. What if they found out about what she was doing? What if someone overheard her telling Ruth?"

"That would explain why Ruth doesn't want to let on about their friendship. She might be afraid of getting involved. But if the police suspected something, wouldn't they have told Dad?"

"You and I both know that the police have been complicit to some degree," Tilly said. Kate's stomach tightened into a knot.

"And of course," Tilly said, "that also means that whoever ran you off the road last night probably did it on purpose."

"If they were trying to kill me, they failed," Kate said flippantly, though flashes of Allen Parks looming over her desk and Chief Gunnison threatening in the high school principal's office were front and center in her memories.

She opened the photo album, turning to the first page featuring her mother and Ruth, their faces radiant. She thought about her mother's death, one of the most painful moments of her life. She and her father had rarely talked about it, and when they had Frank seemed so shaken that Kate usually changed the subject. The idea that someone might have harmed her mother filled her with fury. "I'm going to see if I can get a copy of the police report. If I find out her death was anything other than an accident, I'll . . . " She stopped short of voicing the murderous thoughts going through her head.

"You won't be alone," Tilly said through gritted teeth. She was hugging her mother's journal, tears streaming down her face. "You need to be careful, Kate. You're on their radar again. It makes me nervous."

"Me, too," Kate said, rubbing her neck. A few bruises were already appearing where her seatbelt had cut into her chest, and she felt sore all over. "Well, no time like the present to make myself conspicuous, eh? Let's go get some breakfast and then I'll call the sheriff's office. I'm hoping my car will still be drivable but in the meantime I need to run a few errands and you're my ride."

CHAPTER 39
TILLY

Kate's car was drivable, but Tilly was adamant when she suggested that Kate take Jim's car. His parents had given her the go-ahead to sell it, but it was still sitting in the parking lot at her new complex. It was newer than Kate's car, a hand-me-down from her father, and it wasn't nearly as recognizable. Tilly thought it might provide some anonymity, at least for a little while.

They drove to Las Cruces and then Kate made her way back home, promising to call Tilly once she got back into town and stay on the phone until she was safely locked inside the house with Rusty.

While she waited for that call, Tilly brought out her laptop and browsed local news sites. Clearly she and the assistant district attorney weren't the only ones noticing the string of rapes taking place in town. In sexual assault cases the police were careful about the information they released to the press, so no one had enough information to draw the same conclusions she and Dan Bross had, but she agreed with their reasoning. There was a serial rapist roaming the streets and it seemed that he was escalating.

Kate called, but as soon as she got home she let Tilly go so she could talk to Roman. Tilly could only imagine how hard that conversation was going to be. Her own instinct had been to rush to Kate's side. She figured Roman would be in the same mental space.

Tilly got ready for bed, ready for a break from all the thoughts occupying her mind, but it took forever to get to sleep. She was finally settling in when her phone rang. Given the events of the previous two days Tilly was immediately wide awake, relieved when the number was the clinic followed by guilt at knowing the call wouldn't be good news.

"This is Tilly," she answered. It was Marie.

"Hi Tilly. I know you're not on call this week, but we have a case and Dan Bross asked for you specifically. Can you come in?"

"Absolutely," she said, turning on her lamp and sitting up. "I can be there in about 15 minutes."

"Thank you. The victim is here at the clinic. I'll let Bross know you're coming."

As she got dressed, Tilly wondered about Dan. They'd had a very rocky introduction, but he seemed to have faith in her skills despite only having known her for a few months. And he'd listened when she talked about her theories, a novelty in a field where it was sometimes hard to keep the peace between victim service providers and the rest of the criminal justice system.

When she arrived at the clinic, Marie and Dan were talking in the waiting area.

"What's going on?" she asked.

"We've got a 15-year-old who was attacked in the park. Her mother's in with her," Marie said. "She goes running every evening. With all the assaults happening right now, her mother was spooked so was waiting in the parking lot. When Grace didn't check in, she went looking for her. She saw someone running, and she followed. She found Grace huddled against a tree. The rapist heard Grace's mom calling for her and took off."

"Was he able to . . . " Tilly started, but Dan interrupted her.

"Yes. The attack didn't last long, but it was enough." Dan's expression betrayed his anger. "The mom called 911 so there were police on the scene within minutes, but they didn't catch him."

"All right, I'll go get started." Tilly left her jacket and purse in her office, and then went to the exam room. The victim and her mother were sitting on the chairs against the wall. Tilly introduced herself.

"My name is Diane," the woman said, reaching out a hand to Tilly.

"I'm Tilly Medina," Tilly said, turning her attention to Grace. "Hi, Grace. I'm a forensic nurse and I'm going to be doing your exam tonight. Did Marie tell you a little bit about the process?"

Grace nodded. Her eyes were red and she looked like she was having to work very hard to keep herself calm.

"I'm going to walk you through everything step by step, and if you need a break let me know." As Tilly unpackaged her kit, she noticed a few things about Grace. She was very tall for her age and her body and facial features were very mature. She was fifteen but she looked more like twenty. "Okay, the first thing we're going to do is a personal and medical history."

"Can I get out of these clothes?" Grace asked. "I feel dirty."

"Absolutely." Tilly pulled out a paper sheet and laid it on the floor. "I'm going to have you undress over this sheet so we can make sure to pick up any fibers or hairs that might be on your clothes or skin." She reached into a drawer and pulled out a hospital gown. "You can put this on. It'll be big on you but you can wrap it around good and tight for now. When we get to the physical exam, we might rearrange things a bit. I'll also bring you a blanket. It's a little bit chilly tonight. Your mother and I will step out to give you some privacy."

"No," Grace said, her voice strangled. "I don't want my mom to leave." She took her mother's hand and squeezed.

Tilly smiled reassuringly.. "That's fine, Grace. Whatever makes you comfortable." She stood. "Just crack the door open when you're done. I'll be right outside."

Tilly stepped into the hall and closed the door softly behind her. Dan was waiting at the end of the hall.

"You should probably go home and get some sleep. She's pretty upset. This will probably take a while."

He nodded, but didn't move. "All of the other victims have been adults."

"She looks older than her age. Maybe he made a mistake," Tilly said. Her stomach roiled at the idea of this girl having been someone's mistake. That the trauma that she had endured, and would endure, could be boiled down to misjudgment on the part of her attacker.

"Call me when you finish," Dan said. He looked grim as he left the clinic. Tilly could only imagine what he must be thinking. His daughter Hannah was fifteen, too. Tilly thought about the girl's happy smile from that day in the park, and her anger flared. A few minutes later, the exam room door opened and Tilly headed back in.

CHAPTER 40
KATE

Roman was not happy. It took Kate nearly an hour to talk him out of flying home, and the irony that this was their longest conversation since he'd left town was not lost on her. By the time they got off the phone, Kate was too worn out to do much other than go to bed. But sleep was elusive. The conversation she and Tilly had about their mother's death was nagging at her. She wanted to see that accident report, but she needed to find a way to do it without alerting the powers that be.

Finally, she made a decision. She grabbed her phone and called Angie Lopez, hoping that the detective would answer for once. She'd been avoiding both Kate and Roman's calls for six months, but now that she'd reconnected with Tilly Kate hoped she might be more open to communicating. Kate smiled with relief when Angie picked up.

"Hi, Kate." Angie sounded weary.

"I'm sorry to call so late, but I need your help," Kate said. She filled Angie in on everything that had been going on lately, right up to last night's incident on the road.

"Oh my God, Kate. Are you hurt?" The concern in Angie's

voice gave Kate hope that one day they could be friends again, despite their history.

"I'm a little banged up, but nothing major. They pulled my car out of the desert. It's still running, but I'm driving Tilly's car for a while. Might be good to be incognito for as long as possible. So listen, I want to get a copy of the police report that was filed when my mother died. I'm assuming there was an accident report of some kind. Is there any way you can access that without drawing too much attention?"

Angie was quiet for a minute. "You're thinking there was something suspicious about her death?"

"I'm not ruling out the possibility, though I'm hoping it's not the case. That would make all this feel so much more insurmountable." Kate sighed. "I know these people are dangerous, but it's how brazen they are that scares me. They think they're untouchable." She thought about her father. In the days leading up to his death, when Kate started helping Roman with his investigation surrounding the murder of Gabby Greene, Frank had said something to Kate that suddenly felt much more profound. "Oh, God," she whispered. "He knew."

"What? Who knew?"

"My father," Kate replied, barely able to process what she was now thinking. "We were talking about the case, and my involvement. He seemed especially agitated and he said something about how dangerous these men could be. The look on his face. Angie, he knew. He knew my mother's death wasn't an accident, or at least he suspected. I have to see that report."

"I'll see what I can do," Angie said, the weariness gone from her voice. "Be safe, Kate."

———

Kate was finishing up her work day when her phone rang. It was Ruth.

"I was wondering if you'd like to meet for drinks this evening. My last meeting got canceled so I'm in town with nothing to do."

"Sure. Where can I meet you?"

On her way to the restaurant, Kate texted Tilly. She'd gotten into the habit of letting her sister know where she was. Sometimes it made her feel foolish, but other times it seemed prudent. Regardless, it was the one thing she could do that made both Tilly and Roman feel better about her being on her own.

"Hi Ruth," she said when she spotted her friend at their table. Ruth stood and gave Kate a friendly embrace. She stepped back, holding Kate at arms length, frowning. "Are you all right, dear? I heard about your accident."

Kate winced. "Small towns."

Ruth chuckled. "Yes, news travels fast. Especially bad news." She and Kate took their seats. "I was going to ask you to stay for dinner, but I thought you might be a little bit nervous driving. I know I would be."

"I admit I'm a little on edge behind the wheel," Kate said, a growing unease settling in. She added, "I've been keeping a close eye on license plates and I make Tilly or Roman stay on the phone with me until I get home. It's unnerving, but I won't let this keep me from doing my work."

She wasn't sure why she said it. Kate suddenly felt exposed, as if everyone sitting nearby was a spy waiting to overhear their conversation and report back to some dark shadowy figure. She thought about her mother, divulging her hard-won knowledge about what happened to Tilly. She wondered if that one conversation cost her mother her life. And the fact that she was sitting with her mother's confidante didn't help.

An ache took root. It wasn't just that her mother died. Her whole family was irreparably changed the minute those bastards singled out Tilly, and apparently every moment since. The ache started to burn.

Kate was distracted for most of the evening. Ruth seemed to sense it, keeping the conversation lighthearted and shallow. They said their goodbyes, and Kate made her way home without incident.

She took Rusty for a walk in the desert, relishing the quiet though she couldn't quite keep herself from looking over her shoulder now and then. She kept expecting to see someone driving down her road again, creeping around her house. Returning home, she talked to Tilly briefly and then Roman.

By bedtime, Kate was a nervous wreck.

Without any answers, she was driving herself crazy. Waiting for the phone to ring. Wishing Roman were home. Wondering how she would make it through another two months of him being gone while the pieces of her life continued to fall apart. She teetered between missing her father and anger toward him for not protecting Tilly as well as he protected secrets.

She picked up a book and had finally begun to relax when her phone rang. Caller unknown. For a moment, she hesitated. She remembered the days when her phone rang constantly with threats. On the fourth ring, she worked up the nerve to answer.

"Ms. Medina?" The voice on the other end was shrill and shaking.

"Who is this?" Kate asked, her sense of apprehension growing.

"My name is Lucy. I need your help. Please."

Kate could hear the girl's quiet sobs through the receiver.

"Where are you, Lucy?"

"I'm at my aunt's house, but I can't stay here. He'll find me."

"I'm on my way."

CHAPTER 41
TILLY

Tilly sat back in her chair and closed her eyes, fatigue and gravity conspiring against her. She knew she should go home, but she hadn't slept more than an hour at a time in several days and the thought of being at home alone didn't appeal.

"Tilly?" Tilly opened her eyes slowly. Brynn was standing at the door, a concerned look on her face. She walked into the office and took a seat across from Tilly. "Okay, I've tried not to be too heavy-handed over the past few weeks, but I have to say, you look like you haven't slept in a week. What's going on? And please don't tell me you're fine."

Tilly sighed. "I'm tired. I haven't been sleeping well and I don't want to go home. What more can I say?"

"How long has it been since you slept through the night?" Brynn asked.

"Since Jim died. Maybe before that." Tilly groaned. "It hasn't been an easy transition. And then Kate was in an accident a few nights ago."

"Is she all right?"

"Yeah. Rattled, but no physical injuries." Tilly got up and stretched. "I'm in my new apartment and it's so new and quiet and I feel like I can't relax there. I want to, but I feel so unmoored."

"That's understandable. Maybe you should go stay with Kate for a few days?"

"No," Tilly said. "I need to work. It helps."

"Sounds like avoidance to me."

Tilly smiled. "You sound like Kate."

"Why don't I give you a ride home?" Brynn said.

"That's okay. I'm only about ten minutes away and I'm awake." Tilly started gathering her things and Brynn stepped into the hall to let her close her office door.

"If you can't sleep, give me a call. Anytime." Brynn hugged Tilly. "And you might think about calling your doctor. Maybe they can give you something to help."

Tilly felt better walking to her car, but as soon as she started the drive home she began to sweat. She ended up in the parking lot of the bar near her old house without really remembering the drive. Before worry could take hold she walked inside, took a seat at the bar, and ordered a glass of wine.

Being casual took so much energy. Tilly ordered a second glass, aware that she hadn't had much to eat. She could feel the wine beginning to blur the edges of her reality enough to make forward motion seem possible.

"Tilly?"

Tilly turned. "Hello Dan," she said wearily.

"May I join you?" he asked, though he was already pulling out the bar stool beside her. She didn't bother to respond, instead taking another drink of her wine and letting the warmth buzz through her. Dan ordered a beer and they sat in silence for a while. Tilly was tempted to order another glass, but having Dan there made her self-conscious. She should be home in bed. Instead she was sitting at a bar, drinking alone.

Well, not alone anymore.

"Any updates on the case?" Tilly asked.

"Not yet. We're still waiting on the results from the last two cases. Things are moving slowly." Dan looked like he hadn't slept lately either. He seemed genuinely invested in the outcome of the case. She felt a pang of guilt about always thinking the worst of the law enforcement officers and attorneys she worked with. "It's maddening. We've got a ton of evidence but until we have something to match it against we're dead in the water."

"What can I do to help?" Tilly asked. Dan's agonizing was like an echo of her own inner turmoil.

Dan gave her an appraising look. She could see that he wanted to say something, but was reluctant.

"Just say it," she snapped, immediately regretting her tone.

He hesitated another moment. "Truth is, you're already doing everything you can. Your work on these cases has been thorough. Until our guy makes a mistake, we're stuck waiting." He paused. "And it looks like you're in need of a little self-care."

Tilly laughed. "Nice segue. Don't worry, I know I look like shit."

Dan's cheeks turned pink. "I didn't mean to sound so critical." He stared hard at the bottle in front of him. Without turning to look at her he said, "I don't mean to offend you, Tilly. I know how it is, trying to find normal when your whole life gets upended."

Tilly held her breath. The tenderness in Dan's voice felt like a hot spike to her heart. It poked holes in the wall she'd been trying to construct, allowing her grief to surface. A tear slid down her cheek.

"The only time I feel like myself is at work. It feels wrong somehow, finding comfort in other people's pain. Sometimes I feel like there's something wrong with me as a person."

"After my wife died, I worked night and day. I'd come home, have dinner with my daughter, and then head to my office. I don't think I slept through the night for a whole year. It was so hard trying to help Hannah navigate her feelings, I didn't have the energy to deal with my own."

Tilly could feel his eyes on her, but she couldn't look at him. Not without falling apart completely. When she didn't say anything, he continued. "I don't know you, Tilly. But from what I can see, you're a hell of a nurse." He cleared his throat awkwardly. "If you need someone to talk to…" He let the statement trail off when she nodded.

She kept her eyes trained on the bar top as Dan paid for his beer, said goodbye, and left the bar. She consumed a glass of ice water, waited until the buzz dulled to a hum, then she went home.

———

Tilly slept hard, like her life depended on it, and when she awoke the next morning, she felt heavy with fatigue. She wasn't hungover, but the light coming in her window felt too bright and she couldn't make herself get out of bed. She spent an obligatory moment debating, then called in to work—a first.

She'd been working such long hours that she was ahead on her paperwork. Marie sounded relieved to hear that she wasn't going to come in. Tilly wondered how many of her coworkers had been tiptoeing around her in these past few weeks. She knew Brynn was concerned, and she had to admit that she'd been overdoing it, using work to avoid having to feel anything.

For the past three years, Jim had been her anchor. He'd kept her grounded, listened to everything she had to say about work and life. She'd kept so many things from him, but through his love and support, she'd achieved something that up to that time had felt impossible. Balance. She doubted she would have reconnected with her father or Kate without the stability of their relationship to hold her steady.

Grief took the upper hand. She couldn't push through it

anymore. The weight of the revelations in her mother's journals and the possibility that her mother's death might have been murder was crushing. The loss of her father and now Jim. The concern in the eyes of her coworkers, her sister, and now Dan Bross.

Finally, her mind settled on her last case. She wondered about the attacker—what kind of man he must be to assault a woman so brutally without worrying about leaving all kinds of evidence behind. Was he that confident that he wouldn't be caught? Tilly supposed it wouldn't be the first time an offender believed themself to be above the law. Invincible even. In some cases, that option was best because cocky perpetrators made mistakes.

Was he a man who didn't care if he was caught? That thought was troubling. A person with no fear of consequences could be very dangerous indeed. How many more women would become victims before this man was caught? That thought wrapped itself tight around Tilly's chest, making her breathing feel slow and labored. The weight of it all was suffocating her.

She texted Kate, turned her phone to silent, and went back to sleep.

CHAPTER 42
KATE

It had been a long night.

After receiving the call from Lucy Kate had raced into town, her thoughts spinning wildly. When she arrived at Delia's house, she wasn't prepared. She just powered ahead, ignoring the anxiety that poked at the edges of her determination. Delia opened the door, gesturing for Kate to come in and locking the deadbolt behind her.

Delia's niece Lucy was sitting on the sofa, her face a mask of fear.

"Lucy, this is Ms. Medina." Delia poured Kate a glass of water and then sat beside her niece. Lucy hadn't uttered a word.

"What happened?' Kate asked. When Lucy didn't speak, Delia chimed in.

"She hasn't said much since she got here, and honestly I don't want to waste time. Lucy told her mother she's staying at my house tonight." Delia's eyes pleaded with Kate. "Please take her home with you."

"Delia, I want to help. But you can't expect me to take Lucy with me without knowing why," Kate said, suddenly feeling very conflicted. She'd rushed over without a thought about her own safety or any of the consequences. It wasn't until this moment that she recognized the impulsivity of her actions. She could practically hear Roman's voice telling her to slow down and think things through. And he would be right. She was flying blind. She needed to start leading with her head instead of her heart.

"Lucy will tell you more, I assure you," Delia said. She looked over her shoulder at the front door, clearly afraid. "But you should go now."

Kate was about to protest when it occurred to her that Delia wasn't afraid for Lucy. If Kate's suspicions were correct, Delia might have a lot to fear by standing up for her niece. As if reading her thoughts, Lucy finally spoke up.

"Please, Ms. Medina. I don't want to put my aunt in danger."

"All right," Kate said. "Do you have everything you need?"

Lucy shot to her feet nervously, slinging her backpack over her shoulder, and nodded. She gave Delia a hug, and then followed Kate to her car. As Kate backed out, Lucy sank down low, her head barely visible above the dash. Kate felt a rush of fear.

"Okay, Lucy. I need to know what's going on, right now."

———

When Kate checked on Lucy, she was glad to see the teen fast asleep. Kate had tossed and turned all night. She finally let Rusty climb into bed with her, but even his soft snores weren't enough to settle her. Just before sunrise Kate got up, showered, and took Rusty into the courtyard. While he played she breathed deeply, filling her lungs with cool morning air and hoping to clear her head.

After, she made a cup of coffee and booted up her laptop. She wasn't sure what to do next, but she needed a plan. Her phone chirped with a message from Tilly, who was taking a day off. Kate breathed a sigh of relief. Her life was a series of prioritized worries, and it was nice to put her sister on the back burner for a moment. Especially when she had a runaway teenager in her upstairs bedroom.

Kate thought of Lucy's mother, who was probably asleep at home thinking her daughter was safe with her aunt. On their drive back to Kate's house the previous night, Lucy had finally opened up.

"At first, I thought it would be okay. I mean, when Mr. Garrett approached me to work for him I felt a little bit uncomfortable. I don't pay much attention to gossip at my school, but it's no secret that some girls have been abused. Honestly though, it wasn't just the talk. The way he looked at me felt...wrong. And he stood in the doorway so that I couldn't pass without touching him."

"I didn't think anything could happen at the City office. Vicky and I were working with the clerk and then sometimes we'd go down and do filing for other departments. Or whatever they needed us to do. One day, Vicky came back from Mr. Garrett's office and she looked like she'd been crying."

"Did she tell you what happened?" Kate asked.

"Not then," Lucy said, her voice shaking. "The next few times he came to our office Vicky popped up and followed him out pretty quickly, so I thought maybe there had been a misunderstanding. But then Vicky missed a day of work. Mr. Garrett came to find her and when he realized she wasn't at the office he seemed really mad. I asked him if I could help him, but he said he wasn't ready for me yet."

Kate cringed, a sour feeling taking hold of her stomach. "When was this, Lucy?"

"A few weeks ago." Lucy took a deep breath, her body shuddering as she exhaled. "Vicky came back the next day. She said she had a cold, but I noticed she had some bruises on her arm.

She reached across the desk and I saw them under her sleeve. So when she went to use the restroom, I followed her and made her tell me what was going on."

The look on Lucy's face had Kate seeing red. She didn't know the exact details yet, but she knew the kind of horror that Lucy had felt when Vicky told her story. Kate thought about her sister and her former student Mandy.

"He sold her," Lucy said, her voice barely a whisper.

"Excuse me?" Kate couldn't hide her shock.

"He treated her like she was his property. He took Vicky to some man's house and he sold her. She saw Mr. Garrett exchange money with someone and then he left her there. She was raped, and then Mr. Garrett took her back to the office. That was nearly two months ago and it's been happening ever since."

"Why did Vicky miss work, Lucy? Was she sick?" Kate remembered Mandy's stepfather beating her, telling her she had to report for duty or he'd do worse. She'd seen the defeated look on Vicky's face a few nights ago. It didn't seem like Vicky had much fight left in her.

Lucy's face had gone white.

"What is it?"

"She's pregnant. Vicky's pregnant." Lucy had to choke the words out, and Kate could feel her revulsion growing.

"Oh God. Did she tell anyone else?"

"I don't think so," Lucy said, trembling. "She was so scared." Tears started streaming down Lucy's face. "Ms. Medina, I'm afraid that now he'll come for me."

Kate felt the world tilt. Her insides were at war. She felt instant relief that, so far, Lucy had not been abused. She had a chance to save this girl. But she felt sick over Vicky. When Kate drove the girl home she'd wanted nothing more but to bring her to the hacienda. To keep her safe. And now Kate knew what these men were capable of. What would they do when they found out about Vicky's pregnancy?

Sunlight poured through the kitchen window, and Kate realized her coffee had gone cold. She didn't have the stomach for it anyway. It was too early to make any calls, but she wanted to be at her office anyway so that she would have more privacy and also closer proximity to town. If Vicky was in trouble, Kate was going to find a way to help her.

CHAPTER 43

TILLY

Tilly slept through the day, waking up around dinnertime with a feeling of clarity. Her muscles ached from spending too much time lying down, but the fog she'd been living under for weeks, maybe even months, had lifted. She sat up, stretched, and walked into her living room where she stood in the middle of the room and took in her new space.

"It's a start," she said to herself, and for the first time in her adult life she meant it. For so many years, she'd been running away—from her past, her memories, her family. Tilly knew she could fight when it came to other people, but until now she'd rarely used that power for herself. Her work was a calling that she'd used again and again to avoid having to face the harsh reality of her decisions. It wasn't until her dad died, and the events surrounding her mother's death, that she'd finally started to open herself up to the possibility of really living. And then Jim died, and she'd instinctively began re-constructing all her walls and barriers.

Now, she had a choice.

She could let her grief and anger consume her, driving her to make poor decisions that would keep her at arms length from the people around her. Or she could embrace the tragedy, the pain and the tears, knowing that she would live. That the edges would dull and she would eventually start to feel like a human being again. That it was okay to feel sad and lost. She'd learned last night that she would survive even when it got bad. She could sit with those feelings and then make the choice to thrive despite them, instead of handing over all her autonomy and agency to things she couldn't control.

Tilly picked up her phone.

"Hey, I'm glad you called," Brynn said when she answered. "I just left the office and I was thinking about you."

"Would you like to get some dinner with me? I wanted to talk something over with you."

Brynn paused. "I was going to meet up with Angie. What if you joined us?"

Tilly smiled. "Actually, that would be great. She may be able to help me."

———

Tilly met up with Brynn and Angie at a tavern near the campus. Her face still showed signs of sleep deprivation, but she was feeling better than she had in a long time. They made small talk over drinks while they waited for their food to arrive.

"Well, I'm dying to know what you're up to," Angie said. Her eyes narrowed while she waited for Tilly to respond. "Brynn told me you wanted my help with something."

Tilly laughed. "You don't have to look so suspicious. It's not about anything personal." Angie visibly relaxed. "Not that you're going to like it." Tilly sat up straighter and put on her game face. "You know we've had a spike in assaults lately, right?"

"The police department has been in contact. I hear they're looking for a serial rapist now."

Tilly nodded. "It looks that way. I've done three of the exams now. Same general MO, same plethora of physical evidence but no hits in the database. And the guy attacks in public places, which makes that second point even more disturbing. He's smart. And he's escalating."

"And you're working with the DA, right?" Brynn asked.

"I am. But until we have a credible witness or a DNA match, we're dead in the water. None of the victims can identify him. Their descriptions are super sketchy and he's at least careful enough to wear a face covering. He's not going to stop until he's caught in the act." Tilly began to fidget with her napkin. "So I had an idea."

Angie frowned. "You're right. I'm not going to like this."

"I know." Tilly sighed. "But I've been thinking about the men who raped me in high school. Even if I'd had an exam, I doubt any of them would have shown up in the system. They were all such fine upstanding citizens. And there's something about these cases that keeps stirring up memories."

"You think there's some kind of ring?" Angie asked.

"No. I mean, it's possible, but the details are too similar. If there was more than one guy involved, I think they would have been caught by now. We need a witness." She looked at Angie. "So, I was thinking. All the women who've been attacked so far share similar characteristics."

"They look a lot like you."

Tilly winced. "I know. Not in our faces, but we're all about the same build. Same hair color and length."

"You want to try and lure him out." It was Brynn who said it, and the look on her face told Tilly that she did not approve. "You're being self-destructive, Tilly. You need to see someone."

"I'm not, actually," Tilly said, though she wondered if it was entirely true. She'd always been a little bit reckless, even before her assaults. "I took what you said yesterday to heart, Brynn. I took the day off. Slept. And when I woke up, I could see the damage I'd been doing to myself."

"And you think acting as bait for a serial rapist is a good choice?" Angie asked, the concern evident in her expression. "What would Kate say?"

"I'm sure she would say the same thing you're saying now," Tilly offered. "And, I would remind her that I said the same thing to her last year during that murder investigation. I'm not looking to get hurt, Angie. But I don't want to keep doing exams on girls who've been irreparably damaged, when there's something I could do to help."

"You're already helping," Brynn countered.

"That's what Dan said," Tilly replied.

"Are you talking about Dan Bross?" Brynn asked. "Didn't realize you guys were friends." Brynn looked surprised and maybe even a little impressed. The assistant district attorney certainly hadn't endeared himself to the clinic staff.

"We're not exactly friends, but we have been working together on these cases." Tilly took a breath to anchor herself. "Jim and I used to argue about professional boundaries all the time. It drove him crazy that he was bound by so many rules when it came to his involvement in his cases, but he was also a stickler for those rules. When he saw me getting too invested in a case, or having altercations with law enforcement, he always reminded me that I had a specific role to play."

"He was right," Angie interjected. "These women may need you to testify for them one day. What happens if you become a victim, too?"

"Believe me, I have no intention of ever being victimized in that way again."

The three women sat in silence for a long time. Finally Angie said, "I assume you're going to do this regardless of what we say."

"Pretty much," Tilly agreed. She figured Jim would be

adamantly against this, and for a moment she felt a pang of guilt. Was she being self-destructive? Had a good night sleep given her the energy to argue her way into a dangerous situation?

Tilly was surprised when Angie sighed and said, "All right. Let's talk about how this is going to work."

CHAPTER 44
KATE

Kate woke Lucy long enough to let her know she was going into the office. When she closed the door Rusty curled up on the carpet in front, as if he knew his job was to stand guard over their houseguest. Kate headed into town. She had one morning appointment, and then she planned to return home. She hoped she wouldn't be alone.

Kate knew she wasn't in the best frame of mind to see her morning client, but she tried to put her best foot forward. The minute the client left, Kate was out the door. She drove to Vicky's house, grateful that she knew where the girl lived without having to do time-consuming research. She pulled up to the house just as an older woman was leaving. When the woman spotted Kate, she took a step back toward the house.

"What do you want?" she asked Kate with a scowl.

Kate put her hands out in front of her in what she hoped was a gesture of surrender. "I'm sorry to drop by unannounced. I was hoping maybe Vicky was home."

The woman's hostile expression deepened.

"You have no business here. Go away." The woman began to

advance, causing Kate to take a step toward her car. But the door to the house opened.

"It's okay, Abuela." Vicky stood in the shadow of the door, so that Kate only recognized her by her voice. The girl's grandma frowned at Kate, but she turned and walked toward her own car that was parked on the street.

"Come in," Vicky said. "Quick please."

Kate glanced over her shoulder as she walked in the front door.

"What are you doing here?" Vicky asked. She's allowed Kate enough room to step in the door but she didn't offer Kate a seat. In fact, she stood with her arms crossed, eyeing Kate suspiciously.

"Lucy says you haven't been to work," Kate said. Mentioning Lucy had the desired effect. Vicky's hard expression softened.

"Is she all right?" Vicky asked.

"Yes, she's staying at my house right now. And I was wondering if I could talk you into coming with me. I can keep you both out of harm's way until we can figure out what to do."

Vicky laughed, a cold sound with sharp edges. "Can you keep my family safe, too?"

"Victoria, who is this?" An older version of Vicky stepped into the room.

"This is Mrs. Medina. The one who gave me a ride home the other night." She turned to Kate, all the defiance gone from her face. "This is my mother Ramona." Vicky's mother stepped up next to her daughter. Her face was wary, but she looked like a mama bear who wouldn't let anyone touch her cub without a fight.

Kate hesitated. She wanted to help Vicky but wasn't sure how much her mother knew and she didn't want to make matters worse. Thankfully, Vicky had more to say.

"Ms. Medina has a place for me to stay." When Ramona

started to protest, Vicky turned to her mother. "I can't stay here, Mama. It's not safe for you or Michael. If they think I ran away, maybe they'll leave you alone."

"I'm setting up a safe house," Kate said. "My house is like a fortress in the desert and I have good security."

Ramona sighed. "How will she be safe when she's still here in town? These men are dangerous, Ms. Medina. You have no idea."

"Actually, I do." That stopped the conversation. "Last year, I was attacked while trying to help the police with a murder investigation. I want nothing more than to put a stop to the abuse. I want to help Vicky. And all the other girls."

Vicky looked at Kate with newfound respect, but Ramona looked less than convinced. "Victoria was going to be the first person in our family to go to college." A tear slid down Ramona's face. "Why did this happen to her?"

"I'm so sorry that your daughter was singled out, Ramona. It wasn't her fault, and I wish that it hadn't happened. But maybe Vicky can help me make it stop. And I can help her finish school online, so she can still go to college."

"Please Mama," Vicky said. "I can't stand it if something happens to you. And at least this way, I'll be close."

It took a few more minutes, but Ramona finally relented. Vicky packed a bag and followed Kate out to her car. The street was quiet, but both Kate and Vicky looked around nervously as Kate drove back home.

————

When Kate and Vicky got home, Lucy was waiting at the kitchen table. Both girls cried long and hard, but they seemed relieved to have each other. Kate wondered if they'd been friends before the abuse started or if their friendship had been forged through the horrific circumstances they found them-selves in.

Kate got Vicky settled into the room next to Lucy's and then let the girls have some space. They'd have a lot of talking to do, but first Kate had to make some calls. The first call was to Roman, letting him know what was happening. She knew he'd be worried. Taking these girls in meant an increase in the danger for Kate. She couldn't keep him in the dark, and she would probably need his advice.

The second call was to Angie. She'd been trying not to nag at the detective since they last spoke, but she needed someone in law enforcement to guide her.

"Hi Kate. I was going to call you this afternoon."

Kate had been ready to explain her situation, but Angie's words stopped her in her tracks. "You found the report?"

"I did. You were right, Kate. There was almost no investigation into the accident. The notes are incomplete and if this had been turned in to me, I would have laid into my investigator."

"Who was the investigator?"

"Blake. I haven't heard of him. But the officer who signed off on the report? Him I recognize."

"Tell me."

"It was Chief Gunnison."

Kate sighed. "Of course it was." She was surprised not to fall apart, and then disgusted because she'd been expecting this news.

"Listen, this doesn't mean that your mother's wreck wasn't an accident. All we know is that the reporting officers did a shoddy job."

"Right," Kate said, then laughed. "Come on, Angie. You and I both know she was killed. And we know who did it, at least in theory."

"I'm going to do some more digging," Angie said. "There

may be a chance that we can get the case reopened, but I want to gather as much information as I can before we look into it."

"Thank you, Angie. I appreciate your help."

"So, what did you call for?" Angie asked. It took Kate a minute to get back on track.

"I feel like I'm losing my mind," Kate mumbled. "Sorry, yeah. I have two girls staying with me right now and I need some advice."

Angie paused. "Why are you asking me?"

"Angie, I am truly sorry for everything that happened last year between you, me, and Roman. I really do hope that you'll forgive me someday. But right now Roman is on the other side of the country and it might as well be the other side of the world for all the help he can give me. I need someone in law enforcement that I can trust and I need someone familiar with the situation." Kate wondered if she should have kept things simple, but she'd been waiting for an opportunity to make amends to Angie for half a year and was willing to deal with the consequences.

"Do the parents know the girls are with you?" Angie queried, all business.

"Sort of. The first girl, Lucy, her aunt called me and asked me to look out for her. Her mother doesn't know she's with me. The second girl, Vicky, her mother knows."

"As long as you have their permission, there's no reason the girls couldn't stay with you indefinitely. Have both girls been assaulted?"

"No. Lucy has been approached, but only Vicky was abused." Kate said. "Angie, Vicky is pregnant. I don't know what to do and I'm scared they're going to come looking for her. I think she's safe behind these walls, but the system is untested and they know where I live. How long will it take before they put two and two together?"

CHAPTER 45
TILLY

Tilly and Kate had hit a stalemate. The call had started off well enough, but then Kate told Tilly about the two teenage girls she was now harboring. And then Tilly told Kate about her plan to make herself bait for a serial rapist.

"Are you out of your mind?" Kate shouted. Tilly's head was pounding. Her discussion with Angie and Brynn the night before hadn't gone much better than the current conversation. Despite Angie's best efforts there was no way to guarantee Tilly's safety and by the time she'd arrived home her nerves were jangled. Unable to sleep, she'd had a few glasses of wine. Her throbbing head was the price for another night of poor choices.

Was this plan another one of those? Angie and Brynn had come around, but only because it was clear that Tilly wasn't going to budge.

Kate echoed their sentiments, raising some excellent points. She'd almost had Tilly reconsidering. But then she'd told Tilly about taking in Lucy and Vicky, and Tilly could feel herself digging her heels in.

"Explain this to me, Kate. How is what I'm doing any different than what you're doing?"

For a moment, Kate was silent. Tilly knew she'd hit her mark, but she felt a wave of guilt in response to the fear she heard in Kate's voice.

"You're right," Kate said. "I know exactly what you're thinking, Tilly. But I'm safe behind these walls. Who's going to watch over you?"

Tilly gasped as Kate's words pierced her heart. She listened to Kate backpedal, but it was through a fog of grief and help-lessness.

"It's okay, Kate. I know what you meant. I have to go," Tilly muttered, disconnecting before Kate had a chance to say anything more. She laid her silent phone in front of her on the bed and let sorrow overcome her. As her tears slid down her cheeks, staining the comforter, she marveled at how confident and sure she felt one moment and how broken the next. She looked over at the picture on her dresser—a photo of her and Jim at an art benefit.

Jim's arm was wrapped around her waist, and they were smiling. Happy. They'd been happy. But as Tilly looked at the photo, she noticed something she hadn't before. For all his cheerfulness, Jim's smile looked sad somehow. It had been one of the loveliest evenings they'd spent together, but something weighed on his mind.

She wondered how she'd never noticed before.

————

"Hey," Brynn said from the door of Tilly's office. "Did you want to go out for drinks tonight?"

Tilly thought about the empty wine bottles lining her kitchen counter, and the hangover it had taken her most of the day to work through. "I can't. I have to catch up on some paper-work and then check in with Kate. Rain check?" She smiled, hoping to ease the concern she could see in her friend's eyes.

"All right. I'll see you tomorrow."

Tilly worked until she was alone in the office, and then changed from her scrubs to workout clothes she'd brought along. She pulled her dark hair up into a high ponytail. She'd chosen skin-tight leggings and a rash guard that hugged her curves. Other than her tired eyes, she looked much younger than her years.

She packed up her scrubs and headed out to her car. After dropping her things at home, she headed toward the park that bordered the north side of campus. She stood under a street-light and stretched, taking her time so that anyone around would notice her. The lot was almost empty, but she said a quick hello to the few people she passed as she made her way to the path that led around the circumference of the park.

Tilly began at a brisk walk. It wasn't late, but the darkness was complete. For a moment, Tilly doubted her plan. Doubted herself. Her feet felt heavy on the path.

She quickened her pace, listening to the crunch of gravel with each step. Her heart beat faster. The park was quiet, and only a small breeze rustled the leaves. The path veered away from the campus streets, drawing Tilly further away from people and into the shadows of the cottonwood trees.

Tilly ran from shadow to shadow, her blood pounding in her ears. Anxiety had turned her jog to a full-out run. Her chest felt like it was going to explode and she realized if she didn't slow down, didn't take a breath, she was going to pass out. She slowed to a stop and bent down at the waist, heaving. It was then that she heard footsteps on the path behind her.

She bolted upright and peered into the darkness. She couldn't see anyone behind her and the sound had stopped, leaving her feeling crazy and paranoid. From the beginning of this insane plan, Tilly had reminded herself that there were other dangers that lurked. That she was putting herself directly in harm's way, regardless of the source of danger. She was doing the exact things that she warned her patients about, that she railed against during presentations and classes.

The whole trek around the park would take her nearly an hour and she had barely begun. All her bravado gone she headed back the way she'd come, keeping a slower pace this time and looking all around her. She was nearing the bend when she saw a figure step out from a shadow. She stopped cold in her tracks.

"Stay away from me!" she shouted, readying herself to sprint through the park and toward the light of the parking lot. She realized how unprepared she was. She hadn't even put a can of pepper spray in her pocket. God, she was being so stupid.

"Tilly?" Dan Bross's voice tore through her panic. As he neared, she could make out his face. He was wearing a suit jacket, as if he'd come from the office.

"What are you doing here?" she asked, her voice shaky. Her relief at hearing a familiar voice was immediately overrun by suspicion. She hadn't told anyone where she was going. She wasn't anywhere near the places where she'd run into Dan before. "Are you following me?"

"Yes," he said simply. "I spoke with Brynn earlier. She told me about your plan."

"Great," Tilly said, her anger building. "That's just great."

She started walking faster so that she walked right past Dan, brushing the sleeve of his jacket as she stormed back toward her car. She could hear him behind her, his feet crunching the gravel. When she reached her car, he was still walking behind her. She whipped around. "You've done your job, Dan. You can go home."

Dan locked eyes with her, his expression a mix of frustration and shame. Then he turned and walked to his parked car, a few rows down from Tilly. He was gone before she could even decide what it was she was feeling.

CHAPTER 46
KATE

"We need to talk," Kate said as she laid out the breakfast she'd made for Lucy and Vicky. Both girls were still in pajamas, and the dark circles under their eyes illustrated what Kate already knew—neither was sleeping much. Her first night with Kate, Lucy had crashed hard. But Vicky's appearance had brought with it a buzz of anxious energy they were all feeling. Kate had been meaning to ease them into the conversation, but after two cups of coffee and a lot of worry she was low on subtlety.

"I wanted to make sure you guys were settled in before making you go through everything with me, but now I need to know the whole story so I can keep you safe." *And myself*, she thought. She turned to Vicky. "Lucy told me a little bit about what's been going on but I want to hear it from you. And if you want us to talk in private, we can."

"No," Vicky said, grabbing Lucy's hand. "No, I want Lucy here. We're in this together."

Kate was surprised by the solidarity between the two girls. By all accounts, Vicky had been on the receiving end of the actual abuse and Lucy had sort of dragged her out of hiding, forcing her hand. But all of the defiance Vicky had displayed seemed to be gone. In fact, she looked relieved. Worried, but relieved.

"It didn't surprise me," Vicky said, "when Sam—I mean, Mr. Garrett—came on to me the first time. I'd been doing some data entry in his office, and he asked me to work late one day. And I knew what was going to happen. I've heard the rumors, you know? Everyone has. But it's easy to think that some of those girls asked for it, you know?"

Kate nodded, though the thought made her sad. It was hard to imagine how a person became a victim until you'd had those experiences yourself.

"For a while, it was just me and Sam. First in his office and then he took me places. Like this house. It wasn't his, but we would go there after work and then he'd drop me off at home." Vicky looked at Lucy. "I tried to convince myself that he liked me. And then, I thought if it was only me, then he'd leave the rest of the girls alone. I saw the way he was looking at you, Lucy."

"I know," Lucy whispered.

Vicky breathed heavily, as if the telling was wearing her down. It probably was. Kate remembered feeling drained after telling her sister, and then Roman, about the assault she'd survived.

"It wasn't all bad," Vicky said quietly, her eyes downcast now. Like many victims of sexual abuse, Vicky had been groomed. Garrett had made her think she was special. That they were in a relationship. And by the time she realized her initial fears were right, it was too late.

"It's all right, Vicky," Kate said, reaching tentatively across the table for Vicky's hand. "I promise you can tell me the whole truth and I won't judge you. I want to help you."

Vicky nodded. "About a month ago Sam took me to the house, but there were other people there. Other...men."

Vicky's voice was becoming more of a whisper and Kate

knew they needed to take a break, but she had one more thing she needed to know for certain. "Vicky, I need to ask you one more question and I need you to be totally honest with me."

Vicky's eyes were wide with fear.

"Are you pregnant?"

Vicky nodded.

"Was it Sam Garrett?"

"No," Vicky said, tears beginning to slide down her cheeks. "No, Sam told me to go on birth control, but I didn't. I couldn't. I'd have to tell my mother and I couldn't tell anyone. Anyway, he told me it was a precaution. That they would always wear condoms, like that made everything better. But there was one man...he was never gentle and he started to get more rough with me. The last few times we were together, he didn't wear protection. I would lie there, focusing on this blinking light on the smoke detector, and pray that I could make it through."

Vicky wrapped her arms around herself and started to rock. "I feel so disgusting. Like I'll never be clean again."

"Who was the man, Vicky? Do you know?"

"No," Vicky replied softly. "Sam said it wasn't important for me to know their names. And I don't know if they knew mine. They never called us by our names."

"There were other girls?"

"Yeah. A few. I saw them in passing. We were never allowed to talk."

Kate was filled with dread. "Okay, let's table this conversation for now. I need to go to work for a few hours. There's food in the fridge and I'll stop by the store on the way home. Don't answer the door or the phone while I'm away."

———

Kate was cleaning up for the day when Delia appeared at her door.

"Is this a bad time?"

"No," Kate replied. "I'm packing up for the day. How are you doing, Delia?"

"It's been a hard couple of days. I'm not sure what to tell my sister about Lucy. I told her Lucy got sick at my house, so I was keeping her home. It took a lot of convincing to keep her from coming over."

"How long do you think you can keep her without arousing suspicion?"

"Not more than another day or two. Then her mother is going to insist that she either come home or see a doctor. But for now she's excused from school today and tomorrow."

Kate sighed. "This is complicated." She took a seat at her desk, and Delia sat down across from her. "It's probably not a good idea for you to drop by. I'll have Lucy call her mom later tonight. Hopefully that'll relieve her worries for the moment."

Delia looked down. Kate sensed that she had something more to say, so she waited as patiently as she could. She was anxious to get back to the girls. When the silence continued, Kate decided to jump in.

"I should be getting back to the house," Kate said. She stood and finished packing up her bag.

Delia let out a big sigh. "Someone came to see me this morning. Asking about Lucy."

"Sam Garrett?" Kate asked, knowing even as she said it that Garrett wouldn't out himself in that way.

"No, a police officer. He said he needed to talk with Lucy about a theft at the City office. I told him she didn't live with me and he looked surprised. Like he'd been told otherwise."

Delia's words shook Kate to the bone.

"I think they know, Kate. I think they know you have her."

CHAPTER 47
TILLY

On the drive to work, Tilly shifted between rage and despair. By the time she arrived at the office she had gotten past wanting to punch Brynn in the face, but her mood was still terrible. True to her chosen profession, Brynn did not seem content to let Tilly stew. She showed up at Tilly's door just before lunchtime.

"Can we go to lunch and talk about it?" Brynn asked warily. She looked tired and her makeup couldn't quite cover the puffiness around her eyes.

"What's there to talk about?" Tilly replied stubbornly. "You ratted me out to Bross. I feel like I'm back in middle school."

Brynn stepped in the door, closing it behind her. "What choice did you leave me, Tilly? Angie may be willing to support your scheme, but I can't in good conscience just watch you put yourself in danger."

"Why the hell didn't you say that at dinner?" Tilly was fighting hard to keep her volume in check.

"Are you kidding? I did! You weren't prepared to listen. You'd already made up your mind and you made it clear that you weren't going to take no for an answer." Brynn shifted uncomfortably. "Not that you needed our permission. Did you think I was going to be all right with it?"

"No, probably not," Tilly admitted grudgingly, her anger receding. "Dan followed me to the park and nearly gave me a heart attack."

"He told me."

Tilly felt her cheeks flush. She wasn't thrilled that Brynn was talking about her with the assistant district attorney. Dan was one of the first attorneys she actually liked, despite his gruff manner. She had to admit that she wanted Dan to respect her. She couldn't swallow the thought of him seeing her as some loose cannon.

"I can't seem to get my shit together," Tilly said, caught up in her own internal dialogue. Brynn took a seat across from her but stayed silent, giving her room to talk. "I woke up completely determined the other day. Then, last night in the park, I was terrified. Every bit of resolve I had was gone the instant I heard footsteps crunching in the gravel behind me. It's so frustrating."

"I can imagine. You're trying to find your equilibrium, and you don't strike me as the type of person who sits still well. When you were telling us your plan, I could understand where you were coming from. I didn't agree, mind you," Brynn said with a smile, "but you looked more engaged than I've seen you since Jim passed away."

Tilly nodded, knowing Brynn had a point. But hearing Jim's name on anyone else's lips still felt like a shot to the heart.

"It's probably a good thing I forgot my pepper spray last night. Dan would have gotten a big surprise," Tilly said dryly.

"Lunch?" Brynn said. Tilly was grateful for the subject change. Brynn got up and opened the door, only to find Dan frozen in mid-knock, looking startled.

"Is this a bad time?" he asked, stepping back.

"No, in fact, I was trying to talk Tilly into lunch. Do you want to join us?"

Dan looked at Tilly tentatively. "Is that okay?"

"Sure," Tilly said. "Why not?"

———

They walked across the street to the burrito bowl shop opposite the hospital. After ordering, they sat down at a table near the window. It was an awkward grouping. Brynn and Dan seemed to get along well enough. At least, they spoke easily like colleagues who'd worked together for some time.

"Can I address the elephant in the room?" Dan asked. Brynn glared at him.

"I already talked to her. No need to rub salt in the wound."

Tilly was rethinking her decision to come out with them, but now there seemed to be no way to avoid the conversation. "Go ahead, Dan," she said.

"I'm sorry I scared you last night," he said solemnly. "The look on your face...I don't ever want to see anyone look like that again."

Tilly was surprised at how shaken their interaction had left Dan.

"It's fine," Tilly said, hoping to cut off any further comments.

"No, it's not," Dan said. Tilly braced for a lecture. "Listen, I know how you feel. I want to get this guy off the streets too. And if I could find a way to sidestep the system, I might."

Tilly waited for the but, and when it didn't come she didn't know what to say to fill the silence. Dan was still looking at her with an intensity she could feel. Brynn, on the other hand, was looking everywhere but Tilly.

"Anyway, thanks for inviting me. I need to get back to the office." He picked up his trash and moved away from the table. Tilly looked down and realized she'd hardly touched her food.

She pushed it away, finding that her appetite had left the building. She watched Dan walk out the door, wondering what exactly had just happened. Was he condoning her plan?

"That's not what I was expecting," Tilly said.

Brynn finally made eye contact again. "Yeah, that was intense."

"I didn't realize you knew Dan well," Tilly said, then added, "I guess I didn't think anyone knew him well. He seemed too prickly and at odds with the clinic staff to be a favorite."

Brynn laughed. "He's not my favorite, by any means. But we've worked together for a long time and he's a good attorney. He actually cares about his clients. It's a rare find in this field."

"I know what you mean," Tilly replied. They finished their meal and went back to work. Tilly wasn't sure how to feel about Brynn's interference, or Dan's insistence on addressing things head-on. But it was good to feel cared for. It had been a long time since she'd had real friends.

CHAPTER 48
KATE

Exiting the store with an armful of groceries, Kate was completely thrown off guard when she saw someone standing near her car. Thoughts of her confrontation with Allen Parks a year before passed through her head. Even more so when she realized who the person was.

"Can I help?" Sam Garrett took a step toward Kate as she approached her car. She'd planned on loading up the back seat, but she stopped at the trunk instead. "Thanks, but I've got this." He stood nearby while she unloaded the bags and when she closed the trunk he was smiling at her. If she didn't know better, she would have thought Garrett to be a Boy Scout-type, taking any opportunity to help a person—particularly a female —in need. It seemed incredible that he was playing that role for her now, and for a moment she wondered what he really knew about her involvement.

What to do? There was so much strategy in these interactions and, despite her training, Kate preferred directness. She took a step to pass by him and he moved into her path, showing his hand.

"Please move," she said calmly, even throwing in a smile to

gauge his reaction. His smile stayed plastered on his face, but malice flickered in his eyes.

"No need to be rude, Kate."

"Ah, yes. As a woman, my job is to step aside demurely and let you help me whether I like it or not," Kate said, working hard to keep her tone and expression neutral even as she felt the rage boiling inside. "I guess we can assume that consent is not something you value."

Garrett's face turned red. Kate could see his smile faltering. "I am a respected member of this community, Ms. Medina. What are you implying?" His voice had dropped low enough that only Kate could hear. He was too close for comfort, but Kate was in full fight mode. She leaned a little closer, forcing Garrett to back up an inch.

"I'm not implying anything, Mr. Garrett. And unless you'd like me to say what I know about you here in the parking lot, I suggest you step away. Now."

She slammed the trunk shut and pushed past Garrett. When she opened her door, she turned. Garrett had moved out of her way, but the look he gave her chilled her to the bone. She sat down behind the wheel, locked the doors, and closed her eyes. She thought about the two girls staying at her house and knew that she'd made a mistake. Instead of staying under the radar she had openly challenged Garrett, and by the look of things he wasn't going to let it go.

———

Later that night, after Lucy and Vicky were in bed, Kate called Roman. She told him about her encounter, and then braced for his reaction. She was surprised at the calm in his voice when he said, "Is the security system working properly?"

"Seems to be. I've been checking the cameras at night and before I leave the house. I got a couple of alerts from some coyotes walking by the other night so the motion sensors are working."

"How's the pup?"

Kate looked down at Rusty. He was curled at her feet snoring softly. "He's enjoying the attention."

"Listen, Kate. I need to say something to you and I want you to let me get through it before you freak out, okay?"

A flush of fear and anxiety swept through Kate's body like a cold wave. "Too late," she said weakly.

"It's been eating at me for weeks. Since Jim's funeral." He was silent, leaving Kate time to imagine the worst. She braced herself. "I've been feeling so guilty being here. I love the training but every night I'm lying awake wondering if you're okay and if things will be different when I get back."

Kate's fear turned to agitation as Roman dragged the moment out longer with another pregnant pause. "God, Roman. Just say it."

Roman laughed. "I knew you wouldn't make it." The sound of his laughing both annoyed and calmed her. Her body relaxed despite her nerves. "I know you're sitting over there imagining the worst, and on any other day I'd probably be mad at you for not trusting me. But I realized that I've been underestimating you. I keep thinking I have to be there to keep you safe, and I can't keep thinking that way. I have to trust you to take care of yourself, and you have to trust that I'm coming home to you."

A mix of emotions kept Kate from saying much. And she felt so tired. Tired of always worrying that Roman would change his mind. That she wasn't good enough for him. That she either couldn't cope without him or she couldn't still be her own autonomous person with him. What he was saying—this revelation—was a turning point in their relationship.

"Thank you," she said quietly. There wasn't much else she wanted to say, and the conversation ended shortly after. Kate pulled Rusty's bed closer to her bed. He curled up and was softly snoring before Kate settled in to read. She'd turned off her bedside lamp, when the first alarm pierced the silence of the night.

Kate flew out of bed, grabbed the tablet with her security software and ran into the hallway and up the stairs. Lucy and Vicky were huddled in the space between their bedroom doors.

"I heard something outside," Lucy whispered. Kate could see her hands shaking where she clung to her friend. "Someone is out there."

"Come down to my room, girls." Rusty was whining and growling, dancing in circles near the stairwell. He was ready to attack but Kate's mind was on keeping her charges, and herself, safe. "Rusty, come." She led the girls back into her room and locked the door. Rusty stood at the door, his growl low and menacing. Kate sat on her bed and focused her attention on the security camera feeds. She could see two men, one at the side of the house farthest from the road and the other around the back. They both wore baseball caps, but kept their heads down as if avoiding the security cameras. The thought bothered her. She and Roman had placed the cameras in visible spots hoping to deter any would-be intruders. Kate watched with bated breath to see if this tactic would be enough.

Lucy and Vicky had settled into a corner of the room, their eyes wide with fear. Kate wanted to comfort them, but she was fighting to keep her own anxiety under control. The man near the back of the house disappeared from the screen. Kate zoomed in, but couldn't see any trace of him.

The man at the side of the house was making his way to the front, looking over his shoulder constantly. It's a test, she thought. They were testing her security. She picked up her phone and dialed the sheriff's office. A few minutes later, as the sirens were approaching, the men disappeared into the desert.

CHAPTER 49
TILLY

Tilly returned to the park the following three nights. Each night her resolve wavered. It bothered her a little that no one was trying to stop her from being reckless anymore, but she was self-aware enough to recognize that that probably meant she wasn't doing it for the right reasons.

On the other hand, the crisp night air was soothing and gave her time to think.

The thinking was sometimes agonizing. She analyzed every major decision she'd made since she was a teenager. She mourned the loss of the semi-normal life she'd been trying to create with Jim. And she wondered if she was capable of being normal. After so many years of fury against her abusers and the efforts it took to barricade herself from emotional connection, Tilly found herself lonely.

She had friends. She had Kate. But she felt more alone than she'd ever been. That realization brought tears to her eyes, but it also made her laugh. And her bitterness eased. As she put miles on her pedometer, she worked through emotions she'd been avoiding most of her life. And while she checked in with Kate every day, she kept this process to herself. She told herself it was to keep from burdening Kate further. Really, she wanted Kate to be her sister, not her therapist, and she was afraid that line would be breached.

It was Friday night. Tilly was not on call, so she was planning a weekend trip to see Kate. They were finishing their daily check-in as Tilly started her second lap around the park.

"The sheriff's office didn't see any signs of tampering with the cameras or the locks. No sign that they tried to get in. I'm convinced they were testing the perimeter," Kate said, having explained about the previous night's unwanted visitors.

"And you're okay? Are the girls okay?"

"Yes. I'll tell you more when you get here tomorrow. I don't want to talk about it over the phone."

Tilly was surprised at how confident Kate sounded, given the circumstances. "I'll head up early tomorrow morning. I'll bring breakfast."

"That's definitely an offer I won't turn down," Kate said, laughing. "See you tomorrow. And Tilly, I love you."

"I love you, too." Tilly disconnected, pushing her phone back into the pocket of her yoga pants. She'd been walking along the path during her conversation. Now she was ready to jog. She'd picked up some sports headphones that sat at the back of her head, allowing her to listen to music without being oblivious to her surroundings. She'd seen so many young men and women running with earbuds that blocked out all sound. It made them so vulnerable.

Tilly shivered, picking up her pace. She'd entered the darkest part of the path, and the isolation bothered her. Her eyes swept the landscape ahead. Despite her vigilance, she was caught off-guard when she saw a figure stepping out from behind some nearby brush. His movement was slow and steady as if he'd been waiting for her. Before she could react his arms wrapped her, pinning her arms to her side as he wrestled her to the ground.

It wasn't fear that took hold of Tilly, but rage. Her attacker was strong, but she was determined. She kicked furiously while trying to free her arms, ramming her head back violently and screaming. The side of her skull connected with bone, causing her attacker to loosen his grip while he groaned in pain. She was able to free one arm, and she reached back to claw at whatever she could get her hands on while trying to twist her body so that she was facing her tormentor. Her fingernails made contact with skin, and she pictured herself tearing into his flesh as she scratched.

"Fuck!" he yelled, his voice shrill. He wrenched her arm painfully behind her back, shoving her face into the hard ground. "Stop," he ordered. "Or I'm going to hurt you."

"I will kill you, you bastard," Tilly growled, and then resumed screaming as much as her aching lungs would allow. A gloved hand clamped over her mouth as he pressed her face hard into the earth. He'd managed to straddle her and was putting his full weight on her to hold her down. Her vision began to dim as he pressed into her back, making it harder and harder to breathe.

For a moment, she lost time. The world had grown black and still. Then pain tore through her, bringing her back to the terrifying present. She couldn't move, and it was hard to tell where the pain was coming from. A moment later, the weight on her body was gone and she felt cold air rushing over bare skin on her back. She heard sounds that she couldn't quite place. Yelling. A scuffling sound on gravel.

She breathed once. Twice. And then she let the darkness take her away.

———

A bright light shone in one eye and then the other. Tilly's head pounded and a wave of nausea made her body convulse. A hand gently turned her head while she retched. When she was finally able to breathe again, she opened her eyes and let the blurry world come into focus. She was in an ambulance. A paramedic was sitting beside her, emptying the bedpan she'd vomited into. She tried to turn, but even if the medic hadn't stopped her the pain in her body would have.

"What happened?" she whispered. Her throat was on fire. "Can I have some water?"

"I'm sorry, I know your throat is probably not feeling great but we have to get you to the hospital before we give you anything. A SANE nurse will meet us at the ED."

The nausea was back. "Was I raped?"

"No," a different voice beside her answered. She recognized the voice, but turned her head to convince herself that it was, in fact, Dan Bross sitting next to her in the ambulance.

"Dan?" she said, then winced at the pain of speaking. Dan had a bandage around one side of his head, and his eye was swollen shut. For a moment, Tilly couldn't understand what she was seeing. She started to shake. Had Dan attacked her? No, why would he be with her if he'd been her attacker? The throbbing in her head grew more intense, forcing her to close her eyes against the light. She wanted to sleep, but she needed answers.

"What happened?" she asked, gritting her teeth as she forced her voice to be louder.

"You were jogging in the park. A man attacked you," Dan answered, his voice weary. "He's in custody now. Before you ask, I don't know if he's our guy. We'll need to get you examined and collect any DNA. It looks like you dug into his neck with your nails."

"But he didn't...?"

"No," Dan repeated, his voice gentle this time. "I think he would have, but I got there first."

She opened her eyes and looked at him again, hoping he could guess her next question. He did.

"I've been out here every night this week. Just to make sure you were safe." He sighed. "I'm not going to lie. I didn't think your plan would work so I wasn't staying as close as I should have. I didn't want you to be angry with me for following you." His face was ashen. "I can't believe this happened."

Tilly placed a hand gently on Dan's arm and whispered, "Thank you."

He leaned closer, his face deadly serious. "Please don't ever do this again."

CHAPTER 50
KATE

Kate's heart thudded in her chest. Tilly had arrived at her door, a bag of takeout in hand, looking like she'd gone rounds with a heavyweight boxer. "Tilly, what happened to you?" Kate took the bag and walked Tilly to the couch. Her sister's movements were slow and jerky, as if every step was agony.

When Tilly was settled, Kate gave her a moment to catch her breath. "Tilly?"

"I got jumped last night at the park. I'd say I look worse than I feel, but the asshole really did a number on me. No breaks, thankfully, but the bruising in my ribs is awful. Spent the night at the ED. I actually haven't been to sleep. Just went home, showered, and drove here." Tilly smiled, then winced. She had bandages on her face, and Kate could see angry red abrasions covering most of one cheek. "Before we have the 'I told you so' talk, I'm going to have to take a nap."

"You can sleep in my room." Kate was already on her feet, and though she expected Tilly to argue her sister nodded gratefully and followed her up the stairs and down the hall. Tilly's voice was raspy. Kate remembered the fire in her throat after her attacker had tried to strangle her.

When she returned to the living room, Vicky was sitting at the kitchen table with a glass of milk.

"Good morning. I hope I didn't wake you. My sister got here a few minutes ago."

"No, I was awake."

Kate retrieved the bag of breakfast burritos from the coffee table. "Do you want something to eat?" She offered Vicky a burrito and then sat down across from her. "We need to get you some more sleep," Kate said softly. Vicky's skin was pale and she had dark circles under her eyes. If Kate hadn't heard her pacing last night, she might have thought the girl was sick.

As if reading her mind, Vicky said, "I'm always a little pukey in the mornings. But food helps." She tore into the burrito, but her bites went from ravenous to reluctant. "Okay, maybe not." She pushed the food aside and took a sip of her drink. Kate got her a glass of water and squeezed some lemon into it.

"Try this," she said, setting the glass in front of Vicky. "Might help."

Vicky took a hesitant sip. "Thanks."

Kate studied the young woman's face. She was ashen, which wasn't surprising if she was feeling sick. But she was also on edge. Kate got the feeling that Vicky was working up the courage to say something. Putting herself in work mode, Kate relaxed her shoulders and focused on her food, giving Vicky time and space.

"I think I should go home," Vicky said. It wasn't what Kate had been expecting, and her first impulse was to argue, but she resisted. "Whoever tried to break in the other night was here for me. They know I'm staying here."

"You're safe here," Kate said, trying to reassure Vicky, but the girl shook her head.

"I know you mean well, Ms. Medina. But I won't be safe as

long as I stay in this town, and I can't leave my mother and sister. I can't hide out here forever."

"I can find a place for you to stay. Maybe in Albuquerque? You could finish school online."

"No," Vicky said, the color returning to her face. "I talked to Lucy last night. I'll go back home, back to school. Then Lucy can go home too. I think they'll leave her alone if I cooperate."

Horror dissolved Kate's professional demeanor. "You don't really believe you can keep other girls safe by letting yourself be a victim? Vicky, it doesn't work that way. Even if they don't take Lucy, it'll be some other girl."

"And how does me staying here fix that?" Now Vicky was angry, but Kate could see the emotion wasn't aimed at her. Vicky was resigned to her fate. And hadn't Kate felt the same? Hopeless. Like there was nothing she could do to stop the violence. In working toward opening her safe house, Kate had lost sight of the reality. She'd allowed herself to see the house as a fortress where she could protect all the girls being preyed on, but in doing so she'd forgotten that these girls had free will. Keeping them safe by taking away their agency was not an option.

With a heavy heart, Kate took Vicky's hand. "I don't want you to go, but I'm not going to make you stay. I just want to keep you safe."

Tears streamed down Vicky's cheeks but she didn't look at Kate. With whispered thanks, the young woman excused herself and walked quickly upstairs to her room.

————

An hour later, Tilly was fast asleep in Kate's bedroom and Vicky was gone.

Vicky's mother had come to pick her up, and the entire affair was done so quickly Kate felt blindsided and weary. Lucy had come down to say goodbye to her friend, and now she and Kate were sitting quietly in front of a muted television. Kate couldn't remember if she'd turned it on or if Lucy had, but neither was paying attention.

"Are you okay, Lucy?" Kate finally asked.

"Yes. Well, no, not really." Lucy scooted closer to Kate on the couch. "I've been thinking a lot about what to do. Is there a way to avoid being the next in line . . . without having to compromise my goals? I mean, I took that internship at the City so that I could get into college and have a successful career. Vicky tells me I should quit. To steer clear of these horrible men, but a part of me wants to get right back in their faces" She looked at Kate. "Am I crazy?"

Kate smiled sadly. "No. I know how you feel." She hesitated, but she knew what she needed to say. "In my previous career, I was raped."

Lucy gasped.

"And I let that one horrible incident nearly wreck my whole life. I quit my job. I came here to live with my dad." Kate took Lucy's hand. "I let it defeat me."

"What changed?"

"A girl named Mandy." Kate thought back on the high school girl who had sought her help last year. She often thought of being pulled into a murder investigation as having turned the tide for her, but the truth was she may never have found her way back into having something worth fighting for if it hadn't been for that one girl. And then, all the girls like her. Kate had realized that, despite having followed her dreams and loving her career in the prison, the work she'd done since moving back to Alamogordo had been the most rewarding of her life.

"You can stay with me as long as you like, but if you're ready to go home I'll help you."

Lucy nodded. "Thank you." She leaned in and gave Kate a

hug. "I'm sorry what happened to you, but I'm glad you're here."

Kate's eyes filled with tears. As Lucy got up to leave, Kate noticed Tilly standing in the shadows at the bottom of the stairs. At first glance Tilly's face was a field of bruises and abrasions, but her smile was full of hope.

CHAPTER 51
TILLY

Tilly woke up stiff, and as the day wore on her body felt like drying cement. "I feel like I'm about a hundred years old," she said as she shambled to the dinner table. She joined Kate and Lucy, who were already digging in.

"How's your face?" Kate asked. The scarring across Tilly's cheek was going to be horrendous.

"I'm trying not to think about it," Tilly said. She smiled, but it hurt. Even the smallest movement made her face feel like it was on fire. She'd come downstairs after lunch for some water, and had given Kate a quick rundown of her night. She knew Kate would want to know more but she'd gone right back up to bed, unable to stay upright. She'd been at Kate's house for almost twelve hours, and she'd slept most of those. "I think I can stay up for a while, but the minute I take the pain meds I'm going to be out again."

She looked at Lucy. "Kate tells me you'll be heading home in the morning. May I offer some advice?" Lucy nodded warily. "When these guys are grooming their victims, they rely on the fact that you don't know what you're getting into. And by the time you figure it out, you won't know how to get out of it."

Kate raised an eyebrow, but didn't interrupt.

"You don't have to let them run your life, Lucy. You can choose not to be alone with them. You know what they're after. Just make sure it's too hard to get to you. They'll lose interest."

"But I don't want them to move on to someone else," Lucy protested.

"None of us wants that," Kate said, picking up where Tilly left off. "But right now, the best we can do is try to keep you safe."

The rest of the meal was quiet, for which Tilly was grateful. Beyond the damage to her face, her throat was still sore and raspy where her attacker had held her to the ground. Lucy helped Kate do the dishes, then headed to her room to sleep. Kate made two cups of tea and ushered Tilly back to the living room, helping her prop her feet up on the couch. Then she retrieved Tilly's pain meds and handed them to her with a glass of water.

"Meds first, then we'll chat," Kate said. Tilly complied dutifully, hoping that the meds would kick in quickly.

"Are you taking Lucy home tomorrow?" Till asked.

"Yeah. I need to run into town to grab some groceries, so I'll drop her off on the way. I spoke with her aunt this morning. I guess she explained some of the situation to Lucy's mom. We talked about some strategies for keeping out of Sam Garrett's path. I hope she's okay."

Tilly sighed. "You and I are like night and day on some things, but on this we're the same. I thought I could go out there, pretend to be helpless, and take a dangerous rapist off the street by force of sheer will." Tilly gestured around the room. "This house is amazing. But you can't protect every girl. This is not a fortress and you are not an island."

"I know," Kate said. "Don't worry. I already read myself the riot act this morning, and there won't be any 'I told you so' from me." Kate slid back and put her feet up on the coffee table.

"Intellectually, I know it's going to take a lot more than just me to end this nightmare. Did I tell you about Sam Garrett waiting for me in the parking lot the other day? Broad daylight, and he stands there with a smug smile. Like he owns the place. And I can't help feeling like he does. Like all these living breathing girls are objects to be owned and traded and discarded."

Tilly leaned her head back against the couch cushions. "I was out running last night and I didn't want to be there. I'd already kind of decided that I was out there for the wrong reasons. Reckless. That's what it was. I feel so fucking sad and angry that Jim is gone. But I also feel relief and guilt. It makes it hard to breathe sometimes. I've turned into one of your thrill seeking weirdos who avoid dealing with their problems by taking unnecessary risks."

Kate was quiet. Tilly trained her eyes on the ceiling.

"I kept looking over my shoulder and all around. The guy stepped out of the shadows right in front of me. Pinned my arms and threw me to the ground. He was smashing my face into the ground so hard, it felt like my whole skull would flatten. And he was putting all his weight on my upper back. I couldn't breathe."

"You said he didn't rape you," Kate said, almost as if she were reassuring herself.

"No, he didn't. Though he might have and I couldn't have fought him off. Then Dan Bross appeared and took him down." Tilly couldn't help but smile a little.

"The attorney? From the park?"

"That's the one," Tilly said. "Brynn told him what I was up to and he'd been following me at the park every night."

"That's not creepy," Kate said with a laugh.

"I don't disagree, but considering he saved my life I'm giving him a pass this time." Tilly rolled her head over painfully to look at Kate. "He lost his wife a few years ago, and I think he's been trying to help me through my grief in his weird, socially awkward way." She returned her head to a more comfortable position. "Anyway, I realized something last night. The worst thing those assholes did to me back in high school was to alienate me from everyone. I hadn't formed a single deep connection with anyone until I met Jim, and I always had him at arm's length."

"Same for me," Kate said. "I hid behind my career. And then I took this huge fall from grace and couldn't find my way back."

Tilly slowly sat up and faced Kate again. "We all stumble and fall, Kate. But we have to learn to pick ourselves back up. No matter how scared we may be or how much it hurts." She struggled to stand up and Kate was beside her in no time. "See," she said softly as a tear slid down Kate's cheek."More proof that I can't do this all alone. And neither can you." She smiled. "But we can do it together."

CHAPTER 52
KATE

Tilly stayed with Kate for a week while she recovered and Kate wondered how she'd feel to be alone in the house again. She was surprised to find the stillness comforting. For a few days, she got back into a routine. Her client load was increasing, so she was out of the house more than usual. She decided to bring Rusty with her to the office and it didn't take long before he also got into a routine, saying a quick, non-jumping hello to clients and then settling quietly into his dog bed under Kate's desk.

When Thursday rolled around she decided to go back to her women's luncheon, leaving Rusty snoring happily in the office while she was gone.

When Kate arrived she saw Ruth at their usual table. She'd been so distracted with Lucy and Vicky she hadn't had much time to consider what she'd learned about her mother's death. The older woman pulled Kate into her arms, but Kate was more wary than she'd been.

"Nice to see you, stranger," Ruth said with a smile. "Is everything okay with your sister?"

For a moment Kate wondered how Ruth knew about the

attack, but then she remembered that she'd told Ruth about Jim's death. She relaxed. "She's doing better. A lot of ups and downs, but she'll be okay."

"That's good. I remember when my husband passed. It was a lonely time, but luckily I had the business to keep up with. It kept my mind off the sad things."

"How long did you work together?" Kate asked.

"A long time," Ruth said. "I started as a secretary at the company and then worked my way up. After we got married, we pretty much ran everything together. In fact, I'd taken over management before he passed away so it wasn't much of a transition professionally. Everyone was already used to me being in charge."

"That's great," Kate said, though the dispassionate way Ruth spoke about her husband and the business was unsettling. "Who's the speaker today?" she asked, changing the subject. "I forgot to look on the website."

"Jennifer Thomas. She's the new director for the Women's Health Center at the hospital."

A few minutes later, the program started. Kate listened with fascination as the speaker talked about new initiatives to curb teenage pregnancy and provide reproductive health care to the uninsured.

She agreed with everything the speaker said, but as the women in the audience stood to applaud Kate couldn't help but think about how many of these women turned a blind eye to what was going on right under their noses.

"Kate, are you all right?" Ruth looked at her with concern. "Are you feeling well, dear?"

Kate joined Ruth in laughing, snapping herself out of the downward spiral her thoughts had taken. "I'm fine. I'd better get back to the office. Nice to see you, Ruth."

Kate left abruptly, but she had a stop she wanted to make before heading back to work.

———

"Can I help you?"

Sam Garrett was sitting at this desk. As she'd hoped, his secretary hadn't returned from lunch so she knocked at his door. As she walked inside, she shut the door behind her. The look of surprise on Garrett's face was priceless.

"May I have a word with you?" Kate said. She kept her tone light, but inside she felt like steel ribbons ran the length of her body.

"I'm very busy," he said, shuffling some papers. "Why don't you make an appointment with my secretary." He looked toward the door with a frown. "She should be back any minute."

"This won't take long, Mr. Garrett." Kate walked right up to his desk and planted herself firmly in place. She kept her smile in place, but she hoped that the look she was giving him gave him pause. "I wanted to extend you the same courtesy you gave me in the parking lot the other day." At his confused expression, Kate continued. "A warning."

"You need to leave, Ms. Medina," he said sternly, but he looked uncertain of himself.

"It's funny. I've said those exact words before in my office, and it never seems to keep you creeps from showing up uninvited. Like your little drop-in at the grocery store." Kate lowered her voice. "I wanted to deliver a friendly warning. I know who you are, Mr. Garrett. And I know what you've been doing. And if you so much as lay a hand on another girl, I promise you will go straight to jail. No passing go."

The element of surprise had thrown Garrett off his guard, but Kate could clearly see the moment his arrogance snapped back into place. A slow grin spread across his face. He stood, making Kate want to step back. She fought the urge.

"You're a smart woman, Ms. Medina. You must know that

there's a whole lot of space between what you think you know and what you can prove." He started to move around his desk, making Kate's uneasiness nearly unbearable. Instead of shrinking she took a few steps toward him, stopping him in his tracks. Again, she saw a flash of uncertainty.

"Here's what I know," she said, stepping right up to him and looking him in the eye. He was taller than her, and she knew he could probably overpower her, but her resolve was strong. Besides, he wasn't likely to attack her in his City office, was he? She shook away her doubt. "I know that you all think you're untouchable. But I also know that with every single person you hurt, with every man involved in this atrocity, you're that much closer to being caught. Closer to making a mistake. Look at Benny Parks. He almost ruined it for everyone, didn't he? You may think you hold all the cards, but now that I know you're out there I won't stop until every one of you is in prison."

The tension between them was reaching a boiling point. Every fiber of her being screamed for her to retreat, but she couldn't. She couldn't keep running. It was a lesson she'd learned the hard way last fall when Roman got attacked. It might be in her nature to avoid and to run, but the only thing that could break that cycle was her own resolve. She was also emboldened by the uneasiness which had settled over her opponent.

Suddenly, Sam Garrett's face fell and his shoulders sagged. Kate took a step back, completely confused as to what had happened. She waited for the bravado to return, but it didn't. They stood that way until a knock at the door brought them both back to the present.

"Mr. Garrett? I'm back," his secretary called through the door. They could hear her take a seat at her desk and begin typing. Kate realized she was holding her breath. The Assistant City Manager looked equally stiff and tense. The moment seemed to drag on.

"You'd better go," Garrett said."It's better if no one sees you here." He led her to the door, peeked outside and then opened the door, saying loudly, "Thanks for stopping by, Ms. Medina. I'll take that into consideration."

Without a word, Kate walked past his secretary's desk and down the hall in a daze. She'd expected anger, hostility, and threats. She knew by taking this action she'd started a war and she hoped that it was a war she could win. Sam Garrett's reaction had thrown her off balance. What was it she saw in his face? Was it regret? No, she thought as she walked to her car. It was fear.

CHAPTER 53
KATE

The weekend came without incident. Kate awoke early on Sunday morning and took Rusty up into the mountains for a hike. The sunlight shone through the leaves, creating a spectacular light show across the path. Kate laughed as she watched Rusty leaping over fallen trees as he ran along the path. It was a rare moment of peace.

When they arrived home Kate checked in with Tilly, who was still recovering from the attack but getting back into her own routine.

"Any updates on your case?"

"Not yet. It'll be a while before DNA comes back, and in the meantime he's not talking. But either way, he's been charged with the attack on me. And given that there is a witness, I don't see him getting off."

"That's good."

"Yeah. One less creep on the street," Tilly said. Despite her injuries, she'd seemed calmer and less angry than she'd ever been in her life. Kate knew the road would be long, but she was glad to see both her sister, and her herself, finding moments of solace amidst all the brutality and horror they faced each day.

"So, tell me more about your visit with the City guy the other day."

Kate sighed. "It was not what I was expecting. I thought I'd walk in there, give him a piece of my mind, and then have him gunning for me. His reaction threw me. Not that I don't expect there to be fallout. If he wasn't out to get me, now he will."

"What do you think? I'm guessing you have a theory."

"I do," Kate said, smiling. It felt good to have someone understand her. "It bothers me, the way this organization has stayed under the radar for so long. It occurs to me that the girls aren't the only ones being groomed."

"You're saying the men are victims too?" Kate could hear the disgust in Tilly's voice.

"Not exactly. I'm saying what I saw in Sam Garrett's eyes . . . He was scared, Tilly. Unsure. Certainly not what I would expect from a predator, especially since we were standing in his office. I was the intruder, but something I said rattled him. And it made me wonder if the people higher up the chain have something on him."

Tilly was silent for a moment. "It makes sense, actually. Like in mob movies where the boss has all the power, but his grunts do all the dirty work. We know a lot of men are involved in this, but we don't know how they got involved. Like when Jacob took me to that party, he was a kid. But maybe they were bringing him in. Initiating him."

"And if there was some proof of their involvement—something being held over their heads—like pictures. At Benny Parks' trial, they showed pictures of him with Gabby Greene. I don't remember where those came from, but the fact that they existed seemed odd to me." She paused. "Or maybe video..." Kate said, her voice trailing off as a memory tugged at her thoughts. "Vicky mentioned a blinking light in the smoke detector."

"They don't usually blink unless the battery is low."

"That's what I was thinking," Kate said, her voice breathy from the revelation. "Maybe they're filming the girls. What if the men don't know they're being recorded, Tilly?"

"Or maybe they don't know at first. Then whoever is in charge tells them. Blackmails them. And then they're stuck. It would be pretty damning evidence since all the girls we know about are under age."

Kate sighed. "It's a lot of speculation. I wish Roman was home. If this trafficking ring involves video, the FBI might be more inclined to take on an investigation."

"If it exists," Tilly said quietly. "And if we can find it."

———

Kate was sitting out in the courtyard, enjoying the cool breeze, when Rusty hopped up and barked. Soon, Kate could hear a car on the gravel drive. Keeping Rusty at her side, Kate walked to the gate and opened it. She was surprised to see Ruth walking up to the door.

"Ruth! Hello." she said. She opened the screen door but leaned into the doorframe, blocking the path. This was the second time the woman had appeared on Kate's doorstep unannounced.

"Sorry to drop in on you," Ruth said. She smiled at Kate, but there was something in her expression that gave Kate pause. "Would you mind if I came in for a minute?"

Kate's insides were at war. It felt horribly rude to not invite Ruth in, but Kate didn't want the older woman in her space. She was relieved that no one was staying with her and that she had never mentioned her true intention for the house. "Sure, but I actually have to head out in a few so I'm afraid I can't entertain you for long."

Kate stepped aside, giving Ruth room to move past her.

Rusty stayed glued at her side. Usually, one sniff and any guest became his new best friend. Now he stood silent and watchful at Kate's feet.

"I was just sitting out here in the fresh air. Would you like to join me?" Kate said, taking a seat on a patio chair. She gestured for Ruth to sit across from her. "So, what brings you out my way today? Farmers market?"

Ruth laughed. "No, though I used to frequent the markets. I don't do a lot of cooking these days, now that it's just me, so the produce usually goes bad before I can use it. Actually, I was thinking about you the other day after the luncheon. You seemed very out of sorts, and I thought I'd drop by and see if you're okay."

"Thanks for thinking of me, but I'm doing fine."

"Not too lonely out here in the middle of the desert?"

"Not with my trusty canine companion," she said, patting Rusty's back. The dog remained a statue. "Only two months until Roman gets back from training. In the meantime, I'm keeping myself pretty busy."

Ruth sat forward in her chair. "Listen, I heard something the other day and I thought you would want to know."

"Oh?" Kate said, a chill racing down her spine.

"A friend of mine at the City . . . one of his interns told him you'd been harassing her. From what I understand she's a nervous thing, so I'm sure she's overreacting. In fact I hear she's gone to stay with a relative out-of-state for a while, so maybe the stress got to her. Anyway, you might want to keep some distance from the City office until things blow over. I'd hate to see your reputation tarnished over the ravings of an unstable teenage intern."

Kate's throat was so dry that she couldn't muster a response. Her mind raced wildly. She couldn't imagine either Vicky or Lucy reporting her, so the information must have come from

Sam Garrett. But after her visit to his office, she didn't get the feeling he'd be telling anyone she'd been to see him. Had someone been watching her? Following her?

Kate studied Ruth as if seeing her for the first time. The woman had just delivered this news deadpan. She did not appear to be concerned for Kate, and certainly not for the intern she was speaking about. The words were right, but there was something missing from her demeanor. Something Kate hadn't paid much attention to before. Something hollow.

Ruth stood, her gaze traveling around Kate's courtyard as she continued. "I always told my husband, bless his soul, that sometimes you have to cut ties in order to keep the organization healthy. But sometimes a warning is enough. What do you think Kate?" Her eyes narrowed. "You will heed my words, right?"

"I have no idea what you're talking about," Kate replied calmly. "I've only been to the City office a few times since I moved here, but since I live here I'm sure I'll have to stop by from time to time." She was still thinking about the girls, hoping they were safe.

Ruth's expression stayed neutral, but Kate could see a flash of anger in her eyes. "Well, you're a capable woman, Kate. I'm sure you'll do the sensible thing."

"I'm not sure I understand any of this. But I can handle any accusations that come my way. I'm sure that whatever story you've heard was a misunderstanding," Kate said, and then added, "Sounds like the sort of thing someone would say to deflect attention from themselves, don't you think?"

Ruth nodded, the corners of her lips turned down slightly. She walked toward the gate, turning before she opened it. "I'm glad you've got good security out here, Kate," she said with a smile. "I'd hate for something to happen to you. Or anyone staying with you."

Kate shut the gate, leaning against it and trying to catch

her breath. When she heard Ruth's car kicking up gravel on her way to the highway, she sank to the ground. Rusty whined, sitting beside her and nudging her with his nose. As the cold truth penetrated her thoughts, the world began to spin.

———

"Kate?" Tilly said as she opened her door. Rusty dashed into Tilly's apartment, leaving Kate standing like an apparition on Tilly's doorstep. "What are you doing here?"

"It's her," Kate said weakly.

"Who?" Tilly said, leading Kate into the apartment by the arm. "Kate, you're scaring me. What's going on?"

Kate hadn't allowed herself time to process her thoughts. After Ruth left she pushed everything aside, focusing on one task at a time. She packed a bag and headed over the pass with Rusty while waves of nausea rolled through her, making her feel like she'd vomit if she opened her mouth to speak. She'd kept herself together long enough to make the drive, but now anxiety took hold and she let it. Usually the fear of passing out or dying made matters worse, but right at that moment Kate would have been happy for oblivion.

"Ruth," Kate croaked. "She's part of it." She paused, trying to steady herself. Tilly wrapped a blanket around her shoulders, and Kate frantically searched her eyes.

"Part of what? What are you talking about?" Kate could hear the panic in Tilly's voice, but all she could do was say the words out loud—to take them out of her brain and put them out in the world where she and Tilly could examine them.

"She's been watching me. Every single moment since the day I met her. She had me followed. Those men from the house the other night? She sent them." Kate was hyperventilating, and she knew that soon she would have to stop and breathe. But not before she finished. "She knew about my security system. She knew everything."

"You probably told her about it, Kate. Please calm down. I need you to breathe." Tilly had taken hold of Kate's shoulders and now she leaned into Kate, putting their foreheads together. Kate almost let herself melt into her sister. Almost. But there was one nagging truth still eating at her. She pulled away from Tilly, their eyes locking.

"Tilly, I think she got Mom killed."

She felt Tilly's body stiffen. "Slow down. Start from the beginning."

Kate's panic was finally beginning to fade. She took a few deep breaths and tried to pull herself together. "When I first met her, Ruth talked about Mom and Dad like they'd been good friends. Then she changed her story. She made it sound like she hardly knew them at all."

"You said it yourself, she might be forgetful." Tilly's tone was still skeptical, but frown lines burrowed deep into her forehead.

"I know," Kate said, wishing once again that that might be true. Knowing it wasn't. She needed to help Tilly see. "I was re-reading Mom's journals. And those photos, Tilly. They were together a lot. There are photos of Mom and Ruth with their arms around each other."

"Why did she come to see you?" Tilly asked quietly.

"She said she heard that I'd been reported for harassing an intern at the City."

Tilly laughed. "I guess your visit to Sam Garrett didn't go unnoticed." Then she paused, "But wait, why would he tell her?"

"I don't think he did," Kate said. "If he'd wanted to, he could have called security and had me escorted out of the building that day. He was worried, Tilly." The menacing look on Ruth's face as she left Kate's house flashed across her mind. "She threatened me. A subtle threat, but given all the things she's said and done. Given all the things that have happened . . . ."

"Mom told her about what happened to me and Ruth betrayed her," Tilly said. "But why?"

Kate sighed. "I don't know, but I have to find out. I think she's the key."

CHAPTER 54
TILLY

"Ms. Medina?"

Tilly lifted her eyes from her computer screen and was surprised to see Hannah Bross standing in her office doorway. A mix of concern and wariness coursed through her body.

"Hannah? Is everything all right?"

"Yeah." Hannah smiled. "Is it okay if I come in?"

"Yes, absolutely!" Tilly said, shaking her head and laughing. "Sorry, I'm still a little slow on the draw." She reached up and touched the scar under her right eye. The bruises were taking their sweet time to heal and Tilly still felt self-conscious.

Hannah walked forward and took a seat in one of the visitor chairs in front of Tilly's desk. When she didn't immediately speak, Tilly asked, "How's your dad?"

Dan hadn't been by the office since Tilly's attack. She assumed he was busy with the case, but she worried that he might be avoiding her. After the initial shock wore off, he'd been angry with Tilly. She couldn't blame him, and she found herself saying a silent thank you that he'd been there that night, even if he was angry.

"He's okay," Hannah replied. "Actually, he asked me to stop by."

"Oh." Tilly felt a little bit deflated.

Hannah slid a business card out of her pocket and across the desk to Tilly. The card held information about a grief support group that met at the hospital.

"When my mom died," Hannah said slowly, "It was so hard."

Tilly reached out a hand, but Hannah didn't respond. Instead, the teen seemed to be building to something. Tilly sat back again, trying to be patient.

When Hannah began again, her words were measured. "I missed my mom so much, but I felt like I'd lost both my parents. My dad worked all the time and when he came home, he smelled like cigarettes and beer. I started to wonder if he was mad at me. Like it was my fault that my mom was gone."

"Oh, Hannah. You have to know that wasn't the case," Tilly said, but Hannah's gaze silenced her again.

"I know," Hannah said. Her expression was serious, but she smiled again, like she was trying to reassure Tilly. "But sadness doesn't alway make much sense, does it? Things got bad for a while, and then one day, he came home from work and looked at me like he'd never seen me before."

Tilly had no idea where this was going, but instead of trying to hurry Hannah along, instead she tried to picture the scene. When she'd run into Dan and Hannah at the park, they'd seemed very connected. She tried to imagine Dan, hollow and broken in his grief, looking at his daughter like she was a stranger.

Suddenly she realized she knew exactly what that looked like. She'd seen her father give her the same look. Before she had too much time to consider this, Hannah continued.

"He had a new case. A girl my age had been killed. He told me that when Mom died, he felt like a piece of him died with her. And it took him a long time to see that a part of her was still alive." Hannah sniffled. "I'd never really seen him cry before that. I knew he did—I could hear him in his room at night. But that day he just sat in the room and cried. And then I started crying too and it was the first time we'd both been sad together."

"Why are you telling me this?" Tilly asked softly.

"My dad told me about your friend who died. And your parents. He told me about the case and the night he followed you."

Tilly's face drained. "He told you about that?"

"Well, he told me a bit," Hannah said. "He seems to think I'm too young for all the gory details, but I keep telling him I want to be an investigator. Anyway, do you remember when we saw you that day in the park?

"I do."

"When we got home, I told Dad that you looked really sad. Kind of like we used to look. And so he told me a little bit about your friend."

Tilly was surprised to feel a tear sliding down her cheek. "Jim," she whispered.

"I told him we should bring you with us to our support group," Hannah said. "And he said that you might like it better if I invited you."

Tilly smiled as she wiped away her tears. "That's very sweet of you. Boy, I bet your dad thinks I'm going a little crazy right now, huh?"

Hannah's expression turned serious again. "No. He says you're very brave."

Tilly clutched the business card to her chest. "Thank you, Hannah. I think you're right. I'll come."

———

"And it's okay if I call you?"

Tilly smiled at her patient. "Of course. And if you need follow-up care, we're here for you. We have a great social worker on staff. You've got her information there in your packet."

The young woman, Anne Marie, had come in a few hours earlier following a first-date that had turned ugly. When she realized what was about to happen, her body had shut down, taking her mind to a safe place, away from the violence. She described the attack like she'd been watching it from outside herself. Thankfully the physical injuries were minimal, but Tilly knew from her own experience that guilt and shame could be more damaging than any wound.

"Thank you," Anne Marie said, choking back a fresh wave of tears. "I don't know how you do this every day, but I'm glad you were here for me." She turned and walked toward the waiting room where her mother was waiting to take her home.

Tilly sighed and walked back into the exam room to clean up. She was finishing when someone knocked at the open door frame. "Tilly?"

Angie Lopez stood at the door.

Tilly stripped her gloves off and threw them in the trash by the door. "What can I do for you, Detective?" She smiled, gesturing over her shoulder as she walked by Angie toward her office—an invitation to follow. When they reached her office, Angie closed the door behind her and took a seat across from Tilly.

"How are you feeling?" Angie asked.

"Better," Tilly said. "Starting to look more like myself. I'm going to need some physical therapy for my shoulder." She rolled her shoulder slowly, stretching out muscles that weren't quite healed. "But I'm guessing you're not here to inquire about my health." She gave Angie a rueful smile. "Am I in trouble?"

Tilly had been waiting for some fallout from her recklessness. She'd gotten sporadic updates about the case from her victim advocate, but Dan hadn't been around for a few weeks and both Angie and Brynn had been distant.

"No," Angie said. "But I hope you got that out of your system, because you nearly gave me a heart attack."

Tilly swallowed hard. She'd been bracing for a lecture, and the detective's concern made her feel off-kilter. "No more going rogue," Tilly said quietly.

"Good, because things are complicated. Since Dan is now a witness for the prosecution, he's been removed from the case. And given his position as ADA, the office has basically told him to stay away from the clinic until after the case goes to court."

"What?"

Angie held up a hand. "Before you freak out, the case is being fast-tracked and so it should only be a few months. In the meantime, Dan is handling non-violent cases."

"He must be furious," Tilly said. One thing she knew for sure was that Dan Bross's passion for his job rivaled her own. "So, staying away from the clinic probably means no contact for me, eh?"

"Right," Angie said. "But listen, Dan isn't furious. He's actually perfectly happy to take a back seat."

Tilly eyed Angie suspiciously. "That doesn't sound right."

"That's the other reason I'm here," Angie said. "Remember I said it's complicated? Well, that's actually the good news. You caught him, Tilly."

It took a few seconds for Tilly to understand what Angie was saying. When she did, she felt a little bit dizzy. "Oh my God," she whispered.

"Guy's name is Douglas Murphy. He's married. Two kids. Works in customer service. Squeaky clean record. DNA hits in seven cases including yours."

"It was him," Tilly murmured, trying to wrap her brain

around the idea that her actions, though reckless, had actually worked.

"I can see what you're thinking, Tilly," Angie said sternly. "Remember, no more going rogue. Think about Kate. And your patients." Her voice softened. "Attacking you was what brought him down, but the work you've done with his other victims, Tilly? That's what's going to seal his fate."

EPILOGUE

Kate walked into the event space. She scanned the crowd and saw Ruth sitting at their usual table. The older woman was conversing with one of the usual attendees. When she spotted Kate looking at her, she smiled and waved as if nothing had happened. As if the world in which they'd lived last week was the same world today. But everything had changed, and despite the older woman's brazen attempt to intimidate Kate she was more determined than ever.

Keeping her face neutral, Kate turned away and headed to the front of the room.

"Oh, Kate! I'm so glad you reached out. Your new program sounds amazing. I can't wait to hear your presentation."

Kate smiled. "Thanks Julie. It's not exactly the type of thing people like to discuss over lunch, but I appreciate the chance to speak to this crowd. We'll need a lot of support from the business community to be successful. Especially the woman. The mothers and grandmothers. We'll need everyone."

"Well, I'm sure you'll get it. My husband and I moved here after our girls went to college. I would have loved a program like this back home." Julie blushed. "Actually, I have to admit, they may have had similar programs, but as a stay-at-home mom I was pretty focused on what was happening with my daughters. I'm glad they got through high school safe and sound."

Kate's stomach churned. "I'm so glad. I just wish it was true for all teens. Even in small towns like ours, you wouldn't believe what goes on behind closed doors."

A flash of horror crossed Julie's face, but she quickly plastered a smile back on her face. "Let me make sure everything is set up and then I'll introduce you."

Kate set her bag down and pulled out her laptop. She connected to the projector and started up the presentation. A hush fell over the crowd, the provocative title screen demanding their attention. Kate stood near the podium, nursing a glass of water and doing breathing exercises to keep her nerves in check.

Glancing toward the back of the room, Kate saw Tilly and her friend Brynn slip in and take seats at the edge of the crowd. Kate smiled at her sister.

Tilly's beautiful face was marred by the fading scars left by her attacker. All her physical injuries were healing. And thankfully, since she'd been attending grief support sessions, her emotional state seemed to be more stable.

The trial of the serial rapist in Las Cruces was drawing nearer. And the evidence Tilly had gathered doing exams, combined with her own attack and Dan Bross's key witness testimony, made it pretty likely that the rapist would serve the rest of his life in prison. It was a victory, but the price Tilly had paid was too high.

Kate's own experiences had been more disappointing. After Vicky and Lucy left her house, she struggled to get back to center. Her confrontation with Ruth, and Vicky's subsequent disappearance, weighed heavily on her mind. Though she'd reached out to Vicky's mother, the woman refused to divulge any information. Kate prayed that the young woman was safe somewhere, but not knowing left her feeling very uneasy.

Tilly reminded her constantly that she couldn't save every single person she tried to help, and Tilly's support had finally pushed her toward her current path. The road ahead was bound to be difficult but Roman would be home next week, giving her something to look forward to.

"Kate, are you ready?" Julie's voice brought her back to the present.

"Definitely."

Julie approached the microphone, tapping it a few times though the conversations had stayed quiet. "Thanks for joining us this week. I hope y'all got some coffee and pastries. We have a great presentation today. Kate Medina comes to us with a background in forensic psychology. Having spent many years working in the prison system, Kate now runs a family coun- seling practice here in town. She's also starting a new program to end a particularly awful kind of violence happening in many communities. But I'll let her tell you more about that. Kate Medina."

Amid tentative applause, Kate took her place behind the podium. She saw Angie Lopez make her way to Tilly and Brynn. When they made eye contact, Angie smiled and Kate was filled with hope that some wounds could be healed.

"Thanks for being here," she started. "Since starting my prac- tice, I've enjoyed coming to these gatherings and learning about all the great work being done in our community. My focus is on ending interpersonal violence, and today I'd like to talk with you about domestic sex trafficking."

A few of the nearby audience members winced.

Kate smiled warmly at them. "I know. It sounds terrible, and it certainly is, but my goal is to give you some useful informa- tion and tips so that, as a community, we can all be aware of the dangers and learn how to intervene. Alamogordo is a wonderful small town, and I know that we can come together to keep our most vulnerable neighbors safe."

Kate looked back at Ruth, holding her gaze until the other woman looked away, her face red with barely concealed rage.

As Kate spoke, her audience seemed to relax. And at the end of the presentation, she was rewarded with standing applause and enthusiastic questions from her peers.

Kate walked out from behind the podium, glancing quickly to the back of the room. She saw Ruth high-tail it out of the atrium. Kate smiled. It was a small but important victory in her fight to end the brutality in her town.

I'm coming for you, she thought as she watched the door close behind Ruth, then turned to the sea of faces in front of her and began her work.

ACKNOWLEDGMENTS

Writing a book is a labor of love, and when you write about the darker parts of humanity, it's also a practice in patience and self-care. I am so grateful for all the people who help me along the way, starting with my husband who listens as I brainstorm and reads the earliest, most awful drafts, and then ending here with you, the reader. Thank you for picking up this book and being with Kate and Tilly as they tackle some very difficult challenges.

As an indie author, I rely on all the wonderful professionals who make up my publishing team. To Kim Huther for working hard to edit this book into shape. Your attention to detail is most appreciated. To Carl Graves for designing a book cover that is both beautiful and true to the story inside. And to Mary-Glenn McCombs and all the marketing and publicity folks who make sure the books get into the hands of readers and reviewers.

To Sonja, Michelle, Kaitlyn & Kate–your feedback has been extremely helpful and I am so glad to travel this road with you. Your guidance and laughter make my heart happy.

To my best friend Jessica. Sometimes life really gives you lemons, eh? But when you have a ride or die . . . make lemonade baby :) I know these last few years have been a struggle, but I'm so proud of you and how brave you've been. Remember, being strong doesn't mean you can't cry.

My husband always says that regardless what genre I'm writing in, I write relationship books. This is very true. There is nothing more interesting to me than human motivation and the dynamics in a relationship, whether good or bad. As a student of psychology, I love being with and around people. As a former SANE director, I've worked with victims, families, community members, political leaders, nurses and other medical professionals, law enforcement, attorneys, investigators and a whole host of other individuals involved in the criminal justice system as it pertains to interpersonal violence. It can be a very heartbreaking job, but a lot of my inspiration comes from that time because wherever there is darkness, there is also light. Love. Kindness. Resilience. Hope.

My love to all those people working alongside victims and their families. You make the world better every single day. And a special thank you to nurses–because you are ALL heroes in my book.

Family is at the very core of who I am as a person. I am so grateful to my parents, who always support me and have my back, even when I'm wrong. I have an amazing extended family–cousins, aunts, uncles, grandparents. They've taught me so much about love and what it means to be a family.

My sister is the best sister in the Universe. She's one of my first readers and she makes me feel like I'm doing something amazing with my life which really helps get me through the hard days.

And of course, my husband and my kids. They keep me on my toes and they love me even when I'm weird (which is pretty much always). I have two teenagers and they actually acknowledge my existence around their friends. I see that as a win. Love you guys.

ABOUT THE AUTHOR

Amy Rivers is an award-winning novelist and writer of short stories and personal essays, as well as the Director of Northern Colorado Writers. She was recently named 2021 Indie Author of the Year by the Indie Author Project. She's been published in We Got This: Solo Mom Stories of Grit, Heart,  and Humor, Flash! A Celebration of Short Fiction, Chicken Soup for the Soul: Inspiration for Nurses, and Splice Today, as well as Novelty Bride Magazine and ESME.com. She was raised in New Mexico and now lives in Colorado with her husband and children. She holds degrees in psychology and political science, two topics she loves to write about.

ALSO BY AMY RIVERS

A Legacy of Silence Series
Complicit

———

Standalone Novels
All The Broken People

———

Cambria Series (Women's Fiction)
Wallflower Blooming
Best Laid Plans & Other Disasters

CPSIA information can be obtained
at www.ICGtesting.com
Printed in the USA
BVHW052239240922
647939BV00017B/146

9 781734 516067